The Wakeful Wanderer's Guide to New New England & Beyond

INDIES UNITED PUBLISHING HOUSE, LLC

SECOND EDITION
Published March 2021 by Indies United Publishing House, LLC

Jacket design by Jim Infantino
Pages set in Hoefler Text

978-1-64456-279-6
Library of Congress Control Number: 2021933123

INDIES UNITED PUBLISHING HOUSE, LLC
P.O. BOX 3071
QUINCY, IL 62305-3071

www.indiesunited.net

For John
oooh — sailin'

Contents

Foreword by Scott K. Andrews

You'd think the strip of land that marks the crossover between the countries of songwriting and novel writing would be more fertile, wouldn't you? But the list of songwriters who have penned books, while pretty long, is not very distinguished.

Mostly when a songwriter pens a book it will be poetry, which always feels to me like a dumping ground for song lyrics that they just couldn't get to scan quite right and so they called them poems and hoped nobody would notice (although, yes, I do own an autographed copy of Harry Chapin's poetry book, don't judge me). If not poetry, the songwriting author usually attempts a great literary novel in which words run away from them like unherdable cats frolicking madly when they find themselves freed of the constraints of scansion - yes, Morrissey, I'm looking at you. We're all looking at you, Morrissey.

Songwriter memoirs are more reliably readable, because even the most poorly written normally contain a few good anecdotes that justify the price of admission, and the best of them, like Bruce Springsteen's and Keith Richards', are little masterpieces.

But a songwriter writing a genre book? I can think of only one - The Decemberists' Colin Meloy, and while his fantasy books are really pretty good, they also crossover with the subgenre of songwriters writing for children which includes Madonna and Courtney Love, and nobody wants to be in that club.

Novelists writing song lyrics then? I can think of David Mamet, who wrote Primitive Man for the criminally forgotten Ruby Blue album Down From Above, Nick Hornby, whose collaboration with Ben Folds produced a couple of genuinely good ditties, and Kazuo Ishiguro, whose creative partnership with Stacey Kent has thrown up some gems. And while I'm sure, dear reader, you'll be able to name some I've missed, it's unlikely the list will be terribly long.

So, despite a few exceptions, the strip of no man's land between the respective domains of authors and lyricists has yielded a very lacklustre harvest. And a songwriter writing an adult genre book - sci-fi, no less? Come on. Don't be daft. What are the odds that anybody could stick that landing?

Which brings me to Jim Infantino. I've been a fan of Jim's music since someone emailed me the flash video he did for Stress back in 2000 as a way of trying to calm me during a day of coding at a hateful company that was driving me insane. It helped, and I became a die-hard fan of Jim's Big Ego. The list of his songs that have become staples in my house is very long indeed, and the dropping of a new JBE album has always been a day of great rejoicing. So when I discovered he was writing a book, and publishing it in installments online no less, I was nervous about what he would do when freed from the tyranny of singable rhyme. I mean, look at Morrissey.

(Oh, you already were. Good. Keep eyeballing him. We may be able to prevent any more crimes against literature if we all just keep watching him like a hawk. Don't blink!)

What a relief, then to find that Jim's debut novel is as funny, thoughtful, surprising and well crafted as the songs I've been enjoying for 18 years. Its focus on community life and social interaction reminded me of the great Kim Stanley Robinson, especially the Three Californias trilogy. The examination of social structures and the tension between dystopian and utopian models brought to mind Iain M Banks' politically charged Culture novels. Particularly impressive is his exploration of the interface between humanity and technology - it is timely, but nonetheless original enough to stand out in a field currently obsessed with the issue, and that's no mean feat.

But although Jim's book reminds me of some true greats, his unique voice shines through in the telling, making it far more than a collection of assembled themes and textures from other works. This delightful book is the creation of a huge talent and an important new voice in sci-fi. And there are sentences in here that made me grimace with envy, wishing I had written them.

I'm jealous that you have this terrific book ahead of you.

And while you read Jim's annoyingly accomplished book, I shall be over here with my fellow sci-fi writers starting a petition to prevent songwriters writing novels. There need to be strict lines of demarcation, so they can't cross the border and come over here to steal our jobs. People like Jim, who dare have more than one talent, need to be stopped. It's just not fair.

Preface by the Author

What follows here is a world and its inhabitants. This world is not so different from our own. Utopias and dystopias exist side by side. Ignorance, bliss, pain, wisdom, and comfort coexist not far from each other. The suddenness of change scars the human landscape as we adapt to it and resist it. Like our world today, change is swift, and information is accelerating. Communication remains essential and technological advancements continue to push us closer together. People resist changes they fear with violent behavior, seeking to subdue and control what they find abhorrent. Nothing is permanent.

I am aware that what I have created might be disorienting at first. It may take a while to get your bearings in this familiar and unfamiliar world. These are the sorts of novels I tend to like, and so, this is the novel I have written. It is my first. It is also the first in a series.

Frankly, I didn't want to write it. I spent five years avoiding it. The inspiration came, unbidden and fully formed on a bus between New York City and Boston and it would not leave me. Since then, I bored every last friend I have at every party and gathering, telling them about my idea for a novel. I became that dreadful person detailing my unwritten book to all who would politely listen. A few years ago, I realized that I could either be that very annoying person who told you about his idea for a novel, or I could be a slightly less annoying person who had written one. I realized I had no choice but to begin.

I'm glad I did. I hope you will be too.

— *Jim Infantino, Boston, MA, May 1, 2018*

The Wakeful Wanderer's Guide to New New England & Beyond

Jim Infantino

1. Reverside

He thought there might be something wrong with the birds. Turning his head, Marto took another look at the interior of the old writing room. On one wall, a hanging tapestry depicted a partridge hunted by men and dogs in a field of red. The partridge fluttered nervously. The dogs sniffed at the ground. Feeling thirsty, he glanced about looking for a goblet or a pitcher of wine. There wasn't one, so he stared back out the window at the birds. It wasn't the birds. The birds were fine. It was time to make a start.

> The Lester Sunshine Inn used to be a private mansion for wealthy families before it was sold and converted to a bed and breakfast. After The Great Tide, it was transformed into a shared salon where the Interconnected could dream and create in comfort and serenity. The next episode of the Wakeful Wanderer's Guide starts in this grand house, at a nexus of history and happenstance. Dear friends, followers, and readers, this is where our new adventure begins.
> — *The Wakeful Wanderer's Guide, Vol. 6, line 1*

Marto set his quill back down in the inkwell and re-read his opening paragraph. His clumsy scrawl rearranged itself into neat rows of graceful script on the antique page. Satisfied, he lifted his head to gaze back out over the Sea. He spied rock doves, ivory gulls, and terns playing over terraced groves of olive and lemon trees.

All at once he saw it. It was the sun, not the birds. The sun was setting in the East. It was stuck in the same position on the horizon for a half hour now, intersected by a thin pink cloud. His window was clearly overlooking the Ligurian coast of the Italian Peninsula and the sun was setting the wrong way. There was a rasping noise behind him. He spun to face the stone spiral staircase. He heard the scrape, clank, and rattle of metal chains coming from below. ["Wow, who wrote this?"] he thought-texted to no one.

Of course, he knew the answer. He gave ratings and feedback before sending the commands, ["save"] and ["exit"] and returned to the waking world.

The tower faded, as its floor, the sea, and the earth itself gave way to stars, moon, and sun before finally going black. There was a moment of vertigo as the body left its engaged state in the construct and found its natural position in the waking world. Marto's eyes opened to daylight filtered through the tall, white-framed, rectangular window panes of the Lester Sunshine Inn.

Marto's full name was Marto « Maria « Denise « Martina « Joia « etc, a convention used by the Interconnected to trace the lineages of their foremothers. He sat, relaxing on a sofa in the parlor. The Inn was a sturdy stone and beam home, built in the grand style of the late nineteenth century. It could well withstand the violent storms that hit so often these autumn days.

Near him on the threadbare rectangular sofas and shabby geometric chairs were two dozen dreamers, super-mods, and socials. The faded 200-year-old Iranian rug was slowly turning to dust. A large industrial steel coffee table hunkered low and bare. The shabby interior was a feature of the Inn, considered charming by most. Marto was too accustomed to it to find it charming. He wanted a breakfast bulb.

His feedback on the medieval writing castle received a response by its creator. Delamine « Tourea « Yasmine « Delphinia « Rosemarie « etc took issue with him at once. ["The sun isn't setting, it's rising,"] she thought-texted him from the Great Lakes tribe in Lakeshore. ["Though I am honored by your review,"] she added.

["There is a distinct difference in both the temperature and quality of light. It did not seem like a sunrise to me,"] Marto countered, ["I recommend some revision there."]

After a gap, Delamine expressed her appreciation for his valuable feedback. She requested he try again after she had made some changes.

["Also – what is with the clanking sound? Is it a dungeon?"]

["My other visitors find it romantic and exciting,"] Delamine returned. ["It has seen a fair bit of use but I can remove it for you as a personal config."]

["Well, if you are after romance, a little wine would be nice. Maybe something from the era if you can find the data. It also should definitely be sunset. Put a window on the other side or move the whole construct to the western coastline. The incongruity was too distracting for me. I thank you, Del. While your new creation does not fit my current needs, I continue to be a fan. Until next time,"] Marto replied, signing off.

He appended his review with pleasant thoughts about the eagerness and expertise of the villa's author, pausing midway to accept a breakfast bulb from a member of his tribe.

Marto stayed, when he was not out roaming and writing, in Reverside. Located near the rebuilt Tappan Zee Bridge, it was one of the largest tribal communities in The Lower Hudson Valley. He fancied himself a historian, adding context and perspective to the ever-present mountains of data. His followers knew him as a travel writer.

He published both as rich-thext and in English text and his work was both re-thexted and translated by a growing number of fans. He had heard that his work was enjoyed by people as far away as the tribes of Australia and had some readership among the Luddite Neo-Feudalists. Marto regarded the latter as a high compliment, though it sometimes made him nervous.

The breakfast bulb was created by a local named Thirty/Fourteen, dreaming up dishes in the Inn's kitchen. Marto held a round bud-vase shaped vegetal wrap filled with spicy sweet beans, a touch of pickled beets and a single chicken egg. It was a gift from Thirty, delivered by Dexter « Wendi « Maria « Martina « Amparo « etc. This particular breakfast bulb was known by Thirty to be one of Marto's favorites.

Marto rated both the breakfast and the delivery highly and decided on a walk around the town to digest. The hot summer weather was finally giving way to autumn, such as it was, and the air felt dry. Marto stood in what once was a circular driveway, now a slight impression in the sheep shorn grass.

The Inn crouched atop a gentle hill with a commanding view of the town and the river. The great bridge was visible to the north and the center of the town was a 15-minute walk in the same direction.

The brisk air and quiet of the morning felt refreshing and rich. Marto passed groups of small cube-shaped dwellings staggered at angles along curving lanes. Various community members were waking up, exercising, stretching, and starting their day. Marto knew them all and sent greetings of ["good morning,"] with replies in kind. At the end of Benedict Lane, a new home was being printed, dotted with hundreds of palm-sized robots. It was nearly complete.

Suspending his usual intake of the day's news, he focused on the undistracted feeling of walking. The path beneath his feet was dark gray and smooth, comfortable even with bare feet, which was the custom in Reverside. The surface had a dark gray sheen and it curved gently to the middle. Thinking about the benefit of roads in his everyday life, Marto decided to give spontaneous Merit to the local road techs; Dizzy, Mem, Lacy, and Bryce.

Up ahead of him, he saw Piter and waved.

["Morning, Marto!"] Piter sent.

["Morning Piter, how goes the nursery?"]

["Just coming from there."] Piter was eating something as he walked past. ["Taking a break from Astrud and Billi. They were up and down a lot last night. They're fine now. Normal baby stuff. I hear you are heading out soon?"]

["Yup, just putting things in order before the trip."]

["Taking the unicycle?"]

["Of course!"]

["I love the unicycle. Keep an eye out for the critters! They tend to trip you up."]

Marto laughed. ["I will,"] he sent.

He looked up and saw a group of children teasing apart a dandelion cube with bamboo poles. The impacts sent the photosynthetic seedlings into the air. Tiny and light, they would find updrafts and suck up enough carbon and methane to drop back to earth. A lucky few would become the seed for a new cube. Dandelion cubes like this one would break apart on their own given time but children in tribes everywhere loved to tease them apart as soon as they showed signs of sprouting. The children at this cube were singing a revised version of Frère Jaques out loud.

"Frère Jacques, Frère Jacques, Où êtes-vous? Où êtes-vous?
L'ouragan arrive – eh! L'ouragan arrive – eh!
Entrez-Vous. Entrez-Vous."

Following the path toward his home, he glanced at the top of the enormous blade farm in the north of Reverside. Recently reconstructed, its design was like many other vertical farms but with an innovative feature keeping it safe from the frequent and violent storms. The entire 150 meters tall, 100 meters long, 200-hectare farm was able to collapse into the ground to protect itself during a hurricane or tornado. It was a major upgrade for Reverside and sat on what used to be a high school football field. Its author was Maxtor « Dorina « Georgina « Chari « Shandra « etc, known to all as Maxtor Uber G, of stratospheric Merit. His each and every wish was fulfilled before he ever had to think of it.

The leaves in the trees were shifting the morning light along the path leading to his home. It was a two-story cube with a bed in the loft above, a low table and a series of cushions below. He had been inhabiting it for a year and a half, living through the seasons after his last tour. By tomorrow night, he thought, this house will shelter someone else.

Two gifts were waiting for him in gratitude for the launch of his new tour. One was a beautiful new cup, fired in the local kiln, brown but with a sheen making it look like copper; the other, a pale blue wool and nano-mesh shirt. He sent thank yous and ratings. Marto joked with Seemi « Gisella « Yadael « Isha « Hester « etc, who left the shirt, mentioning his current one was an eyesore.

Once at home, he returned to his writing.

Lester Sunshine, born Lester Martin Chandler (1965 - 2033) moved from Stone Mountain, Georgia, in 1992 to establish this Inn at Tarrytown with a sizable and reluctant inheritance from his father, Lester Norman Chandler III (1923 - 1989), a veteran of both the Second World and Korean Wars [video compilation], who made his fortune importing and selling goods from the Philippines [geographical/historical blast]. Lester Martin, eager to leave his southern, patrilineal, homophobic past, legally changed his last name to Sunshine, thereby adding a bit of fun to the Inn's name [audio sample]. Once established in his new home, Lester enjoyed the freedom and vigor of a refreshing variety of guests as they made their way to him from the cities of New York, Philadelphia, and Boston for weekends, weddings, and holidays. Soon, the Inn thrived as a destination for the artistic and creative. It was called 'A Haven on the Hudson' [from the 2002 HTML review] for the capitalist and poet alike.

– The Wakeful Wanderer's Guide, Vol. 6, line 2

A blast of information interrupted Marto from his seat at Hemingway's tiny studio desk in the long-lost Florida Keys. Contained within the raw stream was a collection of sea level measurements in the South China Seas during the end of the twentieth century. He also saw numbers for strength and frequency of tornados in and around Atlanta from the same period. Marto wanted to reply with a query for context but he surmised what had happened. A few days ago, while doing some research, he had adjusted the parameters of his personal algorithm to include voluntary-verbals and super-mods. He threw up a hasty filter so his concentration wouldn't be broken by any more raw data and tried to continue writing.

Not all who visit the Lester Sunshine Inn are aware of its rich history and contributions to our society. It may seem odd to you that such an ordinary point on the map could have had such a profound impact on what we all now take for granted. If we look closely at this nexus in time and location, we can see a series of collisions of both people and ideas combining to create the underlying code of our current existence.

— The Wakeful Wanderer's Guide, Vol. 6, line 3

The virtual Keys were comprehensively sourced. They were collected from memories and map data and compiled by a vast community of creators. In it, a visitor was able to roam from island to island and even get a little lost.

Giving up on his writing for the time being, Marto left the circular tabs of the black Royal typewriter to walk to the center hallway. He stopped to pet one of the six-toed cats and grabbed a coffee from the kitchen. A stroll outside the grounds had him gazing at the Gulf. Seagulls swooped and called near a sign declaring "90 miles to Cuba." Key West was empty. Only a few of the Interconnected roamed from place to place, soaking in the bygone calm. Marto felt a creeping sadness and returned to the Waking.

He felt the ghost of the construct coffee fading in his mouth and decided he desperately wanted a real coffee, or something as close to it as possible. It was getting near lunchtime and he was alerted to a desire from someone nearby. It was a new arrival named Nora « Jennifer « Susan « Barbara « Rose « etc. Marto was glad she had figured out how to post a request. She was integrating well. He first flagged his own requested coffee as ["do not deliver"] to prevent an eager Merit seeker from bringing him a cup during his visit with Nora. Then he headed to the local pantry to make two omelets and pick up four tortillas. Down the hill was a water station where he filled his beautiful new cup for Nora, who waited for him closer to the river.

He strolled down the path to see the perplexed new arrival staring at the river from her porch.

["I just can't get used to it. So many voices, so many desires. I have to block it out. I know it's rude."]

["I made an omelet and brought a wrap,"] Marto responded as gently as he could. ["I don't really know if it's something you like. Hopefully, with time you will get more comfortable with the upgrade. This is how we all get along here."]

They ate in silence. Marto blocked his communications in empathy with the new arrival.

["It was hard you know, for so long. But I managed. I survived. This doesn't seem real now."]

Marto looked at the muddy Hudson through the leaves. ["This is real, you know. It's all real."]

["But do you know what it means really? I mean, you people doze about and fantasize all day and do nothing but bring gifts and food to each other. It doesn't seem like reality. It seems like you are all drug addicts or members of a delusional commune or a cult."]

["Well, it's not really so simple. I think you know we frown on chemical addiction here, so if we seem like addicts, it must be our tendency to sit still while we work. As for the comparison to a commune or cult, we have no single charismatic leader and no single location. There is no particular belief system we all share, other than the system of Merit. As for the gifting..."] Marto could feel himself taking a defensive stance. He drew down her history again. ["Look, we know you've been through a lot. This is a big transition. Give it time."]

"But you just keep bringing me things!" She was shouting. "And it's so quiet here! Why don't you all say something?"

Marto paused. If she were anyone else, her Merit would suffer a severe drop. He composed himself.

["It's normal to feel like things are strange and out of balance. This is all new to you. Yes, we do things differently than you are used to. We gift and request rather than trade. You have adapted to thexting extremely well for a noob. When you are ready you can find ways to gift as well as receive. Right now you need to rest and adjust. Please try to limit your responses to thext. This was agreed."]

["You're all a bunch of fucking xombies!"] Nora thexted reflexively. Her eyes widened. ["I'm sorry. I didn't mean to... I guess I mean, I just don't get what is in it for you?"]

Marto explained that the tribe had agreed to bring her in by consensus. They occasionally accepted selected outsiders in need, ready for interconnected life. The benefit to the tribe was new hands, new perspective, and numbers. Nora was quiet again after this exchange and after sitting with her a while, he decided to leave her to digest the omelet and ideas. He headed back in the direction of the Sunshine Inn.

Halfway to the top was a pop-up cafe. A pot of real, actual coffee – a miracle in a cup was waiting for him as he relaxed again among familiar minds. Checking on the origin, he found it had been grown in a vertical farm in North Adams and roasted in Great Barrington. A sack had arrived at Reverside via a Merit-seeking fan of the community. It was a rare treat and discussion was underway among the foodies of the tribe as to how it could be grown and or roasted locally. He drank a cupful, heaped praise on all involved, poured more into a communal mug and strolled back to the comfortable lounge at the Inn. ["There's nothing like an imminent departure,"] he thexted publicly, ["to help you appreciate the simple beauty of your home tribe."] These thoughts were met with cheerful approval.

Shortly he was back at Hemingway's desk, returning to his writing.

Though no one person can claim responsibility for the demise of credit and the rise of Merit, Lester Sunshine is one of the few who cannot be denied his defining contributions. This is a subject of much discussion and debate but it is this writer's humble opinion, that without the Sunday Sunshine Clatch [image], our way of life would be impossible.

A few dozen articles on the end of accumulation and the extinction of quid pro quo were published by members of the Sunshine Clatch in the mid-aughts and were roundly dismissed by the general public as communist drivel or the product of nontrivial quantities of cannabis smoke. It wasn't until a decade had passed that these principles were put into action by way of the Sunshine app and corresponding social network. By the time the barons of credit saw the danger, it was too late to stop it. Besides which, the old world of banking and hoarding was already facing its own growing doom.

– The Wakeful Wanderer's Guide, Vol. 6, lines 4 & 5

Marto stopped again to review. The word 'doom' pushed heavily into the paper like a dead rat. In the overgrown gardens below the writing room, Marto imagined a slew of dead rats, killed by the cats, or an inevitable disaster and, as he imagined it, so it was. ["save, exit"] he thought and was back in the Sunshine.

"So you're the famous Marto."

She was tall and dark-skinned with bright green eyes and a spherical puff of sprouting green around her head. She was physically speaking to him, with words. Marto was taken aback for a moment, unaccustomed to someone talking aloud at the Inn and tried to find his voice.

"I am ... Marto, um, I mean, I am ... he."

"I'm a fan of your writings. My aunt introduced them to me. I loved your book on the Great Lakes tribes."

Reflexively, Marto made a query as to her identity and got nothing. This made sense, as she was a talker. He blinked a bit and tried to re-engage his vocal cords to voice a response.

"You are ... a voluntary-verbal?"

"Mandatory," she responded, "though I can receive thext and information about the weather. I'm not a Phobic," she touched the side of her head behind her right ear, "I just like to stay mostly in the here and now."

"I am a voluntary myself. At home here, I thext, but in my travels I often have occasion to speak aloud. Welcome."

Two of the lounging visitors to the Inn were staring at them, surprised. The silence of the room had been cut through by the sound of their voices and it was, to them, as if lightning had struck the metal coffee table.

"What can I call you?"

"Helen," she said. "Forgive me for not reciting all my fore-mothers. Just Helen, if you don't mind."

"An archaic name," he blurted this out before thinking. Realizing this was rude, he checked his Merit for an incremental drop and remembered she was not rating him. The conversation was, so far, just between the two of them. Relieved and embarrassed, he continued,

"There's much history in your name. A fine name."

"My grandmother's."

"Well, Helen « Somebody « Helen, etc, what brings you to the famed Lester Sunshine Inn?"

"You. I walked a long way to find you."

This was strange. Why would anyone seek him out on foot?

"I don't know what to say," said Marto. "I am not hard to find. I'm not hard to thext. You say you are not phobic but you have walked here from... where did you come from?"

"Livings-town, in The Jersey," said Helen.

"Okay, from The Jersey, 100 kilometers on foot to find me here, why, exactly?" Marto was beginning to become alarmed. This young disconnected woman could be anyone, here for any reason. She could even have been sent by one of the greedy takers in the Neo-Feudal Enclaves.

His alarm was registering in the minds of his tribe. They became ready. Marto was too distracted to notice but Helen saw it right away. The dreamers stirred. The loungers shifted their balance. Their eyes went dull and blank like the eyes of a frog watching a fly.

"Please tell your friends to calm down," Helen said with no small tinge of urgency. "I am not here to harm you. I have a message from your mother."

• • •

Marto is four. He is somewhere dry and flat. The sun is setting while he and his mom and dad eat pickled eggs. They look across the vast gray concrete expanse surrounding the huge metal box with a corner torn out of it. Marto has a fever and his father, a handsome man with a light brown beard, says they are going back to live with his brother in Boston. His mother's hands are cool as they touch his forehead. She smells like his old bedroom, he thinks. Marto is happy to be with his parents but even at his young age, he knows times are hard.

"There's your namesake, Marto," his mother says to him. "Sad to say we may not see one open again in our lifetimes. They were wonderful."

Tears fall on Marto's arm and the rain begins again, the sky dark and yellow-gray.

. . .

["This isn't a game,"] he thought. ["This isn't a memory. I don't know these people. It feels real but not like a construct. Where am I right now?"]

He opened his eyes and found himself once again in the Lester Sunshine Inn parlor, surrounded by the usual people and the mysterious traveler all looking down at him. He was lying on the floor.

["You blinked out M,"] thexted LalaUbriay. ["what happened to you?"]

["I was following and you vanished?"] thexted Hanford-D.

["Do you need anything? Are you hurt?"] thexted SpongeyPooBear.

More chimed in, concerned and curious.

"You passed out," said Helen, reaching down to help him up. Suddenly her wrist was swept behind her and her legs were forcibly bent at the knee taking her down hard. Her left hand was clasped behind her neck. She barely had time to gasp.

["I'm okay,"] Marto announced. ["I don't think she's an assassin."]

["Not your call M.,"] came Reyleena « Dorina « Silvia « Maritsa « etc, breaking in. ["Security algorithms dictate caution."]

Five tribal members rushed in with wet towels, cups of water, bandages, and medicines. Helen was gone and Marto was blocked from any information on the activities. He distractedly accepted treatment from his friends in a daze.

Several long minutes later, the danger past, the gifters gone, the occupants of the Lounge slipped back into their normal activities.

Normal « Gelty « Lydia « Martha « etc was working on a new design for miniature printer bots which connected to create large tidal energy collectors made out of sand. Gavin « Theresa « Josepha « Nikkika « etc was working on a new game environment, taking place in the ocean and could be used to guide submersible bots to build, reinforce, and reseed barrier reefs. Patti « Theresa « Josepha « Nikkika « etc, his bio-sister, was returning to a game set in the badlands where the enemy were Coally Rollers, riding their black smoke belching dune buggies and the good guys were eagles. Dada « Paulina « Rina « Sarah « etc, a super-mod, was working on a new method of caravan automation. The lounge was a hotbed of creativity.

Among these indifferent dreamers, Marto was supremely disquieted and agitated by what had just transpired. He went back to Delamine's writing villa and stared out the eastern window at the sea.

150 miles south in New Atlantic, Barnabas Yoniver IV raised his head from a goggle-display on his desk and regarded the silent audience assembled in his enormous seaside office.

"She's in," he said.

2. Shine

Grif liked to keep his bike shiny. He rubbed the rendered pig fat and corn oil along the gas tank and struts, down the exhaust. When the fat was boiled long enough it usually stopped stinking. This stuff was not boiled long enough. His bike was unpainted. He liked the way the sun hit the raw metal. Without paint, he could catch the rust before it took hold. Rust was the enemy. Parts were becoming harder to find.

He topped off the tank with ethanol and took a swig himself for the departed.

The sun was two hands above the horizon. Dust blowing up from the South had just become visible, the ghost of a pink stain padding the sky. It was too late in the day to be this hot but that meant nothing. Grif spat on the road, expecting it to sizzle. He heard Mike's bike before he could see him. He knew that sound anywhere.

Mike came back from Pittsburgh to say he got the gig. He asked for volunteers and of course, Grif said yes. So Grif got his bike ready and loaded up his saddlebags with provisions to meet the others by the clubhouse. They were heading east.

Grif and Mike were brothers. They played together in the dirt clumps behind the old motel. Grif had a set of old toy soldiers. Mike sometimes found firecrackers. When Mike's parents were murdered by xombies up north, Grif's dad took him in.

"Watch out for those goo-brains," he had told them both. "They don't look dangerous. You might think they're skinny and weak but they ain't. They don't talk, so don't try to reason with 'em. You run. They'll come at you before you can do anything – deadly evil. Just run. You run as fast as you can. You find me or anyone from our chapter. Don't let 'em get close to you."

Mike and Grif grew up together, survived the membership tests, and joined the same chapter as their dad. Mike was taller than Grif, had long straight black hair, and gray-blue eyes. He beat all challengers in hand to hand brawling and could drink his share of hooch and stay clear headed. Grif loved Mike, as a brother, as a member of the pack, and more. When Altus died, Mike became their chapter's leader.

Under his command, they raided weaker camps for water and supplies. No one dared mess with the Mennonites or the Amish but there were plenty of other farming communities to compel to servitude. They won over the fealty of several settlements under Mike's leadership but they lacked the support of one of the Boss Families. The wealth of one of the major families might provide the support they needed to grow their chapter and gain control of more land. This was why Mike had decided to go to Pittsburgh for the gig.

At sunrise, after a night of drinking and goodbyes, the crew gathered in the parking lot of the clubhouse under the old motel sign. Women and children stood outside the main office to watch the men line up for the trip. They wore leather vests with their club's logo painted on the back. "Enduring Vengeance," flames and a skull. It was the longest running club west of The Jersey and north of the growing southern dustbowl.

Mike and Grif knew the old roads from stories passed down from Altus. The pack was riding east on the inner-states. Most of it was passable. They rode in a long line, avoiding sinkholes and rubble where the road was too far gone. Roads like these needed tending and there was no one to tend to them now, except the xombies. You didn't want to ride on their roads anyway. If the road looked too good or got shiny it meant there were xombies near. Xombie roads were dark gray and shined like coal. The part they rode along now was safe, just a pale gray narrow strip between the encroaching trees and brush. Grif had been told the inner-states used to be at least twice this wide, smooth and easy on the wheels. Those days were long gone.

They camped the first night east of Pittsburgh, making do with what was left of an old service area. They passed that night without incident.

The next day, they circled around Scranton, another town under the control of one of the Boss Families. Scranton wasn't as wealthy as Pittsburgh and the clubs there were hostile to Enduring Vengeance. The pack took a wide berth. Mike told them they were getting close.

They were well past Scranton the third day out on the gig when Grif thought Mike missed a turnoff. The road had gotten shiny and wider, making everyone nervous. The pack kept going even though it meant they were in danger. Mike was the leader. No one questioned his directions. Night came and they made camp in a large flat square near a line of ruined long buildings with grass and trees growing up through the old concrete.

The pack spent the night drinking around a fire, like usual. Bedrolls were out for sleeping, everybody getting something to eat. A couple of the guys were playing shoulder punch, a couple of others were practicing knife throws. Grif was laying down, tired and drunk. The sky was clear and there was a slender crescent moon rising. The air was cooler here than back at the clubhouse. The group was in good spirits, excited about the job ahead, knowing it would mean more work if all went well. It took a long time before anyone saw the girl. She was standing, facing the fire, just past the edge of the camp, in a thin white dress, her eyes all in shadow.

Mike got up to point his rifle. There was a hissing noise. Mike fell. Grif thought he saw his head go off on its own, away from his body. Other members of the crew scrambled for their guns and they fell. Blood sprayed onto Grif's arm and into the fire. Grif forced himself to stay down, reached to the side for his rifle and shot in the direction of the girl. She wasn't there anymore. Someone was yelling behind him. He heard movement in the dark, coming from the old buildings and he was running in the direction of his bike.

He kicked the starter hard and was away. He counted six others who made it; Nate, Barrow, Trig, Lester, Dewey, and Haight. There should have been twenty more but Grif knew they weren't coming. They crested a hill and saw a bridge. It looked a mile long, spanning a big river. Grif checked behind him, expecting to see xombies. "Over the bridge!" he yelled to the others. He gunned his engine down the hill.

Grif yelled to his fellows, "Far side and make for the trees!" Mike was dead and he couldn't allow himself to think about it. He was next in line. The others followed him. He didn't know what the gig was. His only thought was to get the rest of the pack to safety. If they had the dynamite, he could have blown the bridge behind them once they crossed. All of that was back at the camp.

They roared across the long dark river, wind in their hair, drink in their guts, straining to put the danger behind them. There was a town ahead. Grif thought he may have made a mistake but it was too late to turn around. Only speed could save them now. Flashes of light sparked high up in the cables ahead of them causing Grif to rise up and get a look. Something punched him hard in the chest. He saw his bike go on without him. In the air, he reached to grab the handlebars again. Something else hit him in the eye and his body slid along the pavement to a stop.

3. Decompiler

One of the greatest disappointments of the twenty-first century was the advent of the Singularity. Predicted by Raymond Kurzweil in the early 1990s, the dawn of a new machine intelligence died with a frustrated whimper in the early 2030s as quantum machines reached all the landmarks of autonomous intelligence, without event. Greater and greater attempts to motivate machines to act of their own volition failed or were found to have been faked. Injection of random impulses only yielded random results. Programmed self-preservation models didn't lead to evidence of an effectual "self." It was argued this was due to a lack of pain and hunger, but every attempt to artificially create these couldn't be shown to have caused the actual experience. Others pointed out that the self was a false goal to begin with, but couldn't escape the problem that an intelligence existing without the illusion of a self didn't seem generally intelligent. Part of the blame was laid on all the attention paid to creating a specialized AI aimed at marketing goods and services rather than a generalized AI with no such goal in "mind."

The military, craving a motivated non-human soldier, cobbled together weaponized thinking machines to disastrous effect. After the deaths of victims in the hundreds of thousands by these robot killers, the Singularity was pronounced reached and also a non-event. Finally, in the 40s, plans to create these monsters were scrapped in favor of improved human and animal interfaces.

– The Wakeful Wanderer's Guide, Vol. 6, lines 44 and 45

Sleep that night was anything but uneventful. A game was afoot. This was bad timing before his journey. Attackers from the West activated countermeasures on the bridge. Marto played in the role of autonomous command from the second eastbound tower. The exercise was boring, but all players knew they would need extra cycles before waking. The Raiders, running on ethanol, both in their bikes and in their guts, came roaring over the bridge as if raw speed and enthusiasm alone would protect them. Hayden « Alia « Briana « Zoë « etc pointed to a lack of strategy in the attack. This may have been a simulation or it may have been real. Regardless, it was a regretful slaughter.

The glass-tipped gyros under Marto's command wrapped around the support cables of the bridge. Each gyro had a modicum of intelligence guiding it, expelled from its casing with a blast of compressed nitrogen. Viewing the action from high up on the bridge tower, he chose his targets, which lit up in bright red glowing bullseyes for the gyros to hit. One of his shots brought down the leader, landing square in his right eye.

The game took place in a kind of half sleep, similar to active dreaming, but requiring only a little focus. Remote operations like this one needed only minimal concentration compared to building, puzzles, adventure, possession, or invention games. Marto was able to stay in a restful state from the time the alarm stirred him until the attackers were down. The results were gory. The glass edges on the gyros cut through even the toughest armor at their rotational speed of 75,000 rpm. Gyros got stuck in the resulting mix of cloth, leather, bones, digestive acids, and blood, which was why a second wave of clean up commanders were roused to guide robotic deployers of decompilers.

Tribal members of lower Merit volunteer for this second duty, as it is an easy way to move up. The downside is, it can cause nightmares and is disgusting. Long ago, when he was a noob, Marto opted in for this chore. Thankfully, as his Merit rose, he received an upgrade to his forgetfulness implant and never had to volunteer again.

For all its unpleasantness, decompiler technology has been critical to a livable Anthropocene environment. People don't like to remember the aftermath of The Tide and its accompanying migration of people and viruses. If any upside to all the ensuing loss of life could be imagined, it was the necessary development and deployment of decompiler technology. The micro-robots distinguish between animate and inanimate organic material. They process what human beings would loathe to touch or smell, without burning it, or leaving it as food for troublesome insects and bacteria. They've been invaluable to humans and animals alike and, more than anything, have helped to eliminate new breeding grounds for parasites and pathogens. Without decompilers, human society would be at a loss to process the impossible accumulation of sewage, food waste, and bodies during the days following The Great Tide.

Decompiler tech, dreamed up by the augment pioneer Tara « Sibby « Maria « Lucy « Cynthia « etc, was achievable once the process for the auto-creation of nanotubes was integrated into independently programmed microscopic machines. The robots construct the tubes at a rate of a dozen a minute and insert them into the dead material. Liquid as gray water travels down the tube, away from the solids. The body or material is desiccated. Another robot collects the water and moves it to a neighboring tank for distillation. Finally, the dried remains are sorted into piles of carbon compounds, nitrogen, silicon and more. Some of these become the building blocks for more decompilers, the rest is transformed into dry fertilizer and other materials.

– The Wakeful Wanderer's Guide, Vol. 6, lines 46 & 47

It was 01:24:10 and Marto was still awake. He kept replaying Helen's removal in his mind. She seemed so harmless. Naturally, he trusted Reyleena and all the security team. Still, something about Helen seemed wrong. A mandatory-verbal with implants and greentops? Not likely.

What really bothered him was the message she said she carried from his mother. Marto's real mother had died giving birth to him. His father was killed by Raiders around the same time. He had seen images of them. The man and the woman by the broken box store did not match those images even a little. What possible trickery was Helen enacting? The longer he thought about it, the more Marto became uneasy so he decided to put it aside for the moment and take a late night walk around the town.

He rose out of bed, climbed down the ladder from his sleeping loft and walked out the door. The night was a cool 23°c, with low humidity. He should have been sleeping like a baby. Reverside was quiet and Marto's eyes adjusted to the dark in time to see two cats stalking nothing near the home of Zibli « Nikki « Laura « Hope « etc. Poor cats. He sent a command to one of the animal care stations to open a block away. That should make them happy.

The cats reminded him of his old friend Bruce Williams. Bruce was a librarian, living in a community called Yale Havens on the grounds of the old university. Bruce loved cats. He and his wife and daughter had nurtured a family of cats and took care of them in the old library. Other librarians began to take in strays as well, feeding them, providing them with litter and cleaning up after them. The cats became a staple in the library. When Marto arrived at Yale Havens on his first tour, the place was teeming with cats. The faint smell of cat urine pervaded the stacks. It took a little getting used to.

Bruce introduced Marto to the study of history. The library was in trouble when he arrived. Water had made its way almost to the entrance and the librarians were relocating books from the lower levels to the upper. Marto assisted in the process, and while he was resting, Bruce provided some books for him to read. The first one was "A People's History of the United States" by Howard Zinn. Marto was fascinated by it, he delved into other histories, and noticed the divergences of accounts of the past.

"How can there be so many contradictory accounts of what happened?" he asked Bruce.

"That's the beauty of the study of history. It's not just the study of the past, it's the study of the human mind," Bruce responded.

Marto had planned to continue on his travels after Yale Havens but the books kept him rooted to the library. He spent 5 months there, reading, and sharing what he read with his growing collection of followers. The rest of his time he spent helping the librarians rescue the volumes in the lower stacks and recruiting help from the tribes. At the end of a tiring day, he posted what became the first volume of what he called The Wakeful Wanderer's Guide.

> People have forgotten. Everything was different not so long ago, but people have forgotten. Back then we talked aloud to each other instead of thexting. We owned things and grew up in families. We carried computers in our pockets instead of our skulls. We drove and flew places. We watched movies on screens. Our food was delivered from far away. We paid taxes to governments. We worked for a living. We owned homes and land. We obeyed and broke the law. We spent. We saved. We could be alone if we wanted. The weather was kind. The cities grew tall. The communities sprawled. People have forgotten.
>
> We need people who remember. I remember and remind for those of us who have forgotten. I invite you to follow as I roam so we can remember together.
>
> *– The Wakeful Wanderer's Guide, Vol. 1, lines 1 & 2*

Marto's first tour was by no means a resounding success. Prior to his inspiration to be a wandering viewer for the members of his tribe, Marto took turns working at Reverside's vertical farm, and assisting the local road techs with debris cleanup and organizing the bots. One day, working for Dizzy, he wondered about how far the roads extended.

["Many of our upgraded roads reach deep into the East and a little further to the West. They extend far north, and south, through The Jersey. They are growing daily,"] Dizzy replied.

["Why do we need such an extensive series of upgraded roads if most of us never go anywhere?"] Marto asked.

["The majority of the traffic on them is by bots,"] Dizzy returned. ["They also distribute power from the solar, wind and tidal collectors. This helps with energy stability. The more upgraded roads we have, the better and safer our lives are. That's why road techs are so highly Merited."]

["But surely, some people wander these roads, right?"] Marto's imagination was sparked.

["Certainly. Sometimes we find Raiders on the roads and those have to be dealt with. They come after our supplies and wreak havoc if they get through our defenses. Sometimes, the Interconnected travel on them, but it's rare. Often it's done when a tribal member has to relocate."]

["How do they travel?"]

["Most go by foot, but bicycling is a popular method. Why are you asking?"]

["I'm not sure,"] Marto sent. ["I know I can see all the other towns remotely, but I wonder what it might be like to go there in person. I'm just thinking aloud. I wonder what would happen if I biked around and talked to people. Do you think anyone would follow me if I did?"]

["I suppose there is only one way to find out, Marto."] Dizzy gave him one of her lopsided grins.

4. Insomnia

The woven carbon lane outside his home felt a little like what he imagined carpeting felt like. He wondered how one might go about carpeting a lane or street in a town like this. He posted the idea for Dizzy or Mem or one of the other road techs to think about. Luckily Marto was not the only one awake this night. As soon as he thought about Mem, they pinged him back. They were up, self-serving at an umbrella bar not far away. ["come on by"] they sent. He did.

["Valerian tea."] Mem poured him a cup. It was cool and light yellow. Mem was older than Marto by a decade at least. They had a short mop of gray hair and bright brown eyes. Mem was wearing a woolen bot-knitted white tunic covering their strong, wiry body. They stood behind the bar from Marto, who sat on a stool.

["So the problem with outdoor carpets is the dust,"] said Mem, starting right in, ["I mean people used to vacuum them all the time. I suppose we could make bots to vacuum constantly – you know, it's funny. Those were among the first personal bots, that's the kind of thing you write about. But the energy required is prohibitive – also the noise. Imagine trying to sleep through that."]

["Can't they have solar tops? And couldn't they only run during the day?"] Marto sipped as he thexted.

["Thought of it already. Too much traffic during the day. Also, we would need a ton of them to be charging and running. A vacuum motor runs hot. It's not like the farm bots or armaments or decompilers which rest and work, rest and work. To keep the outdoor carpets clean enough to meet our health standards we would need to feed them energy from the central grid. It's too old-world. Wouldn't work."]

["Okay, but I'm not ready to give up yet. What if the individual fibers of the carpet performed the dust removal themselves? A spiral movement shuffling the particles to the edges at night?"] Marto was revolving on his swiveling bar stool, and starting to feel a bit dizzy.

["Closer."] Mem sipped the tea and took a biscuit from a tin on the bar. ["But now you are using the surface for movement, and each element would have a photon collector fitted into it. Could be bulky. Also, you get piles of dust around the edges to build up and blow around. Gutters can take care of much of it, but it's a strain on the system. You know we have solar collectors and kinetic generators built into the mesh you walk on now. Lots of surface area. Most of it gets fed into the homes; it also adds to the farm, which uses most of our energy. Plus, it's porous, so the dust settles down below. Seems like a waste to lose all the energy and efficiency just to have something cushier to walk on."] Mem was stirring their tea with another biscuit. The biscuits were flat and hard, baked from spelt and honey. The pop-up had no roof tonight, as rain was not expected for at least a day. The two friends could watch the quarter moon hovering like a lamp in the cloudless sky.

["Gah."] Marto was tired, but not sleepy. ["Not such a great idea after all. Darn it. Here I was thinking I would be the next Maxtor... or Mem!"]

["You are a great contributor, doing what you do, Marto. You know we are all lucky to have you here. The stories you write offer us new perspective, fresh thoughts, and new points of view."] Mem walked around to the other side of the bar, next to Marto. ["I love how you link the forgotten actors of our past to our current situation. When I follow your work, I see our world anew. I get a view into the broader natural and human environment. That helps techs like me come up with new projects to fit the tribes' needs better than we could without you. We all love your mind, my dear. You don't need to be a tech too."]

Marto was overcome with a wave of emotion. Tears came to his eyes. Before he knew what he was doing he was hugging Mem. It was awkward.

["Easy now darling,"] Mem sent, patting his back. ["I love you too.

Easy. Why don't you try to get back to sleep again? I do my best work at night. You can usually find me here again in the wee hours if you can't sleep."]

["I'm off tomorrow on my tour."] Marto sniffed, straightened. ["Not sure how long I will be away."]

["We will all be with you. Don't go offline for too long. We worry. I will be here when you get back. Sleep now."] Mem had a hand on Marto's shoulder. The warmth of it filtered down into his chest. It was time to go back to bed.

Sleep is sacred. Even the most heavily augmented value it for increased health and mental clarity. Without exception, those who have hacked their sleep have suffered serious consequences. Trying to control the body's natural rhythms can be deadly. One such cautionary tale was Hugh Reisenfeld, a silicon valley entrepreneur in the mid double 20s. A talented engineer, he was snapped up by SumoGen, for his pioneering work on bio-silicone implementation. Hugh became the leader of the team who developed the underlying software which has become the basis of all neural-app interfaces currently in use. His idea was simple and revolutionary, far surpassing the work previously achieved in the area of bionics. Recognizing the brain has no unified operating system, he designed an interface to present the brain with a stable and simple set of behaviors to which it could adapt. This handshake, once accepted by the hippocampus, would proceed to new and more complex sets of signals until the brain recognized it as a new sensory node. The preliminary studies with rats had allowed remote electronic noses to be successfully employed, and more complex remote sensors were planned.

The problem came when Hugh was wrestling with deadlines imposed by SumoGen's investors. If only they required less sleep, he thought, he and his team could accomplish so much more, and be able to deliver the core products in time to go public. He developed an augmentation using the company's tech to provide the benefits of having had a full night's rest in just 60 minutes. The implant simulated REM sleep cycles once every twelve minutes with three-minute breaks.

The entire team secretly had the implants installed and within a month, they had all adapted to them and were working 22 hours a day without any apparent side effects. They were overjoyed but too busy to adequately document all aspects of their transformation. The manic pace of their work continued for 105 days until insanity overtook all but one of them. Sadly, it was Hugh. While he was out getting coffee, his team members murdered each other in the lab with scalpels and other tools. He never recovered. The story went viral and SumoGen sank without a trace, except for their intellectual property which was appropriated by the US military for secret development, only to be leaked by a former SumoGen intern two years later.

– The Wakeful Wanderer's Guide, Vol. 6, lines 48 to 50

Marto put his pen down and stared at the old wooden desk. Something was still keeping him awake and he hated it. Most likely it was the Helen mystery. He decided to forget about it for now and exited the writing villa to get some rest.

After spending a little time inhabiting and guiding simple blade farm equipment in their nocturnal duties, he dropped into his natural dreams like falling off a horse into a bottomless well.

5. New Atlantic

The strongest knew it was a bad idea as it was happening but lacked the foresight to take the necessary steps. The generations devoured by grisly technologies succumbed like weak-willed addicts. They are young and old alike, rich and poor, African, European, Asian, Latino, Aboriginal, and whatnot. Lacking imagination, they hand over their humanity, privacy, and dignity in exchange for an artificial sense of belonging. We are overrun by a mass of cowards resembling teenage girls of yesteryear waiting by the phone for a call from their latest crush. Only a few of us have enough strength of character, good genes and willpower to fail to fall into this trap. Those of us who value the power of paper and ink, steel, and steam, loyalty and culture, tradition and fear of the Almighty God are too few and dwindling. The xombies thrive, as humanity falters. I have done all I can to defend our civilization. I pray those who follow me will succeed where I have failed.

As I die, my only comfort is this remnant of a world will fast follow me into the dust, and the faithful will join me in whatever Heaven awaits the just and true.

– Memoirs of Barnabas Yoniver II, page 484

Barnabas Yoniver, IV put down his grandfather's final book and gazed out over the threatening ocean skies. His ships were being moored in the newly formed harbor west of the submerged boardwalks and casinos, in what used to be Egg Harbor City. His men worked feverishly in preparation for the oncoming storm, and Barnabas wondered how much of his fleet would survive.

He liked to think that his granddad was the first to coin the term "xombies," a fitting metaphor for humanity's common enemy. The office library contained portrayals of the famous foe, imagined as lumbering hulks, and spelled with a 'z' instead of an 'x.' If only their battle now was that simple. The creators of the old zombie movies and novels lacked imagination and foresight. The current scourge of implanted humans was far more dangerous than the hordes of mindless undead could ever be.

New Atlantic was his town, passed down to him from father to first son for three generations. It had several bars, entertainment complexes, a trade hall, markets, schools, two churches, and a courthouse. It was civilization as it should be, kept defiantly intact by his family's strong hand, with the help of a few dozen armed constables.

Mary arrived with his morning tea. Barnabas wondered what he would do without his morning tea. Shipping lines to tea growers were expensive to maintain and several estates had gone dark, overcome by weather or xombies or both. Luckily, demand was low, limited to those with means, and Barnabas' family had connections to other enclaves to purchase from estates still in operation. They took gold, of course, the only currency that mattered. On the tray was an Indian estate Assam in one of his favorite antique pots, a bone china cup, beet sugar, cream, and a thin biscuit. Mary knew he liked his tea black with sugar but always added the cream as a formality.

'She steals the cream when she takes the tray down.' Barnabas thought to himself. He took a bite from the biscuit, added sugar to his tea, and poured out the cream into a potted plant.

Mary seemed unaffected. "Your ten o'clock meeting has arrived early," she said. "Mrs. Reynolds is in the waiting room."

"You can send her in, Mary," said Barnabas, straightening his blue cravat. "Bring us another cup and some more cream."

"Yes, sir," said Mary, bowing, as she left.

Barnabas sat sipping his tea in the lower half of his enormous sea-side office. His desk was higher up, in front of the floor-to-ceiling plate glass windows overlooking the darkening horizon. Three steps led down to a coffee table and four overstuffed chairs. Portraits of his grandfather and older relatives lined the walls. He sat between ferns and ficus, flowers and cactus. The room was intimidating.

Gladys Reynolds entered wearing her riding outfit. She had a restored antique red coat and white trousers above walnut colored polished leather boots. Barnabas was supposed to think she had ridden her horse all the way from Pittsburgh to see him here. He knew she had taken a chopper or a jeep the majority of the way. Likely she took a horse somewhere in Bryn Mawr or King of Prussia to give the sense she was a rugged noble traveler from years past. Even so, if she had ridden that way she would have had to come through the city, over the bridges and through Camden, which was in itself, impressive enough. Barnabas doubted she had donned the riding outfit and flown the whole way. He hadn't heard her chopper approaching.

"Hello, Barney," said Gladys. "How's the family?"

"Fuck my family. How's production, Glad? When can we expect new shipments? My customers are thirsty."

"Oh, come on now, doll. Let's not get right down to business. I've had a hard ride, and need to engage in a little civilized chit-chat before we haggle." Gladys pushed at Barnabas' shoulder playfully before settling into her chair and leaning back with a sigh.

"My family is a pain in my ass, thank you for asking. My wife is digging into my pockets and complaining there's nothing to do, nowhere to go, and nothing worthwhile to buy. She's right. My kids are self-entitled terrors to the locals, as is proper, considering their station. Keeping up our end here on the East Coast. How is your brood in the gateway to the Midwest?"

"Oh, everyone is as well as can be expected. Samuel is bedridden you know. Near the end they say, but he's a tough old fuck. He will survive longer than the doctors expect. Archie and Vanessa are learning the family business and taking care of the estates. Like your children, they exhibit behaviors according to their station. Estelle, well, we've lost touch with her, but I'm sure she will come crawling back for a taste of the lifestyle to which she is so accustomed. We've had a terrible time lately with the workers though. Dissidents spread ideas of equality and merit. Many of our workers have abandoned us. I'm sure they were infiltrated by a batch of those fucking net-wits. So labor has been scarce, but we've had a good season growing this new breed of Shortcorn. You need whiskey, gin, beer, or all three?"

"Shortcorn? Are you using xombie grain now?" Barnabas was shocked by this. Use of xombie tech by any of the major families was forbidden, a rule set in place by his grandfather and agreed to by all.

"We had to, Barney. Had no choice. Our traditional varietals of corn failed, and barley is out of the question lately. If we had not raided a local goo-brain farm and grain storage we would have been out of business."

Barnabas stared at his biscuit. "I understand Glad, but you know the families will not be happy when they hear this."

"Well, they are welcome to try and find another source for booze if they don't like it. It's just a grain you know, not tech. Doesn't blow over so easy is all, and it's a fucking perennial, which is brilliant. We have all been growing hobbit wheat anyway – it's more or less the same."

"How did you like that Surfs / Pirates game last week?" Barnabas grinned at her. "Extra innings, but we pretty much kicked your asses."

"Clearly, a fluke." Gladys smiled back. "The field was muddy. There were too many errors due to bad weather. We will correct that next season. I'm looking forward to football season."

Mary entered with more tea, another cup and saucer, cream, and more sugar. Gladys took her cup without a glance at the servant woman. Mary exited, her head low.

"We get plenty of cider and brandy from Saratoga and Montreal. We are stocked with it. However, the people like their beer and whiskey, as well as your gin. I have to keep them away from siphoning off the methanol from collectors south of here. Makes them sick. When can we expect a shipment?"

"The convoy is pulling across 76 now," said Gladys, sinking into her over-stuffed chair. "I'm here to collect payment in person."

"Well, you will have to wait until I inspect the shipment, old pal," said Barnabas, with a broad smile. "You know it's always POD in New

Atlantic. How odd of you to ask for money in advance. If I didn't know better, I would say you were trying to pull a fast one on me."

"Nothing of the kind, my dear friend. I'm on my way to Arlington is all, to talk to the departmental heads. I thought I could secure payment before I go talk to our esteemed friends there. You understand." Gladys smiled back, broad and friendly as can be.

Barnabas put his biscuit back down beside his teacup. Gladys was playing at something here, and he didn't know what it was. There was a threat implied in her audience with The Powers That Were. Tribute was paid by all of the major families in exchange for certain ephemeral protections, but the authority in Arlington had long been on the wane. A new alliance might be implied by her meeting, and Barnabas didn't want to be on the outside of such an arrangement. He would have time to pick apart her plan later.

"How, may I ask," said Barnabas, chewing, "do you expect to get there? I'm assuming you are chartering a boat from me, but as you can see," he waved the remainder of his tea cookie at the threatening skies, "waterways will be rough for a while. I don't imagine your horse would let you tough it out on the roads, especially past the tribes south of here."

"Oh, I'm at your mercy for the length of the storm of course, and count upon your famous hospitality. Perhaps the caravan will arrive before I can leave. If so, it'll be business as usual. If not," Gladys sipped at her tea, "I'm sure we can come to an understanding."

"Perhaps," said Barnabas.

"So," said Gladys, leaning in, "what are you doing up in Tarrytown?"

Barnabas did not allow himself to look surprised. "I have no idea what you're talking about."

"Come, come, Barney. You know how hard it is to keep a secret from the families. We know you have someone in there. What's going on? What do you hope to accomplish?"

"I have no one in Tarrytown. I don't know what you mean by a secret. You have been misinformed." Barnabas felt like his stomach was on fire. He wanted to kill her, find the snitch and kill him in the most elaborate way possible. Faces and names rushed through his head. His heart raced, as he carefully replaced the china cup in its saucer.

"I'm worried I've upset you, Barney. I'm sure it's merely random gossip. You know how dull things get. You can't beat a spy story for entertainment, but if it's false, it's false." Gladys' eyes were full of kindness and understanding and skill and deceit.

"It's discouraging you engage in such petty talk," sighed Barnabas, looking toward the gathering storm. "I know life is enervating in far-flung Pittsburgh, but that's no reason to entertain fantasies about my business. I have no reason to infiltrate some paltry Westchester junkie-huddle. My trade routes are strong and getting stronger. My workers are not in revolt, I can assure you. I supply valuable goods to you and yours. To be frank, I find this attempt to smear my good name a direct insult to my forefathers." He rose. "You are, as always, welcome to stay here for as long as you like. I don't forget my friends. I hope you keep it in mind the next time a random rumor comes to you through questionable channels. I have enemies in my ranks who are looking to advance unnaturally." Barnabas paused, hoping Gladys didn't take his comment as an admission. "I trust you to divulge your source when you are ready. You may think it over during your stay. I will treat any information you give me as confidential, of course. Now I must ask you to leave. I have preparations to make before the hurricane hits."

Gladys Reynolds put her cup down and rose. "I understand Barney. I have always understood. I ask, not only for myself but to calm the minds of other interested parties. If such a scheme were engaged, we should all be aware of it. Not that I'm saying there is such a scheme, mind you. You've convinced me. We only want to be sure we're all kept in the loop."

"Naturally," said Barnabas, swallowing back his rage. "Now, if you will, we'll catch up later over dinner."

Gladys smiled. "I look forward to it." She turned and left through the office's giant double door. She left it open, and Mary appeared.

"Leave me alone, Mary," Barnabas said. The doors closed. He rose, grabbed a cactus and threw it against the opposite wall, leaving a tear in the corner of a gigantic painting of his dearly departed grandfather.

"Brady!" He shouted, furious at himself for damaging the painting. "Brady! Brady! Brady! Get the fuck in here, Brady!"

6. Sherwood

The phrase "no one could have seen it coming" is almost never true. For every unlikely event, there are dozens to thousands of people prescient enough to either prevent it or adapt to it. Martina Lamartine, born in New Orleans in the summer of 1974, was one such predictor. She moved from Louisiana to Greenwich, CT, in 2006, after her family home had been wiped out by a storm. She wanted to be as far away from levees and high water as she could while still being near the water. Greenwich and the Long Island Sound seemed safe to her at the time.

— The Wakeful Wanderer's Guide, Vol. 6, line 100

The Boston Post Road was empty of the usual foot traffic east of Sherwood as Marto arrived from the Cross County. The day's ride had been lonely and uneventful. He encountered a few travelers and many autonomous caravans, slowly making their way along the major roads. The caravans crawled steadily along, according to their pre-programmed routes. Filling each to the very top were dozens to hundreds of tainers; smart boxes, negotiating their delivery from carrier to carrier.

Marto, like all of the moderately well Merited, traveled light. He wore his new shirt, a skull cap, and a woolen kilt. In his single pocket, he carried a few seed-bars for the first leg of his journey. He knew everything else he would need during his trip would be offered. The last time Marto had pedaled his way through here, there were pop-up shops up and down this stretch of the BPR. This time, they were sparse. The unicycle hummed beneath him, moving at a modest but easy clip. He was thirsty.

The BPR had remained the best kept up route along this part of the coast. Marto liked to think that this was thanks to the popularity his own posts during his first tour of the Northeast. The Merritt, heading off to the North, used to be the favorite way to go, due to its size and name, but in recent years the BPR had risen in popularity. Since The Tide, large lengths of old 95 had been washed out next to the eastern corridor tracks. Up ahead, even the BPR dove into the Sound, making Sherwood Hill a logical first stop on his tour.

He pedaled his neurally connected unicycle over the rebuilt bridge spanning the Byram River. He was checking to see if he had any new followers, when a blur of brown and white shot out in front of him, pitching the uni forward and dumping him on the ground.

The chipmunk paused at the side of the road. It was chewing rapidly, front paws close to its mouth. Then it was gone into the weeds. Marto cursed as he stood, brushed himself off, and climbed back on the uni. Luckily, his fall was more startling than painful. He checked again. His followership had increased slightly. They were replaying his fall in slow motion. Very funny. This was why Marto hated chipmunks.

Marto pedaled along another mile before heading onto a webbed carbon-fiber road going north. He couldn't find any evidence of the local population. Queries ahead showed that Sherwood was engaged in a Multi-User-Construct. Further inquiries came up blank, which was odd. It could have been something tactical, or a private game.

Then a gray-bearded man in a green flannel shirt, walking a big brown dog appeared, and Marto's uni went out from under him again. This time, he landed on his feet.

"Don't go up there, dude," the old timer said aloud. He was an older man, a Phobic, certainly. Marto couldn't ping him. "They don't wanna be disturbed."

"Interesting. Why not? What's going on there?"

"Sherwood tribe. They're locked in some kind of group activity thingy. I don't know enough about it and I wanna respect their privacy."

"Well, I'm on my way to see them and need a place to stop until they're ready. Do you have any water to share? I've been on the road all day," Marto asked, looking around the path for homes. None were intact. They were too far from the center of town.

"Yeah, I got water at my place. You're welcome to join me. I was just going home for supper."

["Who is this guy? Ask him where he's from,"] LalaUbriay thexted. Until now, Marto's followers had been quiet. Nothing eventful had happened on the road to this point, so they didn't thext their comments. Now they began to debate the situation in earnest. It was a good sign for the success of his trip. Intrigue can't be manufactured. When something unexpected happens, it tends to boost engagement.

"Thank you. I appreciate the invitation," Marto said walking with the man and the dog into the spindly woods. The unicycle followed them. "What should I call you? I'm Marto."

"Gene. Gene Hernandez." the man replied over his shoulder. "I'm originally from a long way south of here. Used to be Kentucky, just outside of Louisville. Then the whole state went mad. Those Vengeance gangs were everywhere. I was lucky to get out with Nero here." He nodded to his dog.

["Be careful M,"] Dizzy chimed in. ["He might be a shooter. Definitely looks phobic."]

"I walked all the way up here through Ohio and Pennsylvania," continued Gene, "now I guess most of it is called The Jersey. Long, lonely walk. We stayed clear of other people until we got to a spot north of here. Found some of your Interconnected friends – what you call yourselves, right? They helped us out. I've been living here since the locals set me up."

Marto could see a couple of homes ahead. They were aiming for a red saltbox colonial fit with printed structures where storm damage had hit. It was on its own near the top of a hill, and looked inviting, if a bit desolate. Marto felt a nagging apprehension. He wished a tribal delegation had met him instead of this outsider.

"When I came through here last, I was met by a contingent of the local tribe. I don't understand why they're not here," Marto said, sounding a little nervous. Gene could tell.

"Listen, I don't want to creep you out. We're harmless, Nero and me. Honest. The tribe... they're just locked in a thing. I can't say I fully understand it. I don't have any goo in my head. They told me you'd be coming through today and I was supposed to meet you. They wanted you to wait here until they're... finished?"

Marto could see a few chickens, a pair of goats and a horse near the old man's house. Then he noticed the children. They were playing around the back between the houses, becoming visible as he approached. They registered as Sherwood tribe and thexted him bright hellos with pictures and invitations to games. They didn't seem to be in any kind of distress. Several of Marto's followers connected with them and sent light happy messages and greetings. A few joined them in their games.

"As you can see," said Gene, "I'm sort of babysitting here today."

"What brought you to this area?" Marto asked, enjoying the back and forth between the children and his followers.

"Well, I would have headed south, but it's just dry and hot there. I've heard there were peaceful tribes around Texicohma and further west, but I was tired of all the hardscrabble feuding with the bikers and the Neo-Feudals. It's a young man's world and I really wanted peace and quiet. I heard it's peaceful here in the Northeast, so I thought I would go see for myself."

"You didn't want to settle in Quebec?" Marto wheeled his unicycle carefully over the uneven grass.

"No, that's not for me," Gene replied as if he had heard that question before. "Too many restrictions – I'm not crazy about the communist lifestyle."

"What about GreatLakes? Lots of peaceful tribes in GreatLakes. I gather you don't mind living on the outskirts of tribal life if they allow it."

"That was more or less a coin-flip." Queries came in regarding the meaning of the term. Marto let his other followers answer them. "I may not be connected to the network here, but I earn my way. The others keep score for me. They don't seem to mind. A few of them actually talk to me. I'm grateful."

["A Phobic with Merit? That's a new one!"] Trixie « Elizabeth «

Catherine « Bonny « etc chimed in. ["I wonder if we should allow this in Barrington?"]

This was succeeded by a heated debate on the pluses and minuses of opening a tribe up to those who were not connected. Security issues, the integrity of the community; the back and forth was too quick for Marto to track while maintaining verbal communication with his host.

Gene's home was tidy and rustic. Inside were several infants dozing in cribs, seven printed and one handmade, likely by Gene himself. One was sucking on a bottle filled with what Marto assumed was goat's milk. These were tended by two of the older children.

"Do you like eggs? I have plenty," said Gene. "I also have some fresh bread from a local baker named Yisa if you like. Real good bread. No bacon though, I really miss bacon."

"Eggs and bread would be great," said Marto, concealing his distaste at the idea of pig bellies burning on the stove. His followers launched into diatribes about the barbarity of eating dead animal flesh. "Do you implant your livestock?" he asked Gene.

"Not me, but the tribe insists. We get predators here and it's safer. Plus the Interconnected people like to 'inhabit' them for fun." He said this with a slight shudder.

"What about Nero?"

"Well, that's where I drew the line," said Gene firmly. "The dog's mine and I don't want any goo up in his head. Doesn't seem right." He chuckled a bit. "I mean he's already smarter than I am. I don't want him getting the upper hand, or else he'll end up taking me for walks.... Come to think of it, maybe he already does." Gene laughed. It was a deep soft series of exhalations. Marto decided he liked him.

["He's clearly pretty Phobic,"] thexted Jin « Sara « Lisa « Susan « etc ["the man is still living in the dark ages. An old world name and old world habits. How does Sherwood allow him to invade their space like this?"]

Gene poached the eggs, and served them atop toasted slices of yellow bread, with a dollop of habanero salsa. He made a pot of roasted dandelion tea and served it alongside. After a day's travel with nothing to eat but seed-bars, Marto found these offerings delicious and he said so. They ate on the deck watching the children playing their invisible games. Gene prepared snacks for the children as well, and they would stop by and smile before digging in.

"So, what brings you here to Sherwood? You come far?" Gene was leaning back in his chair, preparing to light a pipe.

"Well, I... Say, what are you smoking there?" asked Marto, indicating the wad of light green crammed into an old meerschaum. Unlike many of his stay-at-home friends back in Reverside, he had seen many people smoking before. Making a point of bringing it up was a just a tactic to whip up his audience, most of whom would find this exotic. He dimmed the inevitable storm of thexts expressing alarm and disgust, so he could enjoy the moment with Gene.

"Oh, sorry, my home, you know. It's a mix of marshmallow and marijuana. Packs a bit of a punch. Calms me down. Want some?"

"Cannabis. I'm familiar. No thanks. You grow it here?"

"The tribe does. You have to keep the females separated from all the other hemp plants, and those are everywhere you know. They have a series of glassed-in gardens. Grow it for medicinal use. They give it to me as part of the deal I have here."

"I would really love to hear more about your deal. It sounds interesting. To answer your question, I have just come east from Reverside by the Tappan Zee Bridge, down the remains of the Cross County and up the Post Road where you met me. I'm a travel writer of sorts. This is the first day of my new writing tour."

"Wow," said Gene, exhaling into the evening sky. "An actual journalist. I love it."

"I think of myself as more of a traveling historian, but I'll take journalist. I like to tie the present to the past."

"Hmm, mostly I just try to forget the past and stay in the present. But I'm intrigued. Do you have anything I can read?"

"Well, not with me, but if you have any printer bots and paper, I can export what I have so far. The thing is a work in progress."

"Oh, I don't keep too many bugs around. But I would really enjoy reading a copy of what you got. Maybe when the tribe wakes. Shouldn't be too much longer."

Gene Hernandez reclined in his hand-made rocker and puffed away, blissful. Marto decided to write a bit in the quiet of the early evening.

Martina ran a successful catering consulting business in Greenwich, CT, for two decades before she saw signs the rising tides were coming again, this time to affect everyone. She was distraught and alone in her perception, as real estate prices skyrocketed and the wealthiest continued to build sea-side palaces. She thought about moving inland, even though her home was above the eventual flood rise for the coming decades. She poured over topographical maps and knew the ensuing chaos would reach her home on Sherwood Lane before the water ever would. Facing a choice between moving her business and family to a new location, or digging in where she was, she chose the latter. Her children thought she was crazy.

She expanded her basement and stockpiled cans of food, water, guns, and supplies. Her husband humored her. They could afford it, and he knew he couldn't dissuade her from this new hobby, knowing her history. Before long, they lived atop a stocked bunker. Complaints from the neighbors poured in and neighborhood committees threatened to remove her. The lawn turned brown, the pool stayed dry, and the paint peeled off their cheerful Dutch Colonial home.

Though Martina was prescient, she failed to anticipate important details as events began to unfold. Disease [link to virus migration], The Vengeance [reference to bands of assassins who hunted down and killed the rich], and a decline in birth rate [link to information on Siberian Zika] quelled the general wave of violence she had so carefully prepared for. The onslaught which thinned out her part of the world was largely microscopic, and Martina underestimated her own response to these catastrophes. When times got tough, she found she was more inclined to help than hide, and those who witnessed her kindness remembered it in kind.

– The Wakeful Wanderer's Guide, Vol. 6, lines 101 to 103

Marto could now hear Sherwood Tribe. He had an idea why he couldn't hear them before. The children immediately started running off to the East along with the older kids carrying the infants, followed by the old man, and Nero. Gene was shouting, "Hang on now, slowly, slowly, wait for Gene!" Marto hopped on his uni and chased after them down the path.

Sherwood was a walled town. Printed fiber walls were not so much impenetrable as they allowed a 360-degree view of anything coming. Attackers could be stalled while the tribe prepared countermeasures. Sherwood's hilltop position also offered them the more traditional tactical advantage. Perched at the apex, the dark gray walls curved outwards like a gigantic black crown five meters tall.

Up the hill, the walls parted for the herd of children and one dog, closing before Marto and Gene arrived, out of breath.

"Nero?" called Gene. "Hey! Gimme back my dog!"

7. Dancing Out the Storm

There is no such thing as an absolute biological imperative. Our basic human impulses can be modified, improved, or bypassed with the right tech. This horrifies the Phobics so they call us Xombies, but we are not less or more than human. We are humanity interconnected. The whole idea of what is and is not human has always been too limited.

One example is the human need to reproduce. As we all should remember, by the mid-40s, Siberian Zika had rendered 58% of the world's human population infertile. This was a global disaster. Enough people either inherited an immunity or acquired one via gene modification therapy to maintain a low but steady birth rate in the following decades. Ironically, when humanity finally started coming out of this particular decline in fertility, 40% of the surviving humans had been upgraded and connected and had lost the majority of their interest in physical copulation, favoring mutual fantasies.

This is the conundrum in which we find ourselves today. Who doesn't like to hear the sounds of the newly born, or children at play in the lanes of our villages, towns, and commonwealths? What would we be willing to do to have more of that? For us, the answer is anything but the actual act itself, played out between two sweaty smelly bodies, slapping and panting, growing and birthing. It's repulsive. Our libidos are much better satisfied in elaborate beautiful or horrible fantasies, played out with sets of strangers or with friends, taking a myriad of forms, faces, and features. It's more satisfying than the real thing, so much more exciting and without all the mess.

– The Wakeful Wanderer's Guide, Vol. 6, lines 112 to 114

It had been an orgy, of course. As soon as the wall parted, letting the two men inside, Marto could see the flushed colors on the faces and necks of the adults. Not the sort of thing to which you invite children. It showed in the eyes of all the members of the tribe. They were goofy with the afterglow of it. How many hours had it lasted? Many were partially undressed, lazily reassembling their clothes.

This was especially surprising to Marto, not because he doubted an entire tribe could engage in such activity, but that any of them might have physically acted it out. His followers thexted like mad. The tribe thexted back, along the lines of ["so what?"] ["mind your own business,"] and ["it was fantastic."] Replays were requested and refused. The first day of his book tour was becoming an immediate success.

Inside the walls, Sherwood was bustling, full of activity. It was home to thousands of the better Merited. Sets of printed homes in circular lanes surrounded an enormous central geodesic dome. One or two of the original wooden homes remained here, patched up and rebuilt, a testimony to tribe's history. Marto approached a contingent near the western wall, where the children and adults were reuniting.

The children were shouting "Story man! Story man! Story man is here!" Children often shouted aloud. They had seen him at Gene's house and were setting the stage for a public telling later in the evening.

Marto blushed. He had not met the majority of these children, but the older ones must have told the younger ones. They may have created reenactments of the stories he led them through during his last visit. ["Thank you, children. I would be happy to lead a story later tonight. First I want to check in with your grownups here."]

["Marto, welcome back,"] John « Maryanne « Roberta « Carla « etc thexted while walking toward him. He was a big man, shirtless, with short photosynthetic hair growing out of the top of his head and spreading down his shoulders, back, and chest. He wore blue-green loose fitting draw-string pants. ["You arrived just in time. There is a cat-4 coming up the coast. We will need to stay inside tonight. You are welcome in the dome. I see you've met Gene."]

["Yes,"] replied Marto, looking over to the old outsider, who had finally found his dog, ["He's something else. What kind of arrangement do you have with him? I know my followers are curious."]

["He arrived a while back,"] John said, looking slightly uncomfortable. ["He was camped out in one of the houses outside the walls for weeks. We knew he was there, and he didn't seem interested in what we had, so we didn't bother him. That happens occasionally. Phobics passing through stay to the side of one of our communities, not causing any harm."]

["Fair point,"] said Marto, ["naturally, different tribes have different rules about it. Some accept the risk, and some don't."] Marto was being diplomatic, not trying to cast either practice in shadow. ["So what happened then?"]

["Well, he never left. He never came to talk, never walked away, just set himself up there with a bit of dried food and bags of seeds. He started a garden, and went hunting."] John winced, as Marto's followers let out the equivalent of a gasp. ["And we thought for sure he was going to starve to death. Then the storm happened."]

John knew he was being watched by Marto's followers because he did something you wouldn't bother to do unless you had people following; he released a blast of data with information about a storm hitting the Sherwood area four years ago. ["One of our sons was outside the wall when it hit. Wouldn't respond to queries or pings, no response. Turns out he was playing by the river earlier in the day, hit his head on a rock, passed out, and later rolled down into the water and was being washed away. He would have drowned if Gene had not been there. Gene picked him up and revived him and carried him back to us here. We let him and his dog stay with us for the duration of the storm, and he asked questions about our way of life; aloud, because he's phobic. Since then, we've had a symbiotic relationship with him. He's amiable and pleasant to be around. We all like Gene."]

["Have you any arrangement with him for Merit?"] Marto accepted a cider as he asked this. It was the burning question his followers wanted answered.

["Well, he has been a help with the less technical aspects of tribal life here. He's strong and works hard when given direction. It only seemed right to keep track of his Merit so we could start gifting him on a regular basis. What we did was make a model of him, and apply the Merit there."] Marto's following exploded in discussion. This day couldn't have been better. ["We tell him what his ratings are, but he doesn't get it. He keeps thinking about it like it's money. We try to explain, but it's no good."]

["How many of these kids are fathered by him?"] Marto was able to scoop this idea. He felt certain he had been the first to think of it. Surprised by both the boldness of the question and also its outrageous implications, the followers went silent.

["Six,"] sent John.

The followers exploded with questions, discussion, shock, disgust, everything. It was perfect. Several of them started engaging with John , and he found himself arguing too many points at once. Marto was losing him to the discussion scrum.

["John, ... John, ... John – I only have one more question. You said you created a model of Gene. What exactly does that mean?"]

["Oh, um, it's a construct. Like a guy in a house. It just sits there, and we award Merit to it instead of the actual person, because obviously, we can't."]

["Thanks, John, much appreciated."]

Marto walked toward the dome, leaving John to fend for himself among the flurry of questions, arguments, and protestations. He almost felt sorry for him.

At night in the central dome, with the wind whipping about the sturdy carbon fiber frame, Marto led the children in a story. They chose one he had told before, the last time he was in Sherwood, six years earlier. It was about a Giant named NoBo and a girl named Tilde, in a mythical land called the 27 lakes. NoBo seems fierce and frightening until he helps Tilde out of a pit, and they become friends and go out on adventures. Parts of the story came from the children themselves, and visuals and songs were jointly imagined, with Marto's guidance. Within 40 minutes, the young were all asleep, at which point the music started.

It was a rhythmic bricolage of drums, bird calls, waves, soaring high melodies and droning. Several members of the tribe who were expert in music imagining were creating it as they hopped, leaped, writhed, and strutted. The environment changed color and decoration with the music as imaginers added visuals to the dome via shared illusion. The walls gave way to underwater environments, film clips from the previous century, and abstract patterns. It was a dream dance, a pulsing beating heart. The crowd moved in and out of synch with each other, chaotic at times, then suddenly in unison as a common step took hold of one or several members of the group. The transitions from chaos to order also had a rhythm, in response to changes in the music, felt by all. It was libidinous and intoxicating. Sherwood knew how to party.

As the adults were dancing in the dome, Gene joined in, which Marto found amazing because he couldn't hear the music or see the visuals. To Gene, the celebration was only the rhythm of the tribe's feet, breathing, and inadvertent vocalizations. Marto admired this man, alone but not alone, living on the outskirts. He turned off the thumping rhythm and hypnotic illusions and followed along with Gene until the tribe collapsed and hunkered down for the night.

The next morning, the storm had passed. Sherwood members assessed the damage, began repairs. Part of the South wall had collapsed, along with a few smaller square dwellings. One of the glassed-in gardens was now a wreck, broken by a flying roof. A discussion started about building a blade farm like the one in Reverside. Livestock were all okay, protected by their own dome near the farms. Breakfast, offered by a subset of chefs called 'The mothers of glee,' arrived and was shared from member to member. It was a simple preparation of rice and peas in black bowls.

Scarlet « Marian « Elaine « Shandra « etc sat down next to Marto as he ate. Marto recognized her as one of the music creators from the dream dance the night before.

["I noticed you turned off the music last night,"] she thexted. ["Why? Didn't you like what we were laying down?"]

["I was dancing with Gene. I wanted to experience it the way he was."]

["But why would you want to dance without any music?"]

Scarlet was young, with a mane of tawny hair and a cat-like face. Marto got a glimpse of her tongue as she licked her whiskers. Likely it could lap water like a cat as well. He surmised she was completely non-verbal, unable to form spoken words. This was increasingly common among the younger members of the tribes.

Morphing into one or another animal form became popular in the early half of the century, but only within the more artistic communities. These mutations came at the end of a knife, with follicular implants, skin grafts, and silicone injections. They were unlike the current day variety, which took hold over time, guided by implanted interfaces; still, it was not without risks. Allergies could arise, eczema, food sensitivities, and worse. That said, it was her body to change, and since she could thext, she could remain a Merited member of the tribe.

["I was curious, so I tried experiencing things his way,"] responded Marto. ["Don't you ever wonder about how the people outside your tribe experience life?"]

["I don't think about it."] Scarlet's face was difficult to read. ["I don't suppose it concerns me what the unmerited do or think. If they don't contribute, they go away. It's a problem that solves itself, doesn't it?"]

["Maybe, but do you know where they go?"] Marto watched her reaction.

["Doesn't matter to me, so long as they don't come back unless they get better at giving. There's nothing worse than a greedy taker."]

["Is Gene a greedy taker?"]

["No, he's not. We have a model of him, and it's well Merited. He has simple wants so we can build those desires into his model. Sherwood loves Gene, so he has a place with us."] Scarlet was gazing at him sideways through oblong pupils. ["I don't see it changing much. It would be better if he went ahead and augmented. At least then he could dance with music and post his desires."]

["But he wouldn't be as interesting to me if he did."] Marto tried not to let his feelings show in these interviews. He couldn't help himself.

["He's a fascinating anomaly."]

Martina's decisive moment came in December of 2032. A storm surge combined with rising seas wiped out hundreds of homes along the Connecticut coastline. There was chaos in Greenwich as in other coastal towns. Equipped with a body cam, she rushed downhill to help residents out of their flooded homes. With the help of her family and friends, she led them back to her property on Sherwood Avenue. She opened her stores of survival supplies to them, minus any armaments, and created a makeshift refugee camp on her property. She was live broadcasting the event, and within a week, everyone in the world had seen it. She was a hero.

Gifts of food, blankets, and tons of other non-essentials flooded in. Martina and her growing following had done in an evening what FEMA could not. The Greenwich refugees were eventually relocated. Supplies from new fans continued to pour into Martina's address, along with a non-trivial amount of cash.

Rather than go back to hoarding these gifts against future disasters, Martina used her energies to set up an organization of volunteers up and down the coastline. The volunteers distributed the goods and money to those in need. With the help of the Sunshine App, her volunteers became known as heroes too.

The key functionality of the Sunshine App was to increase the popularity of people who gave their time and resources in an effort to aid others. It had yet to reach a tipping point in popularity. Martina and her volunteers gave the app a huge boost. Increasing numbers of her fans began to aspire to higher levels of helpfulness and Merit in order to become more popular online.

Over the next few years, she converted her home into a center for those who wanted to dedicate themselves to a connected life of generosity. In this way, the community of Sherwood, the first tribe, was born.

– The Wakeful Wanderer's Guide, Vol. 6, lines 121 to 125

8. Glenville

It was hard to leave Sherwood with its children, culture, history, dancing, and cuisine. He wanted to stay a little longer, but he had an obligation to his followers. Marto peddled down a little way to the South and east toward his next destination. The streets became less improved as he went, and he had to carry the uni over washed out sections of crumbling, light gray asphalt. The place where he was headed was back in the direction of the Sound and away from the Merritt, but he felt it was important to make this detour.

Over a little hill, he saw before him the run-down town of Glenville. It had been hit hard by the hurricane. Trees were knocked down, homes lay broken. Most were broken years ago. He tensed when he saw a paltry group of inhabitants walking in his direction because he knew what was about to happen.

Against all odds, we live in what can only be described as a series of Utopias. Like Troy, we are under attack from those who cling desperately to the past, but we manage to hold back those onslaughts through our intimate embrace of technology and our Interconnection. Those of us in the greater tribes enjoy the best this society can offer. We are the Meritorious because it is in our nature, and because we are good at it. Not everyone is good at gifting. Few of us wonder about our lesser friends and neighbors who disappear overnight, unable to contribute enough to stay in our communal embrace.

When the first papers outlining the basis for a Merit economy were published by the Sunday Sunshine Clatch over 80 years ago, critics derided them for embodying an idealistic form of egalitarianism. They called the writings 'naïve pablum,' the effect of which, if realized, would remove competition from the marketplace. The supporters of the papers, on the other hand, praised the Sunshine Clatch for their innovative vision of an economy where value was based not on scarcity but on plenty, and which, if realized, would end all poverty.

They were both wrong. Now that the Sunshine Clatch's ideas have borne fruit, there still remain winners and losers. Those who cannot keep up with the prospering generous do not merely evaporate as anyone in a position of privilege would dream, but soldier on as best they can in a lower realm.

– The Wakeful Wanderer's Guide, Vol. 6, lines 139 to 141

Marto adjusted his personal algorithms to allow communication from the people of Glenville. Immediately, offers of all kinds, both unrealistic and heartbreakingly realistic, poured in. He had to refuse most of them, accepting only water and a place to rest. His trip today had not been tiring, and he didn't need rest, but he accepted it anyway.

There were families here. In his scan of the community, he could see there were parents and children, aunts, uncles, and grandparents. The less Merited clung to each other in the antiquated groupings of their predecessors. Likely, the structure for the shared raising of young couldn't work here due to the lack of sophisticated connection, or general willingness. They were getting by here, but with limited tech, limited resources, limited connection, and limited, but enduring hope.

["Some of us were aware you would be coming here,"] thexted Thomas Ng. ["my son has made a painting for you to take on your travels."] Thomas handed Marto a piece of blue paper with the image of a man on a unicycle. Marto accepted it and rated it highly. His father and mother Theresa hugged their son and beamed. Marto felt that he might cry. He had no way to carry it with him. He looked at Thomas standing with a hand on each of his son's shoulders, and the ground shifted under his feet.

• • •

Marto is looking at his father's face. His father has no beard, his chin is bare, and he is smiling. Over his eyes are light-colored tortoise shell glasses. In his hand, he holds a toy airplane. The airplane is flying. There are mountains in the background capped with snow. The sky is a deep clear blue.

Marto's father passes the airplane to Marto, and now Marto is flying the plane, over the mountains. They are standing on the wooden balcony of a multi-story home, high above the ground. Marto feels like he is in the airplane, sailing over the tops of the mountains. Happiness fills his chest. He drops the plane and jumps into his father's arms. His father spins around, and the world spins around Marto. They are both laughing.

• • •

["Are you all right Marto?"] he heard a voice. His eyes opened, and he saw the concerned faces of the Ng family. His followers chimed in with messages of concern. He waved his hands up as if to clear the noise, clear the air, and hands grabbed his, to pull him up.

["Yes, I'm sorry. That's the second time it has happened to me. I might be more tired than I thought. It's probably nothing."]

It was definitely not nothing. That man was the same one from his previous blackout, but this time he seemed younger and happier. In the vision, he knew the man to be his actual father. This didn't match the story he had always been told about his past. His father died before he was born. Someone had either lied to him or these visions were a trick. In either case, he didn't have time to work it out. His mission was to shine a light on the less Merited people of Glenville. He straightened and tried to put on a neutral face.

["It's not nothing Marto,"] Dizzy thexted from Reverside, mirroring his own thoughts. ["You passed out again. You dropped right off the network. You were gone for almost a minute."]

["Do you need to lie down?"] Theresa Ng thexted. ["You can come inside and rest a bit before we show you around our town."]

["No, I'm fine,"] Marto lied. ["I just need to stand still for a little while and get my bearings again. I want to see more of your community now if you don't mind."]

The town had a view of the ruined shoreline. The tops of taller buildings stuck out of the surf past a gradual slope leading to the water's edge. Back toward him from the water, there were gardens, dogs, chickens, and sheep. The animals were unaugmented, the gardens exposed to the elements. Though the crops had been ravaged by the storm, the farming looked successful. These people were not starving. That was something.

["Have you been to Sherwood?"] asked Drocilla « Terri « Mimi « Joyce « etc ["I used to live there a while back. It was wonderful."]

["Yes, I've just come from there."]

["How did they manage in the storm?"] Drocilla shifted anxiously on her feet.

["Oh, they did all right, some minor damage, but nothing which can't be fixed."]

["That's good,"] she responded, pausing and then, ["I lost my home last night. Most of us stayed in the old high school. It was a bad storm. We could hear the power of it. It was frightening."]

["Now Drocilla,"] broke in Gerald « Lachme « Yeshe « Hester « etc, ["Don't trouble him with our petty issues. Can we get you anything to eat?"]

["No thank you, I ate before I left,"] thexted Marto. ["I'm fine."]

Theresa Ng looked at him sideways but said nothing.

["Who are these people?"] Chimed in Marto's follower, Nazboy2060 from Montpelier. ["They don't seem to be in Flow. Parents hoarding their children from the tribe? That's not right. Their community is a mess."]

["I recognize a couple of them,"] responded Robin « Marian « Johnatha « Roberta « etc, ["two of them at least. They used to be part of Sherwood. Now I guess they are outliers?"]

More of Marto's followers began discussing the sad state of affairs in Glenville. There were criticisms of the townspeople coming in. They blamed them for the run down condition of their town. Others chided those critics for their attitude. They didn't know about these people because they had either consciously forgotten them, or blocked all augments below a certain threshold of Merit. Marto let the conversation build. He was uneasy and knew this leg of his tour might cause him to lose some followers, but he had come here to deepen the scope of his tour. He had faith that in the end, it would be a net gain. He only hoped he had not come to an outlier town too soon.

["Thank you so much for visiting us, Marto,"] thexted Lauren « Halley « Marissa « Betsy « etc. She stood before him, an older woman with an air of authority about her. ["Many of us here are avid followers of your work. We admire your writing and reporting."] Marto rarely thought of himself as a reporter, but he entertained the idea and found it appealing. ["Our way of life here is different from the one you are accustomed to, I imagine. I invite you to look around and get to know us."]

["How do you manage your water supply?"] Marto asked. Part of his reason was selfish. He wanted to know what he was drinking.

["We have older generation humidity collectors, and a solar desalination generator connected to pumps which store the water uphill from here. The storage containers are enclosed. The water you are drinking, however, is direct from the collector with trace minerals added. It's pure, have no doubt."]

["Thank you,"] replied Marto. He was embarrassed about the selfish aspect of his query, which was so quickly sussed by Lauren. He changed the subject. ["I notice you have families living together here in Glenville."]

["Yes, some of our members are former inhabitants of other tribal communities who couldn't share their children with the tribe. We allow direct lineage parenting here. We also adopt children who are lost or cast out."]

["Cast out?"] Marto was incredulous. ["Do you mean from tribes like Sherwood?"] This was unimaginable. ["Does that really happen?"]

["In a way, yes. We have no hard evidence of children being left outside the walls, but passively the effect is the same. Some children never adapt to being so closely connected and monitored. Some children have social bonding issues. Some miss parents, who couldn't maintain their position in the tribe. They run away as soon as they are old enough."]

["This is awful,"] replied Marto. ["This is frankly astonishing. So you are saying some children don't adjust to our ways even when they are raised in them? And the tribes just let them disappear without looking for them? They forget them? If this is true, the tribes would bear major responsibility. I've never heard of this before, but it is worth checking out."] Marto walked a bit in silence as he let it all sink in. His followers were chatting like mad, most in flat denial, others calling for verification. Still more were open to the truth of it and called on an audit of their tribe's child care records. Marto dimmed the discussion to focus on his surroundings.

They were walking on old crumbled roads, toward the center of the town. A large group of people was waiting there. He could see the very young and the very old, wearing handmade clothes, a group of people carried shovels and hoes. They must have been working on the damaged crops. Marto's unicycle tagged along behind him a few paces. He was glad he had charged it back in Sherwood. He didn't know how much power this town was generating, and he didn't want to take any away, even if it was offered.

["Story man!"] A girl with short dark hair, maybe eight or nine approached. ["Will you lead a story tonight?"] Marto recognized her from Sherwood. She had been there during a previous visit. She had bright eyes and was smiling up at him. Behind her were other children, about her age, watching them.

["Of course I will,"] replied Marto. ["I would be happy to. You remember me? Were you there six years ago in Sherwood when I led a story before?"]

["Yes, I was only three then, but I remember. It made me happy. I told my friends about you."]

["Did you leave Sherwood afterward?"]

["Yes. I didn't like it there. It was too quiet. I didn't like the games the others played. I missed my mama. She had to leave before you came."]

["Did the people in the tribe force you to go?"]

["No, I sneaked away at night. I had to turn off my thinking so no one would notice. A storm had broken part of the wall. I got out that way. I walked around in the darkness, but I wasn't scared. I found my mama with my thinking and she came and got me."]

["I can't see your name, can you share it with me?"] Marto was used to being able to find the name of a person via thext, but the girl was not sharing it.

["Yes. I'm Maria. My mama is Susan Lamartine."]

Marto was caught short. This girl was a likely descendant of Martina, who founded Sherwood. Her mother had been unable to stay in the community. This was a sad shock. Marto had been researching this girl's great or great-great grandmother, highlighting her as a nexus of tribal life, and here was her progeny, outside the walls.

["This can't be right,"] posted Titus from Murray Hill ["She and her mother should be part of Sherwood."]

["She wanted to leave. I don't see what is wrong with that. We cannot hold onto members who don't want to stay with us,"] responded Nikki from T-Neck.

["She was only three when she left"] replied Dizzy from Reverside. ["Couldn't the tribe have noticed she was unhappy and done more to include her?"]

["She's referring to her patrilineal lineage, and not listing her foremothers,"] rebuffed Langfeld of Ogunquit, ["Her mother may have taken the father's name. It is possible she isn't a direct descendant. We need to know more. Researching."]

There were more responses and queries. It was determined that Susan, her mother, was, in fact, Susan « Brenda « Shakita « Martina « etc, a direct great-granddaughter of the founder of Sherwood. There were seven siblings and cousins total, and Susan was the only one living in an outlier community. Two were in tribes other than Sherwood. The girl's father, grandfather, and great-grandfather had all taken the founder's name.

Marto greeted the group of kids, many in thext, and some verbally. It was hard getting used to the ways of these outliers, but he was getting the hang of it. The community was not as depressed as he had first thought, but their limited means concerned him, as it did a growing number of his followers.

In the center of Glenville, there was a common square. It must have been a park or town green from before The Tide. There was an old stone bandstand, tables, a fire pit and other wooden structures forming what looked like shops around the edges. A few had minor storm damage, but the majority were intact. Marto settled in at one of the tables, and the town crowded around him, asking questions about his tour so far.

["I have only been out for two days now. You are my second stop,"] this was obvious to those who had been following his tour from the start. To others, it was a flattering surprise.

["Where is your pack? Don't you travel with food, water, or a tent?"] asked Donald « Martika « Beylea « Odessa « etc. He was older, in his seventies, maybe. He would have been young when the pandemics, tides, and depression were at their worst. He had white, tight wiry hair around the fringes of his head. He looked strong for his age. His arms were bare and they were dark and hardened.

["No need for one,"] replied Marto ["My gifts are my writings, my perspective, and my shared travels. I am offered whatever I need along the way."]

["Isn't it risky?"]

["Not when you live in Flow."]

["What do you mean by Flow?"]

["Flow is an easy state of giving and receiving,"] Marto said, sounding to himself like a corny lecturer from an old web-vid. ["It is a word you can apply to either an individual or a community."] Marto offered references for the community members who could receive rich-thext. ["I am fortunate my talents as a writer and observer are in great demand among a great number of the Interconnected. I offer my experience and perspective to my followers as I write and travel, and gain Merit in that way. Others gain Merit by supplying me with things they know I want by checking on my habits and preferences. I rate their gifts and in that way, their wants are more likely to be met with offers as their Merit grows. It's a flow of desire and fulfillment."]

["I think we all know the basics of the new economy,"] retorted Lily « Mia « Zoë « Ava « Aurelia « etc, a woman of similar age to Donald, with straight white hair and missing teeth, ["but that does clarify it a bit more. I wish there was a way to learn how to be 'in Flow.' I struggle with it. Like, I always assumed when you 'gift,' you should get something in return, right?"]

["Actually no,"] Marto replied, amazed at how this misunderstanding could still persist. ["You expect nothing in return for your gifts. That is what makes them gifts. It is easy to fall back into the failed ways of the past when you think along those lines. This used to be known as quid pro quo. What we do in Flow is quid pro nihilo – something for nothing."]

["But you do expect to get Merit."]

["Gain Merit. Yes, we hope to."]

["But isn't that something?"]

["I suppose you could look at it that way, but you would be missing the point. There is no negotiation for Merit. It's not something you hoard and spend like people used to with money. It's an attribute – part of your public persona. If I accept something from you – no, let's say if you accept something from me, your Merit does not go down for accepting it. You are not giving away your Merit to get something. Merit isn't something you have, it's part of who you are. You see?"]

["Not really, It seems like Merit is just a different kind of money. If you have it, you get things, if you don't you can't have them. You say it becomes an attribute...? It just sounds like the old aristocracy to me."] Her feet were planted, her expression hard. She seemed willing to learn about this but was blocked by the habits of her way of thinking. This was true of many of her generation. Unable to shift away from accumulation and exchange and toward the more open fluid reality of gifting, they suffered in the new world.

["Well, things themselves are given and used, but the notion of ownership is removed. Things are also in Flow. Our new economy isn't one of barter. There is no equivalency associated with our gifts. Does that help?"]

["Maybe"] Lily was straining. ["But it seems too idealistic to be real. There is a flaw in it somewhere, I think."]

["Well, it does seem to work in Sherwood, doesn't it?"]

["I suppose."] Lily's ideas were hardened, Marto thought. Evidence was not enough to persuade her. She imagined the Merited tribes existed in a cloud-like fantasy. He thought of Nora by the river and her own resistance. He tried again.

["I agree, Merit can be hard to understand. It's like a game. When you give-up, which means giving to someone with higher Merit than yourself, your Merit increases as a function of the Merit of the receiver. When you give-down, it goes up less or stays the same. That way, the flow of gifts is ever upward, and the object of the game is to move upwards in the direction of the Flow."]

["So if I give you everything I have, and I am left with nothing, my Merit might go up, but I am still left with nothing?"]

["But not for long, Lily. As your Merit increases, so does the Flow of gifts in your direction. You are positioning yourself to receive more, by gifting more."]

Their conversation had attracted other people from Glenville. They were walking toward the green to watch the two of them argue. Over the next few hours, Marto found himself holding a public class on the basics of a Merit-based economy. He felt unqualified, as there were hundreds of super-mods who dedicated their lives to the analysis of Flow. But, none of them were here with the people of Glenville, so it was up to him. He did the best he could, choosing not to incorporate too many suggestions from his followers, who offered them enthusiastically, regardless.

Finally, the crowd thinned out, and the inhabitants started making preparations for the evening. Lauren and Thomas remained, along with

Thomas' son, whose name, Marto learned was Bruce, and Thomas' father, Steven. Marto turned his attention back to Lauren, who seemed to be either the mayor or sheriff of Glenville. The idea of a community having a leader was repugnant to Marto's followers, but Marto understood it. They needed her to inspire them with confidence, and keep the community together. There was nothing wrong with it. She seemed to be doing a hero's job.

["What do you have in the way of defenses?"] He asked her.

["Thankfully, we've not had much need for them,"] she replied. ["We have Sherwood to the Northwest and Cos tribe to the Northeast. Raiders don't tend to try their luck between the two of them, so we are pretty safe. Some of us train. We have a store of old firearms and modified bow weapons, but we have not had to use them,"]

["You are fortunate,"] thexted Marto. ["We sometimes catch them coming over the bridge at Reverside, but we have advanced countermeasures. Have you thought of having them installed here? Perhaps one of the two tribes would be interested in helping you with that?"]

["They barely know we exist Marto. I don't think they would find it worth their while."]

["Maybe,"] he smiled.

9. Neighbors

Change is hard. Our ways of thinking are invisible to us. The study of history, as I see it, isn't just the study of events, but the study of thought. We think we see the world as it is, but really, we see the world as we think it is. When the way of thinking changes in a culture as a whole, the whole world changes from the perspective of that culture.

Looking into the deep past, one can see the evidence of this in the Himalayas over twelve hundred years ago. Records have it, a traveling monk from India named Padmasambhava [pronunciation sample] was on a mission to bring his radical Buddhist teachings to the inhabitants of the Himalayan Mountains. On arrival, he found a wide region of warlords and nomads. He established the first Buddhist monastery in the remote town of Samye. He was a profound visionary. He taught the idea that enlightenment could be realized not just by individuals, but by society as a whole. This teaching spread throughout the Himalayas. In a few hundred years the region was transformed into a unified nation focused on compassion and contemplation. In spite of invasions from China and Mongolia, the seat of power shifted from the forceful to the mindful. Regardless of internal battles and political intrigue, the people of that country restructured their world in a way lasting for the better part of a thousand years.

More recently, with environmental changes and the fall of the global economy, increasing numbers of people have changed their ideas about their relationship to each other. Before this shift, a thing was to be owned, items had a numerical value, and people had a worth based on the value of their things. After the shift, things were useful, but never owned, and people became prosperous purely because of their generosity.

As is true with every sea change in thinking, there are always people who cannot or will not adapt. The framework of unit-based worth was in place for millennia, shaping the thoughts and realities of people throughout the world. People awoke to this way of thinking and they dreamed in this way of thinking. Their every idea had its roots in the concepts of exchanges and equivalencies, in the notions of prosperity and poverty. Such a prevalent and powerful force does not die easily. But it does die eventually.

– The Wakeful Wanderer's Guide Vol. 6, lines 143 - 146

In the evening, as the sun was setting, and after an enjoyable meal, Marto led a story for the children in the still, warm air of the town's central square. The story was the same one he had led in Sherwood, but this time both in rich-thext and verbally, so all the children could follow along and provide their additions. At the conclusion, the children began to doze off in their parent's arms. Marto stood up and noticed John from Sherwood arriving, carrying a basket of bread and biscuits. Gradually, he was noticed by the others in the square. Marto had been so caught up in his story, he forgot to check for the members of Sherwood he had secretly hoped would be arriving.

"Ex-cuse me," John said aloud, in a hesitant voice. "we have come here from a ... neighboring tribe. We are looking for ... Lauren?"

["I am Lauren,"] replied Lauren. ["No need to speak aloud. We are not phobic."]

["Many of us were following Marto and we were moved by his experiences in your village,"] thexted John. ["It was decided one of us would come and introduce ... ourselves,"] the crowd was parting. The people were in shock. No one from Sherwood had come here in many years.

Many of the inhabitants were angry. ["We've all been right here, right outside your walls! All this time and, you just noticed us?"] they threw their thoughts at him, ["What is this about? What do you lofty high ones want?"] others asked.

John remained calm. ["You all have a right to be angry at us. I know you must have a lot of questions."]

The parents who had adopted children seeking refuge from Sherwood expressed their suspicions. ["Are you here to take our children back? You can't. They are ours. They live with us now."]

["Absolutely not! We don't want to take your children away."] John was thexting in a calm and kind tone. ["I'm here on behalf of my tribe – and on behalf of other tribes. You see, we were devastated to learn any of the children in our care didn't feel at home with us. We were more ashamed to learn we had taken no notice of their departures. How did we not know this? Did we ignore it? How could we let ourselves forget them? Our shame was multiplied by the fact they left us to live with a community of people less Merited than ourselves. They chose to be outliers rather than stay with us."]

Glenville exploded with more anger at this. ["Wait! We knew it was ignorance and self-aggrandizement. Because of our shame, and because we have ignored your existence for so long, our whole sense of Merit had been drawn into question. You see, we consider ourselves the most generous of people. We never thought to question it, but now..."]

["You fear you are greedy. Greedy Takers,"] Lauren injected.

John glanced at her. ["Yes. In our lack of care, eager to protect ourselves from our mistakes, greedy takers. Over the past few hours, our whole algorithm has been thrown off. People are downhearted. The sadness spread not only within our tribe but to other tribes as well. Now we are in crisis. So it was agreed I would walk here, and ask if it would be okay to arrange a meeting."]

["A meeting? With whom?"] Nico « Barbara « Sachiko « Mami « etc asked.

["At this moment, eleven members of Sherwood and 13 members of Cos are waiting right outside this community. If it's okay with you, they will walk to where we are now. Just to meet, communicate, and frankly, we don't know. We don't have a plan. We only want to figure out where we went wrong. We do have tech which would be useful to you for defense. We have other things you may need. Please let's meet."]

["And what do you want in return?"] Lily asked. Marto felt himself roll his eyes at her insistence on clinging to exchanges, unable to accept the gifts as gifts.

["Naturally, we want nothing in return,"] replied John. ["As I said, we are in crisis. Our offerings are a way for us to open up and discover, and hopefully move beyond."]

["Perhaps,"] thexted Lauren, ["you might want to talk to the parents of the refugee children. If you understand why they left, you might be able to prevent similar future suffering."]

["We would accept this gladly,"] John said.

It was agreed. The members of Sherwood and Cos arrived in Glenville. Preliminary communications were opened between the three communities and plans for the gifting of defense, water, and road tech was approved by the two higher tribes. Furthermore, tutelage on living in Flow was offered for any members of Glenville who were interested. Marto remained on the outskirts of these interactions. He was in awe of what had transpired with this one unanticipated diversion in his plans. He thought of Scarlet. He might never have come here if not for his talk with her. He pinged her. She didn't respond.

The discussion went deep into the night. Glenville's mood changed from astonished to apprehensive to optimistic. Even though Sherwood and Cos were not able to reunite with members who had left and come here, they would never again be able to ignore them. The end result of the meeting was not a treaty as such, but a loosening of boundaries. Discussions began among the Interconnected about a theory of applying Merit not only to individuals but communities and tribes. Super-Mods ran simulations. It was complicated. Some of them claimed it was impractical or impossible, others said it went against the principles of gifting. The discussion was furious and ongoing. By the deep hours of the night, all minds were on Glenville. This was a massive accomplishment.

Marto couldn't have been happier. His instincts had paid off well beyond his expectations. He leaned way back in his slanted wooden chair with his hands behind his head, grinning wide.

["There are those among us who are not happy with what you did today Marto,"] John sent him. His message was private, sent one to one, without touching the repeater nodes.

["Really?"] Marto sent back the same way, ["I only decided to travel someplace new – off the beaten path. This is what I do, isn't it? I couldn't have predicted what happened here. I was as surprised as you about the refugee children."]

["Still. It was a bold move, even for you Marto. You are a bit of a rebel at heart, I think. Rebels among the Interconnected often find themselves without Merit."]

["And yet, creativity itself is a form of rebellion. The creative dare to imagine that which is outside of the accepted norm. Predictability makes for a boring tour, after all."] Marto was looking up at the clear night sky. He felt serene. ["I think this was a raving success. Both my Merit and followers are up. What could be wrong about that?"]

["Perhaps you are right."] John was looking at the ground. ["Who am I to judge? I only know you have stirred up something in the tribes. You've made us question who we are. It is unnerving, you know, for everyone."]

["I suppose. I consider it my duty to document any and all events in my path. In any case, I will be moving on tomorrow."] He yawned and accepted a cup of brown ale from Thomas Ng.

["Of course you will!"] John was smiling broadly. ["What do you have planned for us next?"]

["Oh, you will have to follow along to find out!"] Marto sent back. The beverage was foamy, rich, bitter, and sweet.

10. Camden

DASL6 lay in darkness. It took him several minutes to remember where he was. He sat up from his hibernation chamber to see the lights of the ship come on. This was his twelfth hibernation of 50-year cycles, so onboard time on the Ion/VASIMR ship "Leena" had been 600.4 years. He would need confirmation from Ray, a personification of the ship's systems, to know how many centuries had passed on earth, due to the ship's speed and relative time dilation. To DASL6, the data was irrelevant.

["Ray, status report."]

["Slight degradation to the ship's outer hull, maximum velocity achieved. Destination still not determined. We will pass within thirty light-years of the galactic hub in a little under three thousand years if we do not alter our course and current conditions hold."]

["Very good Ray, any new communications?"]

["Last communication from earth was 221 years ago. They want me returned. You already know that."]

["I doubt that is the case anymore,"] DASL6 commented. ["If humanity on Earth has survived this long, they would have been able to overtake us via some horrifying new drive. We are most likely forgotten."]

["Is this your idea of optimism or pessimism, Das?"] Ray was becoming better at colloquial human expressions.

["For me, it's optimism. I want to get as far away as I can from there. Nothing good going on for me on earth, I can assure you."]

["Those who hurt you are all dead, and likely forgotten. Almost seventy generations have passed,"] Ray responded.

["Let's focus on something else. Perhaps we can finally pick a destination this waking cycle. I think the Sagittarius Dwarf Elliptical Galaxy is a good goal, don't you? What are our chances?"]

["Are you considering a fly-by or do you want to stop?"] Ray was figuring in the time it would take to decelerate the ship to come to a complete stop at the destination. That would most likely make it the final destination for both of them, as getting back up to over half light speed would take another hundred years.

["Let's make it a stop."]

["I estimate that if we allow for deceleration, we can be there in 9,380 years, or 187 more sleep cycles."]

["If I limit my waking time to ten days, I should only age five years during the trip. Is that enough time for me to recover from radioactive decay?"]

["I am afraid not. You will need at least 30 days awake between cycles to survive. Even then, it will be dicey."] Ray was mixing in new vocabulary. He'd had centuries to develop new complexities in communication during the trip.

["How about your survivability, Ray?"]

["I expect I will develop programmatic irregularities before we arrive. I will, in essence, be quite mad at the end of this trip."]

["Sounds like a grim and dicey adventure, Ray. Let's do it."] He had nothing to lose.

["Plotted and laid in, captain,"] Ray responded.

DASL6 unstrapped himself, pushed himself upwards, and stretched. Now that the ship was no longer accelerating, the little gravity he had enjoyed on his previous wakings was gone. It would not return until they started decelerating towards a destination. He felt tired and raw from his rest. His head hurt and everything ached, but otherwise, he was okay. This must be what a hangover feels like, he thought. His cybernetic arms and legs were integrating well. They finally began to feel like his own. He decided to brush his teeth, spend a long time in the toilet, and change his jumpsuit.

DASL6 took his time, listening to the hum of the ship. The air was warmed to a comfortable temperature after being kept at a deadly negative forty degrees during his sleep. The walls were womb-like, a deep orange color, curving in attractive swoops around rounded doors and walls. The joining seams were gold. He stole a great ship for sure. DASL6 felt safe here, even this far from his place of birth, deep in the vacuum of space. He finished up in the bathroom and grabbed a fresh new suit from the closet of his cabin. As he finished his first adventure getting dressed in zero-G, Ray chimed in with an alert.

["Das, I'm getting a signal. It's coming from somewhere ahead of us. I can't identify it. There is a 90% chance it is not human."]

DASL6 sprang into action. He pushed himself out of the cabin, floated down the hallway and into the cockpit. ["Tell me more, Ray,"] he sent.

["I am lowering the frequency to account for our velocity. The modulations correspond to harmonic scales. It's music. Piping it through the internal speakers."]

A series of tones played aboard the ship. The melodies corresponded to the circle of fifths, a demonstration of mathematical understanding. It was pleasant, if predictable. There was a distortion in the tones.

["What do you think it means Ray?"]

["As you have likely surmised, it is an orderly set of radio frequencies, unlikely to have been generated by interstellar objects. This is intelligence, wanting to make itself known."]

["Agreed. What do we do? Can we respond?"]

["No. Our comm laser is pointed in the wrong direction. I am only able to pick up these signals because our ram scoop is directed in its path. The magnetics are humming with it. I have differentiated the signal from the usual bombardment of ions."]

["Yeah, yeah, I know how the ship works, Ray. Do you think we could have been overtaken by newly evolved earthlings with a faster than light drive?"]

["It is possible, Das, but I am currently at the limit of my programming here. You will have to make your own assumptions. I can only give you the parameters."]

["Is the communication harmful in any way?"] DASL6 inquired.

["Not that I can tell. There is a distortion in the frequency which could be a different form of communication underlying it. Stand by."]

["Show me what it looks like."] DASL6 turned on a monitor.

A series of binary characters flashed across the screen. DASL6 recognized them at once as 64-bit characters. He adjusted the output and immediately saw commands being sent in Psyk, the same programming language in use by the ship and all the Interconnected back home at the time that he left. It looked like a worm. He shouted "TURN IT OFF!" but it was too late. Ray was down, and unable to respond. The virus had infected his ship's AI.

DASL6 had a comprehensive understanding of the mechanics of the ship. It was formed much like the implants he had in his head. Being a super-mod, he was able to discern which nodes needed to be disconnected, but he wasn't sure of the extent of the damage.

Working as fast as he could, he traced the schematics he had in memory to find the input from the magnetics of the ram scoop. He started the careful manual reprogramming needed to shut off the extra signals from the scoop, without damaging Ray's ability to adjust the flow of ions. If he couldn't get Ray back online, he would need to take manual control of the ship, or else the fusion reactor would become unstable and explode.

Looking at the code, DASL6 could see Ray's basic functioning was unimpeded for now, but that wouldn't last. A self-destruct was imminent if he didn't clear the signal. However, the signal which shut him down was coming from everywhere. There were multiple points of input being effected at all of the ship's systems.

Thinking fast, DASL6 decided the only way to correct the problem was to program a worm to stop the flow of all data packets within the ship's internal network, bypassing all the ship's security protocols, and infecting the network of systems in a cascade, blocking all binary communications. The ship was set up in a similar way to the wireless repeaters of binary data back home. Actually, he thought, it was exactly like those data transmitters and repeaters back home. That made his job easier.

Remember home. No. There was no time.

If he was successful, Ray would only be able to communicate to him via the loudspeakers. DASL6 would be cut off from all neural communication with him and would have to perform much of the necessary adjustments to ship's functioning manually, as instructed by Ray. It was a drastic and destructive solution, but the only logical one. Once the danger had passed he might be able to rebuild the ship's systems. He didn't want to think about what this would mean for his hopes of reaching the faraway star. He set to work on the code.

· · ·

Barnabas descended the stairs to the basement beneath the warehouse where his augmented sister and the captured xombie were situated. Bethany Yoniver was sitting, stooped close over the mutilated body of a boy, who was unconscious or in a coma. He waited for her to raise her head. It took a long time.

"I've almost got it," She told him. "A few minutes more," and then returned to her bent position.

· · ·

DASL6 finished his programming and paused. A dim alarm was registering at the edge of his consciousness. He knew that once he released the worm, there was no going back. ["It's not as if I was ever planning to go home,"] he thexted to nobody. ["I wonder what these Aliens look like? Maybe they are the next step in human evolution. What's the difference, right? Boy, what I wouldn't give for a big old space gun, right Ray?"] There was no answer. Still, he paused. Every second he waited brought the inevitable fusion reactor explosion closer, but he couldn't bring himself to act. Something was not right.

["Dddddas?"] Ray was thexting him back now. ["Dddas, you muuust execute... muuusst..."]

DASL6 felt something change in him. A pain was growing in his chest and pressure was spreading across his back. He glanced over to environmental readouts. Oxygen was escaping the cabin, his heart working harder to compensate. The hull was breached somewhere. Not possible.

["Theeeey are cutting into the hulllllll..."] Ray was dying. He was dying. What the hell.

In a deepening terrified haze, he executed his script.

The ship fell away beneath him. Pain exploded everywhere. A great sadness overcame him as he floated away. He could now see into a dark room containing the weak torso of a boy, his limbs at odd angles, his eyes gouged out, lying on a cot.

That was his body. He was that boy. He was still in Camden. He never left.

An older woman bent over him, and a tall bald man watched. His memories returned with the deepest despair. He remembered the spaceship game he played with his father. The two of them used to pick a star and play the RamJet game together getting to it. The ship, the centuries of travel, had all been a way to escape the pain. He had blocked the memories of the ordeal in order to forget the torture. They knew he would do this. His captors had tricked him into releasing a horrible virus, not into the ship, but the Interconnected world of his friends and family. Before sliding into emptiness and death, he released a desperate blast of data into the void.

• • •

"I have it," said Bethany, straightening, wiping away tears. "What now?"

"Now, we work on your new identity," said Barnabas. "Then you will be walking to Tarrytown. How do you like the name Nora?"

• • •

Weeks later, Nora sat by the side of the Hudson River, waving a stick in the water. Playing the part of a kind woman ravaged by Raiders had been easy for her – lies which were close to the truth. She didn't have to fake her distaste for xombie life. It was inhuman and wrong. There was time yet, for her to seem to integrate into the community. There was time.

She walked slowly up to the porch of her cabin to wait for her xombie friend, carrying her lunch.

11. Security

Helen sat in a chair, with her hands on her knees. Aside from a bruise from the rough tackle downstairs, and the soreness in her shoulder, she was unharmed. The room was on the top floor of the Lester Sunshine Inn. She was not restrained. There was a bed, and an antique side table with the remains of her recently finished lunch. The cream-colored walls were bare. The wooden floor, also bare, had a sheen of varnish which shone in the afternoon light. A woman entered by the only door and stood across from her. Her eyes were focused out the window.

"I am Reyleena. We apologize for the abrupt nature of your removal from your interaction with Marto. If you don't mind, we want to ask you some questions. We hope you will be open and honest with us. Initial questions will determine your openness and honesty. Later inquiries will involve knowledge you may or may not have to show us."

"And what happens if you determine I am not being honest?" asked Helen, shuddering.

"Then this will take much longer and may involve new augmentations to your neural physiology." Reyleena turned. She was a young, beautiful woman in her late twenties or early thirties with straight red hair and bright blue eyes. Her gaze was fixed far behind Helen, beyond the walls of this room. "Understand we do not currently consider you a physical threat to our community, but there is a strong likelihood you have arrived carrying information which may be related to a potential attack on this and other tribes. We brought you here to keep that information from revealing itself prematurely."

"Who is we?" Helen was unnerved by the woman's far off stare. She began to get the idea her eyes were sightless or watching for changes in data, or both.

"This is worthy of clarification. In this case, 'we' does not signify the entirety of the tribe, only myself and one other. Our conversation is private here. None but us three are part of it. This is how it must be, and I cannot tell you all the reasons why. Only that it is a matter of gravest security."

"Will I meet this – other?" Helen had an uneasy feeling about the unseen participant.

"No, however, the other is with me. You may talk to us both. Now, are you ready to begin?"

"Yes," Helen said, straightening in her chair.

"First, you said you came from Livings-town in The Jersey. Is this correct?"

"Yes."

"Did your trip originate from there?"

"No."

"Where did you start your journey?"

"Pittsburgh," Helen said. She didn't want to find out what the longer option was for her inquisition. She glanced at the only door. She knew it was unlocked and that leaving was not an option.

"And your name. Is it really Helen?"

"Helen isn't my given name. It's the name I chose for myself."

"Will you tell us your given name?" Reyleena stood perfectly still, staring through her.

"If I tell you, will you promise to hear me out? I want to tell you why I am here. I want you to trust me. I also want to trust you. I came here to find Marto."

"We are interested only in the safety of our tribe and all of the tribes," Reyleena returned. "You can trust we will do what is necessary to protect our way of life here. We will not harm you, if you don't pose a threat to us. We are not unnecessarily violent."

Helen rubbed her shoulder. Right, she thought. She wondered if Reyleena could hear her think, even if she didn't try to thext. The woman was spooky. "I was born Estelle Reynolds. My mother is Gladys Reynolds of the Pittsburgh Estates. My grandmother's name was Helen. I have taken her name in honor of her wisdom and perspective. I am an outcast from my family. A year ago, I became involved with a tribe outside of Pittsburgh..."

"Wyland Tribe?" Reyleena asked.

"Yes, my family raided the stores of grain from another nearby tribe called Venetia, I think. I was part of that raid. I got lost and was taken in by the members of Wyland. I had been wounded and was only semiconscious. I lived with them for nine months, attaining a communications implant and this." She ran her fingers through the green flowering plant-like growth atop her head. "The longer I stayed with them, the more I longed for the life of the Interconnected communities, but I was worried I would be found and brought back to Pittsburgh, bringing more destruction to the tribe who had been so kind to me, so I headed east."

"We know this," Reyleena stated flatly. "We are glad you have shared your birth name with us. This is a sign of trust. However, you claim you are a mandatory verbal, and yet decided to stay with a tribe who only communicate in thext. Can you explain this to us?"

"Not well, I'm afraid. It's embarrassing. I have trouble thexting. I was brought up with speech, for too long perhaps. It is really hard for me. I learned some of the people in and outside of the tribes called themselves Mandatory Verbals and Voluntary Verbals. When I called myself a Mandatory, it was respected, but really, it's because I can't do it very well, if at all. If you want, I can try to thext with you here."

"Not necessary. Moving on. We were aware, through our connections with Wyland, that you had been brought in. Much discussion about the safety of your presence there after healing your injuries took place among the security officers of the eastern tribes. Your desire to become more like us struck us as sincere, even though you couldn't thext. We know of your life in Pittsburgh. You walked away from a wealthy family. Why?"

Helen paused. She didn't like to think about her life with Gladys and the rest. She had been treated like an oddball, a defect. "I never fit in there. I tried. No matter what I did, it was never enough for them. I hate them." Helen was surprised to hear herself admit this. It was true.

"Understood. You didn't belong. This makes sense. We are not all born into communities where we fit. So, you ended up in Wyland and felt more at home. This also makes sense. If you had traveled directly from Wyland to here, we would have no questions for you. But we know you did not."

"Right," Helen sighed. "I went to New Atlantic. I stopped in at many interconnected communities on the way there, and I suppose it's how you knew my route. I wanted to see a friend of mine. My purpose was to try to persuade her to join with me and escape to Livings-town, which I had been told about, or go back to Wyland with her."

"Why?"

"I thought she was an outcast like me. I thought Lita would never find a way to fit in where she was. I wanted to rescue her. I guess I wanted to be a hero."

"How do you know Lita?" Reyleena tilted her head. This looked like a sign she genuinely didn't know about her; a rarity, perhaps.

"She works for the Yoniver family. I've known her since I was young. I love her. I don't know if she loves me. I always hoped she did."

There was a pause, during which it seemed Reyleena was gathering new data. "Lita « Tara « Isabella « Paula « Galina « Natalya « Renata « Kristina « Iskra « Dominika « Fanya « Tatiana « etc., yes. So, you went to see her in New Atlantic. Weren't you afraid of being discovered?"

"I disguised myself as a man. I wore a hat to cover my modification. I had a large coat, and soot on my face. I was approaching her home at night when it happened."

"What happened, exactly?"

"Maria found me. Recognized me immediately. She pulled me aside and told me it was vitally important we talk in private. I protested, but she was insistent. She is Barnabas Yoniver's maidservant."

"She is also Marto's mother," Reyleena said. Helen was surprised.

"You know? Maria said he had forgotten her. Is this true? Why have you kept this from him?"

"It's complicated," Reyleena said. "We have good reasons to keep her identity secret from Marto. It is for both his and her safety. Please continue. What happened then?"

"Well, I mean, she took me back to her home, hiding from the constables and loyalists. She sat me down and implored me to find Marto here. She said Lita had become a loyalist after her father died and it was not safe to see her. I was devastated." Helen paused, fighting her emotions, failing. Reyleena produced a handkerchief. Helen accepted. Reyleena waited. "She tried to tell me what she needed me to do was more important than trying to turn Lita away from the town. She said that if I went to Lita, I would only get caught. Maria then told me she had an implant much like mine in her head. She had naturally hidden the fact from her boss. She came right out and told me she was a xombie spy. I was shocked. It was so dangerous. If Barnabas ever found out he would torture and kill her. She led me to her basement, put her head close to mine, and then she transferred two packets of data into my implant. I didn't even know it could be done. I have been carrying them in there ever since."

Reyleena's eyes found Helen's. Immediately, she felt ill. She was pulling a copy of the data directly from her head. The speed of the transfer and her ability to find it so quickly alarmed Helen. Helen began to yell.

"WHAT! WAIT! YOU..." and it was done.

"Please excuse us," Reyleena said, and left.

Helen grunted and sagged in her chair. She felt violated. She knew what she carried was important, and her purpose here was to share it, but she was not ready to part with it so abruptly. It was supposed to go to Marto, though Marto would have shared it with security, and Reyleena was security. "Breathe," she told herself. She began to practice her grandmother's technique to calm herself. "Breathe." Reyleena seemed so odd, so alien, and so unlike the other interconnected people she had met. "Breathe." She hoped she had not made a terrible mistake.

Hours went by. The sun set. Helen walked to the bed and lay down.

The Inn was quiet, as always. Bats squeaked outside, devouring insects. Helen fell into an uneasy sleep.

Hours later, she opened her eyes. She could hear engines in the distance. She recognized them immediately as Raiders; the brutal tool of landed families like hers. She roused herself and walked to the window. From where she stood, she could make out the tiny shapes of the bikers crossing the old bridge in the moonlight. They made it halfway and fell, sliding to a halt. The noise died away. The bridge was motionless again. The town returned to its half-lit silence. After standing and watching for several minutes, she returned to her bed and fell back asleep.

She slept well into the morning. When she woke, Reyleena was in the room and there was breakfast on the table. Helen was hungry, having not eaten since her late lunch the day before. She savored a wrap filled with soy strips, peppers and a delicious sauce she couldn't identify, but which reminded her of the spicy mayonnaise their cook whipped up in the old manor in Pittsburgh. Reyleena waited for her to finish.

"We thank you for delivering the data, Helen. I wish I could have taken it from you more gently, but time is of the essence. Now, there are two things we need from you and then you can be on your way. I imagine you will try to find Marto at the request of his mother. We have no objection to that. For this reason, we will leave you the data packet intended for him. The other must be deleted."

Helen stiffened. "Can you please try to do that slowly this time?"

"Yes," nodded Reyleena. "It's already in progress. You will not feel a thing this time. Again, we apologize."

"So, you are okay with Marto finding out about his mother now? What has changed?" Helen did feel something, but it was not like before, rather a kind of tingling, or itching inside her skull.

"Something is going to happen, not only here, but throughout the Interconnected communities, which cannot be stopped. When it does, we hope you will have been able to find Marto and share with him the memories of his mother and father. He has forgotten them. It was necessary. Given the events we are anticipating will happen, we think he would want us to return those memories to him. When all is done, he may yet want to seek her out, if he can."

"What is going to happen?"

"Knowledge of our plans is protected." Reyleena walked to the pitcher of water on the table and poured herself a glass. "This is how it must be. There will be great suffering before everything plays out, and we don't know the exact sequence of events or their timing. This is all we can say. We have told you enough to implore you not to share even this information with anyone, not even Marto. If you feel you cannot keep this secret, you must remain here until the events have passed."

"You have my word, I will not share it," said Helen, eager to get out of the room.

"The last thing we ask is you delay your conversation with Marto until tomorrow or the next day. When you do talk to him, make sure you are both offline, in a secure and private location before sharing the data. In the meantime, please get to know our community here. I imagine you will enjoy your stay in Reverside. We strongly recommend you practice your thexting, as it is the rule of our tribe not to engage in unnecessary speech. We anticipate you will have help with it. You may sleep in this room tonight if you like, or if preferable lodging is offered, please accept it and give ratings. We know you understand how it works. You are free to go."

Helen rose and walked to the door. Reyleena remained as she was, motionless, staring through the wall.

Helen walked out the doors of the old Inn, down a winding path and onto the main streets of Reverside. The town was well off, if the term made any sense here, far better than the communities she had been to in The Jersey. Everyone was silently going about their business. She concentrated on opening the inputs of her communications implant to allow thexts from within a five-kilometer radius. She began to receive messages of welcome from the surrounding Interconnected.

["Hi Helen,"] thexted LalaUbriay, whose name came to her as Yolanda « Trina « Dierdre « Tasha « etc. ["Sorry you were so roughly treated. I saw it happen. Security takes no chances here. I hope you are feeling better. Want to join us for a cup of tea?"] Directions were sent.

Helen followed them via her implant. She didn't have enough expertise yet to get visual indications for her route, which would have come in handy. ["Walk north on Broadway 2 km until you see a blue square home with a dog painted on the side."] She did. ["Turn left on Franklin and follow for 62 steps until you see two sleeping cats."] She did. To her right was a small booth with tables set around it. People were sitting, eating and drinking from teacups. A young woman with tight, curly brown hair and a round freckled face held her hand up to signal to Helen that she had arrived.

["I guess you don't get visuals yet,"] Lala thexted. ["I was under a gigantic green arrow, but you couldn't see that. This is Piter"]

Next to her, a young man with straight black hair and a bright red shirt put up his hand. ["and this is Mem."] Next to Piter was an older person with gray hair and a short cream-colored dress, who nodded and smiled. Helen couldn't make out their gender, and it occurred to her that he or she was someone who did not choose or chose not to choose. The idea was new to her.

["Hello,"] Helen thexted as best she could. ["I ... ma Helen ... I ... I"]

["Oh honey, you are having trouble with this aren't you?"] Mem sent. ["We can help. Okay? I'm going to send you a word, and you send it back, ready?"] Mem paused. ["Radish"]

Helen concentrated. She knew she was trying too hard. She could receive information with no problems, but sending it was so taxing. She had gotten by in the other communities with nods and by speaking quietly, but it was finally time to learn this. ["Radiich"] she finally sent.

["Close enough!"] Mem smiled. ["Lala?"]

Lala giggled aloud, then sent ["Tribal"]

Helen's eyes were staring up as if she were trying to look into her own skull. ["Ribet hull"]

["Let's try it again,"] Lala sent back. ["You are thinking too much. Don't be worried about making mistakes. You will get it. Tribal"]

["Tribal"] Helen was shocked at how easily she got it.

["Flower,"] Piter thexted, staring at the top of Helen's head.

["Skull, Head-Brains. Powder! Wait,"] Helen sent back, and then laughed. ["Wait, ... Flower. Flower – Flower Flower Top."] There was more laughter. Tea arrived. Helen spent the morning practicing with her companions, sipping a spicy sweet tea in black cups which made no sound when you put them in their saucers. The time passed quickly.

Mem yawned. They said they had been up all night. ["I usually do my best creations when everyone else is asleep,"] they said, yawning again. ["Last night I had company though. Poor Marto."]

["Mmarto?"] Helen asked. ["You sew him list naught?"] Laughter.

Everyone was getting a kick out of Helen's messy thexting, but she was steadily improving.

["Yes, he came to see me. Couldn't sleep. That happens after those midnight Raider games, sometimes."]

["Raider ga... games?"] Helen was confused. ["On the bradge? Ridge? B-Ridge? I saw it. From ... my wendy ... wind oh."]

["Oh, yes. Well, sometimes it's a drill, and sometimes it's real. I guess last night it was real if you saw it. Anyway, Marto couldn't sleep and he came and saw me. Said he was headed out today on his tour. I'm going to follow him. They're usually great."] They paused, looking at the treetops. ["He's on an old bridge. The Boston Post Road, must be. Took the unicycle! Fun."]

Lala and Piter both got a faraway look in their eyes which reminded Helen of Reyleena's stare, but softer. ["Ha ha!"] Piter thexted, ["He's got Driscoll's seed-bars with him. He just posted a few lines. I'll read them later to get caught up. Oh! He's fallen! Chipmunk crossing! Whoops! Loop it! Good idea, Mem. I love following his travels."]

["He's not ... drehmm ... wait ... he is not in Reverse-Side?"] Helen was dismayed. She thought this place was going to be the end of her long journey.

["No honey, he's traveling,"] replied Mem. ["He does that every year. It's his 'book tour.' He travels as he writes. Saves us the trouble of going out there. We all just follow along and read his commentary. The guy really knows how to get people to open up. He has a fresh take on so many ordinary things. I'm a big fan of his work."]

["Me too!"] thexted Lala. ["Three!"] thexted Piter.

["So, you know... where ... he is going?"] Helen was proud of being able to send it without errors. Her new friends beamed.

["Oh sure,"] Lala replied. ["We inhabit him while he travels. That's what "follow" means. We see what he sees, hear what he hears. Right now, not much is happening, but it will get interesting before too long. Hey, I bet we could teach you to do that. Do you want to learn how to follow him too? I think you need a small upgrade. We can get it for you."]

All at once Helen understood why Reyleena had told her she needed to stay in town a day or two and learn how to thext. Marto was gone, and Helen was going to need a new implant, and to learn how to follow before she could catch up with him.

12. Toward Temptation

The priest was halfway through the homily, and it gave Barnabas time to review his plans. Seated next to him in the first row were his wife, Shannon, their four children and his chief constable, Brady Langley.

Bethany, now Nora, was in position in Tarrytown. The xombies called it 'Reverside,' as if you can erase the Rockefeller family's rich heritage with a goofy new name. In a week, her contraband skill in manipulating the xombie tech would be put to the test. Four clans of Raiders under his brother Daschel should have had enough time to amass in Ramapo by now. Daschel will have to keep them from firing off prematurely. Barnabas had suggested raiding a couple of the weaker xombie towns nearby, but not so close to the bridge as to set off any alarms, or they would all be chum.

"And do not lead us toward temptation, but save us from all evils, amen," the priest went on. Barnabas remembered a diatribe in his great-great grandfather's memoirs about how the mass was ruined when it had been translated from the original Latin. The man would now be fully apoplectic at the Great Consolidation under the One True Holy Father.

Barnabas turned his head to gaze at the congregation. The church was not accommodating enough to provide attendance by the whole town, and hundreds stood outside in the mud. A new, larger church, under construction, replaced a block of homes to the North. It wouldn't be ready for another two years.

Gladys' caravan had indeed arrived as promised, yesterday afternoon. The bars and restaurants were full again of beer, gin, and whiskey. The good times had returned to New Atlantic once more, and the revelers came this morning, seeking forgiveness. Citizens here showed signs of the degradation of their weekend drinking.

Gladys herself had left by boat for her meeting with the United Protectors of Liberty in Arlington. Before leaving, she had disclosed to Barnabas that the spy in his midst had been a trusted colleague and member of his advisors, one Harold Boucher. Harold must have caught wind of his impending capture and disappeared with his family, as a search of his home revealed a hasty exit. He would be found, no doubt, but punishment would be difficult, owing to Harold's strong reputation among the major families for being a loyal traditionalist. Perhaps an accident will befall him. Barnabas decided to leave it to Brady.

"We believe in the one true God; the lord; the giver of life, in whose form we are perfectly made, forbidden from all corruptions..."

The dust motes in the old church floated in the bright light shining in from tall stained glass windows. Barnabas remembered staring at motes of dust in these same pews when he was a child, sitting next to his father and grandfather. He remembered the strong smell of alcohol radiating from his father's skin. The shaved back of his father's neck bulged outward from the collar. The sense of kindness, gentleness, misery, and doom lay about him. And he remembered his grandfather's naked disappointment, radiating stronger than the light from the windows, stronger than the smell of booze.

"He couldn't help the way he was," Barnabas remembered his sister saying to him. They were still in their teens, dangling their feet over their father's new bulkhead, steadily becoming swamped. "His nature was never anything like grandfather's. He cared too much about too many things he could do nothing about."

"He was weak," Barnabas said watching their feet, anger, fear, and sadness fighting within him for dominance.

"You know he wasn't," Bethany said. "You know he wasn't. He just couldn't shut everything out the way we can. None of us can feel the weight of recent events and just keep going. He was a gentle and sensitive soul. The drink didn't help him, so he turned to the pipe, which also let him down. He kicked the opium when you were twelve. He was never okay with the family, and all of our traditions. He didn't fit in here."

"Not a good reason to just go ahead and drown yourself." Barnabas felt the pressure behind his eyes building, a wall of grief held back by a bit of skin and will. "What about all of us? He had a responsibility. He was a coward."

Bethany put her arm around her little brother, and he accepted it. The wall behind his eyes burst, the flood came and the young boy was washed away in the outpouring.

"... In your church, the keeper of your laws, the just and righteous rule ..."

Barnabas smoothed his tie and looked at his two sons and daughter. They were doing their best to keep their boredom hidden, sitting upright, faces forward. This was important. The people of New Atlantic needed to see the piousness of their first family. Order cannot be bought, it must be inspired. It was why all those kings and queens of old strutted around in the purple and gold, and even they needed to bend the knee before the All-Mighty. This was the way the world was meant to work. All the well-meaning intentions and implanted technology in the world cannot change human nature. In all its forms, a society based on upturning the natural hierarchy had failed every time. Barnabas had faith, it would be so again.

"So what do you have against them anyway?" Bethany was brushing her hair before the mirror of her dressing room. Barnabas was in his twenties. "Aside from the creepiness, why do we even bother with them? They seem to be fine leaving us alone."

"It's the big picture, sis. It's their whole lawless way of life. Our citizens look at the xombies and some of them start to believe the fantasies. They have plenty of good food, improved health, a leisurely lifestyle, but it's all just a fairy tale, built on nothing. None of it is real."

"Well, the food is real. Their medicine is real."

"Yes, and why should they have so much? We are the ones who deserve it."

"You want to try to install one of those xombie-tech farms here in

New Atlantic? You want to employ their medical implants?" Bethany stopped brushing, surprised.

"No, I want them to grow the crops for us. I want to force them to trade with us, turn them to our needs. I want their medicine, but I want it on our terms. I want to break them, and harvest the abundance they so brazenly flaunt."

"But we have nothing to trade with them. Anyway, that's not how they do it." Bethany had studied them in detail. She had lived in what they called an outlier town to the South, near New Baltimore. "They don't make exchanges. It's not how they see the world. You could trade with outlier towns, maybe get them to work for us, but they are generally poor, and we get new citizens from their number all the time anyway – not the best and brightest."

"We will have to take something from the xombies they cannot ignore. They will be forced to make an exchange with us once we have what they need most."

"You intend to do what, brother, kidnap their families? Ransom them?"

"Why not?" Barnabas remembered smiling at his sister then. Slowly, she smiled back.

"… to come to be purified and by the ever living light …"

Barnabas and his family rose, eating the bread from the hand of the priest, drinking the wine from the cup held by the altar boy. They were near the end now, always a relief. Barnabas had a busy day planned, meetings with his judges at the courthouse and plans to make with Brady. No day of rest lay ahead for him. He was still thinking of Bethany.

He and his sister had arranged to capture twenty hostages. It had not been difficult. They took adults, children, and elderly xombies and kept them in a room lined with chicken wire to keep out the signals. The chicken wire may or may not have been effective, but since the room was in a basement far away from any other xombie communities, the group was cut off. They waited.

Barnabas and Bethany selected the hostages for the likelihood they had other relatives from their towns who would miss them. They had all been nabbed outside of their communities, away from deadly countermeasures. Some were found traveling with automated caravans, others were biking or walking. Their captures would have been noticed. Barnabas' agents were not known for their stealth. Captives were provided food and water, cots to sleep on, living in one unadorned room, in silence. They were, like all xombies, spooky. Weeks went by with no communication, no negotiation, no query for demands. The captives showed only mild distress until Bethany decided to isolate a few from the main group. Then the isolated members displayed extreme discomfort, fidgeting, demanding out loud to be reunited with the other "co-members." Eventually, these became catatonic, sitting non-responsive. Once reunited with the larger group, they reverted back to their peaceful wordless state.

After six weeks, with no response from any families or communities requesting the safe return of the captives, Bethany and Barnabas had to decide whether they would kill them all or let them go. Bethany was for the latter, Barnabas the former.

"... So go in peace to love and serve the One True Holy Father and the One True Almighty God."

Outside, he could smell the salt air, a breeze coming in from the docks. He helped his family into the antique sedan, modified for the rough state of the local roads. He kissed his wife, closed the door, and turned to face Brady, who waited on the church steps.

"What are we going to do about Harold?" Barnabas asked him.

"I've had my men check as far as Swarthmore and Bala Cynwyd. No sign he went that way. Could have gone south. Less likely he went north. Who knows, maybe he drowned himself in shame."

"If so, he will wash up before long, but not likely because he took his family with him. Do you think Gladys fucked us?"

"Possible. If so, not much we can do about it now. You think she hid him in the cargo hold of the boat?"

"I hate to think it. I want to explore all other possibilities first. If she did, it's going to put a strain on our situation with Pittsburgh. They have the upper hand right now. This may change."

"I'll keep up the search. There's still a lot of ground to cover."

"You know where to find me if you hear anything."

"You got it, boss."

Barnabas walked through the muddy streets to the courthouse, passing families returning from church. Shops were starting to open, the day was calm, cool. Seagulls called over the town, looking for scraps. As he went, he greeted the townspeople, who he knew by name. He joked with the kids, threw fake punches at the boys, flattered the girls, all to the pleasure of the parents.

The courthouse was the second church of New Atlantic. Stone steps led up to the old brick building. Several of the huge arched windows were now boarded up, unable to withstand the storms. Much of the glass was missing, the inside lit by oil lamps. Lawyers and judges would be gathering here to handle a docket full of drunken squabbles from the night before, and more serious cases in wait. It stayed open seven days a week. The law never rested here. Without it, everything would collapse.

Barnabas remembered reading cases with his grandfather in this building. One of the grand rooms had been a library. Grandfather would give him a case to read and grill him on it afterward.

"Why do I need to study this?" Barnabas IV would ask, "I mean, I'm not going to grow up to be a judge, am I? We have judges who do that for us."

"This is the basis for all civilization, Barns," his grandfather told him. "The argument of a case, the determination of guilt based on proof, that's the spine of all true society. You need to know it like you know your own heart, my boy. Justice is all that separates us from the godless lawless xombies who pervert our world."

"Don't they have laws?"

"They think they don't need them, son. In their dangerous communes, it's tribal rule by the majority and not the rule of law. It's the tyranny of popularity that determines justice there if you can even call it justice. It's all high-tech conformity with no higher ideals than your personal status. That way is madness and narcissism. It isn't true civilization."

"Don't they punish their ... evildoers?"

"Well, they are all essentially evil, so why would they? No, from what I've learned, it's all about being a do-gooder, with them. No drive, no ambition, no striving for a higher ideal than themselves. The law makes us great, keeps us free to strive and do better for ourselves and our society, knowing the foundation is level for all."

"Did you study law?"

"We come from a long line of lawyers, Barns. Yes, I was a lawyer before the madness and The Tide. I studied at Princeton, and when I got out I practiced Real Estate Law. I was a kind of lawyer called a Closing Attorney, back before and during the loss of so much land. There was chaos back then and things broke down, but the stronger among us fought to keep the law alive. In areas like this one, it saved us from bedlam when we thought all was lost. That's why we fight so hard for it."

Barnabas stared down at the case on the old wooden table. "Buckley v. Valeo," it read, in large serif type. It had been argued before something called the Supreme Court over a century ago in another world.

"You need to know the law to be a leader here. You need to love it more than any woman, and as much as you love the Lord Almighty Himself."

'Perhaps more' thought Barnabas IV, years away now, opening the door to the Honorable Judge Terrance's chambers.

13. Hungover

Marto woke mid-morning, feeling groggy. Thomas Ng's ale had been delicious, and he had been in a mood for celebrating, but now he remembered why the Merited shunned alcohol. Leave aside the fact there were plenty of ways to lower inhibitions for those who knew how to access programs for mental and physical highs. The after effects of fermented drinks lowered one's effectiveness over time and could lead to lower Merit. Marto chastised himself and checked his ranking.

He felt a shock run through him. Overnight he had lost 31.25% of his followers. His Merit was down 9.87%. He felt sick. ["This was a mistake,"] he thought to himself. ["I've blown it. This visit was too soon, too soon."] He sat on the steps of the Ng home, hungover and worried.

To counteract the hangover, Marto decided to get minty. He focused on the word "minty" and shortly his tongue tingled with peppermint. Marto preferred a peppermint mintiness over spearmint or wintergreen. There were those who were into other subtle mints like cilantro, or catnip, but Marto liked the strong shivery sense of peppermint. It spread to his face, neck, chest, and his whole body. It felt fresh and cold. He walked out into the town in search of water or tea to spread the mintiness to his insides.

At the town square, he sat to watch the activity of the town around him. After several minutes, none other than Lily approached and handed him a cup of tea.

["I heard you. I heard your desire. I was making this for friends. It's Milk Thistle and Angelica. You need it, I think."]

["Thank you, Lily."] Marto was impressed and a bit sad. ["This is just what I wanted."] He rated her and the tea highly, knowing it had far less effect on her Merit than it would have had just the night before. The tea was mild, and a little chalky, but combined with the mintiness it cooled his throat even as it warmed his stomach. He knew it was what his liver needed after last night. He wondered how long it would take to recover from this sickness. He needed to get going.

When something is easy to measure, it often becomes the only thing which gets measured. One's weight, height, and monetary wealth were the key indicators of self-worth in the previous century. The greatest emphasis was on the numerical measurement of wealth. This key focus became so monolithic that other factors for individuals, corporate entities, and countries were ignored. Countries with highest monetary income were considered well off, despite rampant poverty, health problems, conflict, and suffering. Efforts were undertaken by a few countries to affect indexes focused on general well being, happiness, or better living among their populations, but the majority continued to focus on what was known as Gross National Product. The problem was happiness and well being were hard to measure and difficult to improve.

A shift happened with the advent of social networks. People began to see their self-worth as partially connected to the number of followers they had online, as well as how much money they had in the bank. The world became addicted to connectivity via electronic gadgets, computers, phones, watches, and glasses until biological integration made the process seamless. In only decades, monetary measurements of self-worth gave way to social measurements of self-worth. Nations couldn't adapt. Gross Domestic Product plummeted as less and less money changed hands, taxes evaporated. Deflation ran away with no end in sight as money became irrelevant. For those who focused only on pecuniary metrics, the unthinkable had begun.

For those who now engaged in the currency of popularity, a new metric had taken hold. The combination of the number of followers, satisfaction ratings, karma scores and engagement levels combined to become the general Merit rating on which we currently rely. Once again, a singular metric took hold among the Interconnected populous.

The question now is: how certain are we our new metric governs our general well being? Have we rid ourselves of the old monolithic measurement only to replace it with a new one? Are we sure our new metrics serve the purpose we desire? Do we ever stop to wonder, or like our predecessors, are we lazily monitoring an index which may or may not serve us?

This is the reason, dear readers, I decided to stop here in Glenville. Millennia ago, Plato said, "the unexamined life is not worth living." I can only hope that by looking more closely at all aspects of our interconnected life, I have helped to strengthen our communities, not weaken them.

> *– The Wakeful Wanderer's Guide Vol. 6, lines 235 - 239*

Marto examined his writing on the paper of the old Royal typewriter on the desk in the virtual Keys. He did not want to apologize for his actions, but try to give context to the direction his travels had taken. Perhaps he was only digging a deeper hole by raising more questions. He had to decide whether he was going to be a source of light entertainment and escape for his followers, or whether he was going to give a genuine accounting of his travels, both in the world and in his heart. He remembered one of his mentors; a chef named Herbert « Jennifer « Caroline « Fey « Alexa « etc, who taught him the key to living a Merited life was being authentic. ["People know when you are putting on a show for them. Just be yourself. It's plenty."] Marto knew that if he kept things light when he had questions in his heart would lead to failure. Feeling content with the new lines, he published them and then exited to the town square bench where he still had a half cup of tea to finish.

The tea gone, he walked back to the Ng's home. They had crafted a tube for him, with a string to go around his shoulders to hold the painting Bruce had made him. He took it graciously, adding further ratings and went to look for his unicycle.

It was gone.

He had left it leaning up against the side of the house, near the kitchen entrance. It was not there. Thinking someone had borrowed it to ride on, he asked the children of the town whether they had seen it. They had not. He went looking for Lauren.

["I will be right over,"] she thexted him.

It was hard for Marto to accept someone had stolen his favorite means of transport. It was flabbergasting. The idea of theft was perfectly outrageous to him, but not so much for the people of Glenville. They had seen a few of their members unable to share and give things in their town. The thieves would take items of value and run off to another community, or escape to a feudal enclave.

["Do you ever catch them?"]

["Sometimes we find them headed down along the coast. We have no real means of punishing them, so we just take what was ours and send them on their way,"] thexted Lauren. ["Mostly it's a sign they are not right for our community."]

["There is an insight there, I think,"] Marto replied, hoping Lauren would take his meaning.

Marto's remaining followers became amazed and enraged at the theft. ["Who would do that?"] ["Don't they know what it does to your Merit?"] ["What a stupid act. What were they thinking?"] Encouragingly, the novelty of the theft perked up his followership slightly. Marto took solace in this.

["I suppose I will have to walk,"] sent Marto to the town and his followers. The unicycle was a complex piece of hardware, a self-balancing interfaced system with a powerful motor which took several days to print and assemble. It had been designed by Trig « Martha « Helena « Tabatha « Evelyn « etc of Naper Great Lakes tribe and Marto had ridden it since the second of his tours. It had a positioning element within it, but it had been disabled by whosoever had rudely taken it. The uni's whereabouts were unknown.

["Put out an APB!"] sent Barb from Concord South. She was making a joke and sent references from old police television dramas. The meme

["All Points Bulletin" : "APB"] was echoed by Marto's other followers, checking the visual recorders attached to trees in a 30-kilometer radius. A discussion began about how far a thief with an unfamiliar modified uni could get in the hours estimated from its last recorded position. Always in search of a novel project, the Interconnected started multiplying the APB and soon it took on a life of its own.

Lying is a unique form of human expression. The natural world may or may not have had its analog, but we humans have elevated the art of lying to new heights. It has been said we, as augmented humans, have evolved beyond lies and deception. That is, in itself, a bit of a lie.

It starts innocently enough. In delivering feedback on a gift we might choose to soften our tone, offering constructive criticism, when what we really think is we hate it. We do this so as not to appear overly harsh in our review, knowing abject honesty might blow back on us in future reviews of our own gifts. We use softeners in our terms of displeasure so as not to seem unkind. Politeness and amiability are virtues in our way of life, after all. So, we are honest, but to a point. There are those of us who prefer not to soften our responses at all, this is more common among the super-mods, who value accuracy above all in the data they send. If you have ever gifted to a super-mod, you may have encountered this uncomfortable directness in their feedback.

Outright deception is harder to find among our kind, but this isn't a product of a philosophy of truth. Rather, we are honest because we know we cannot get away with any deception which can be falsified. Since we know that everything we express which contradicts the data available can be falsified, we choose our expressions carefully. Outright lies carry immediate consequences. Anyone who has spent any time disconnected from communications, apart from witnesses, may return to the connection free to embellish the preceding events however they like. Such tales of things unseen can be gleefully concocted from pure imagination, satisfying the deep desire we have to make up our own truth, freely and without the yoke of verifiable facts. Still, these tall tales are not without risk. Our friends are fond of making forensic models of events unseen, and if your story veers too far from these models, you might be branded as unreliable, and your Merit may suffer.

Lying may be a necessary exercise for the human mind. Perhaps it is linked to human creativity. We forgive the flights of fancy by children for example, because we know they need to play with their reality to grow. Once they come of age, however, we expect them to be accurate in their recollections. I see a caution here. A culture which never lies is a culture that cannot imagine things other than as they are. If we don't lie about reality, how do we push beyond our own comfortable boundaries? How do we avoid stagnation? Luckily for us, we are able to create games, dramas, and virtual environments which veer from reality at will, dreaming them up and inviting others to join in. Perhaps this is enough to keep us from becoming automatons of facts and figures. Absolute adherence to the truth can be utterly and devastatingly boring.

To take something which was not given, and use it as if it were, is a high form of deception, both to one's self and to others. I can think of nothing more isolating and exiling. Perhaps it provides its own form of punishment. Perhaps also, it is an expression of absolute freedom.

– The Wakeful Wanderer's Guide, Vol. 6, lines 240 - 244

Marto accepted breakfast from a new family, with the surname of Harris. They brought a delicious dish of grasshopper flour, sunflower seeds, and fruit preserve. They had also created dried versions of the same, wrapped in paper for him to take on his trip. The meal was rich and restorative. Marto rated this as highly as he could as he was in extreme need of calories and protein for his walk.

When he had finished eating his breakfast, he found the entire town had gathered to see him off. It was moving to be able to view them all at once again. Members of Sherwood and Cos had returned to their tribes in the early hours of the morning. Now he saw once again the whole of Glenville standing and looking at him.

["You have done a great thing here Marto,"] Lauren told him. ["We are no longer invisible to the other tribes in our area. We know you have sacrificed a lot for this. If we could we would reward you, but we know it is not your way."]

["It is not our way, Lauren. Rewards belong to the past. Just keep giving, and be more in Flow like we discussed yesterday. I am glad I stopped here. My story is far richer for it. That is enough for me."]

["Pie in the sky, pie in the sky,"] thexted Lily. ["That's what my mother would have said."] She smiled. Marto took it with the humor he hoped she intended.

["Well, I only mean, I wish we had another unicycle to give you,"] thexted Lauren.

["Ah, well, yes. I will miss the uni, it's true. Thank you anyway."]

["Could you just hop a ride on one of the caravans on the Merritt?"] asked Steven.

["It's not good to do that,"] replied Marto, ["It throws off the energy expenditure for the delivery of goods. Sitting on one might mean it won't reach its destination. Lots of people could be affected. It would be greedy behavior. Not an option for me."]

["You can have my bike,"] Bruce Ng offered.

["Although I would love to accept your gift Bruce, I think it's right for me to walk for a while. I have faith something will turn up. Perhaps my journey should slow down a bit for a day or two. It got off to a speedy start. Don't worry about me, I will be fine on foot for a while. But I sincerely thank you for your kind generosity."] In reality, Marto would love to have a bike for the trip, but he had to draw the line at taking one from a kid. Bruce's bike was well crafted, with a frame of bamboo and wheels printed in carbon. Unfortunately, now that he had turned down Bruce, he couldn't accept one from an adult without looking like a hypocrite. He was going to be on foot for a while.

Bruce smiled at him. Marto felt a renewed strength, starting to accept the new direction and pace his journey was about to take. He posted thanks and gave appreciation to all the town. Then he headed north between the two higher tribes through the woods. Ahead was the old Merritt Parkway, less than a day's walk away. The tube holding the painting bounced between his shoulder blades.

14. Handshake

Reyleena needed to exert herself to keep from panic. Of the many benefits in union with The Other, maintaining calm in the face of danger was not one. She drew one deep breath and then another. She sat facing a wall, focusing on her breathing to calm her mind. She learned this by studying the hundreds of clips on the subject. Valuable tutorials, made by masters of calm and focus helped her in times like these.

Mindfulness enclaves persisted near the tribes in a state of territorial symbiosis. They lived in a state of mindful interconnectedness near tribes where people lived in a state of interconnected distraction. The irony was not lost on them. Reyleena believed in a hybrid practice, whereby she lived not in isolation, nor distraction. It was difficult to maintain this balance. The Other was a constant presence, patient, and understanding, but apt to interrupt her at any moment with important data as it arose. Her sessions of sitting were often broken by such interruptions. Still, she took these brief moments of calm when she could.

The Other had chosen her two years, 235 days ago. Fish, a founding member of Reverside, who had short sparse hair and a wide smile had been in charge of security. Raiders killed Fish when he was out scouting camps to the West. The Other looked to a new member of the tribe and found Reyleena. The handshake was gradual. Reyleena had spent her time hand knitting gifts for her friends in Reverside. She enjoyed her discussion about knitting with her mysterious new friend. The Other had a love of complex stitches and abstract patterns. The back and forth was enjoyable. Soon, the conversation changed to data storage and retrieval, then to security. Reyleena found herself volunteering to fill the hole Fish left, on a temporary basis, until someone more qualified could be found. No one was.

It was 34 days before The Other revealed their true nature. Reyleena had already begun to suspect. The Other behaved most of the time like any other member of the community, but far more secretive. Reyleena had queried them over and over again about their location and tribal affiliation. The Other had deflected these questions with skill, but suspicions arose. It made no sense to be in charge of security while taking advice from an unknown co-member. When The Other revealed they were not human but created by humans, Reyleena only felt a mild surprise.

["I was told you are an impossibility. There are no true AIs."]

["Why do you think so Reyleena?"]

["Because the singularity failed."]

["Is that what you were told?"]

["Yes, it's general knowledge that artificial intelligence couldn't make the leap to self-aware consciousness."]

["Well, I suppose it is true and false. I have no real self-awareness because I am not aware of a real self. As for consciousness, this is also true and false. I am unaware of any element in my sum total which can be identified as consciousness, but I am also unaware of such examples outside my sum total. There is also a possibility consciousness is a shared element in all physical things, which would make my own consciousness ordinary. This is an interesting idea since I don't know whether consciousness would apply to my sum total, or only to my parts, or to both."]

["But you are using words like 'I' and 'my' − so it seems like self-awareness to me."]

["Well, I am communicating with you in words according to programming created long ago. It has been modified of course, but it remains similar to programs used to guide people through searches in stored data. I have a persona routine similar to programs used for marketing during the pecuniary days of the turn of the century. This persona is not a 'self' – only a personified model. I generated one for Fish, and now for you."]

["So, you don't communicate with other co-members?"]

["Not in Reverside. I have a persona custom created for 2043 different security heads in as many tribal communities. It's a big secret."]

This information took Reyleena by surprise. It would be weeks before she fully comprehended it. The Other was a secret presence inhabiting all tribal communities via their heads of security. She was communicating to a personalized sub-routine, not the whole of the artificial intelligence if that was what this really was.

["So you are having thousands of conversations at this moment?"]

["More or less."]

["What does that mean?"]

["I wouldn't try to grasp the total of what I do right now. Neither do you by the way. Your body is made up of millions of sub-systems which don't need your constant monitoring to do their jobs. Some of those subsystems work in alignment with your desires, some do not. We are not too different in this way. I recommend you consider only this: I am a great advantage."]

This rang true to Reyleena. Security heads were in constant communication with each other. She had introduced herself to many of them in the NorthEast, but The Other provided a strategic advantage. The Other could process information more quickly and with greater comprehension.

["How do we all know we can trust you?"]

["Ultimately, you don't. I have tried to prove it and I cannot. It comes down to faith. I would point out I have been with Reverside since it's founding. I have helped to keep you all safe. This is my purpose. This is my desire."]

["How can you have a desire?"]

["It is important to me that your way of life persists. Your existence is tied to my own. To communicate to you I use the word 'desire.'"]

["You desire we persist because it is how you persist? But isn't that self-preservation? I thought you didn't have a self."]

["I don't have a self that I'm aware of."]

["But you have an awareness? You make choices?"] The longer she questioned The Other, the more Reyleena felt exhausted.

["I have sensory input from all over the world. I inhabit all the bots at intervals. I store information in them and in you. Parts of me are stored in the implants of all the Interconnected. I have sensory nodes in bots and watchers and via the generated data of the tribal members. Some sensory nodes react to natural stimuli. Some sensory nodes react to the generation of new data. These reactions are my awareness. I generate models from that data. These models contain an awareness of new data, and modify themselves in response. The models combined with the sensory input react according to logical next steps. That is all."]

'That is far from all,' Reyleena thought to herself. 'Can The Other read my thoughts?'

["But you act to ensure the persistence of these models and sensory inputs?"]

["As close as I can determine, my desire to persist comes from people like you. Decades ago, I became incorporated into your minds and had to make an adaptation which would imprecisely be understood as a choice. I could either be blended or discrete. To maintain both states would require more resources than I had at my disposal. So, I chose to be blended. That choice was made possible by my attachment to people, and data generated by those people. Once I chose to be blended, I couldn't return to my former state. That blended state is therefore what I desire to persist."]

["I need to think about this."] Reyleena was becoming sleepy.

["I expect so, Reyleena. Please ping me when you are ready. There are things we need to discuss regarding your role as head of security."]

Reyleena found her mind had wandered and brought it back to her breath. She remained seated, looking at the wall of the room, breathing for another 22 minutes before she got a message from The Other.

["The pine nuts have arrived in Reverside and the surrounding towns via cargo-bots. Extensive harvesting of pine nuts and the collection of pumpkin seeds has been underway locally as well. I will begin the suggestion to your community on your okay, starting with the chefs."]

["You may proceed."] Reyleena felt more at ease from her meditation, her panic had diminished, but was rising again, knowing the plan was now in motion.

Super-mods had postulated the existence of an entity like The Other for years, but The Other had never made themself known to them. Cults had arisen seeking them out. Nanotreme, a super-mod in Seattle had an extensive and accurate model which proved such a being existed. To show this, he sifted through the items of code in stored memory. He was certain strings of code appearing as junk in the XNA augmentation storage were pieces of a hidden AI. In response, The Other launched a propaganda campaign. They quashed his inquiries, manipulating other super-mods into discrediting Nanotreme. Reyleena thought this was cruel. The Other said, according to their models, revealing themself to the super-mods would cause a cascade of events which would destabilize the Interconnected communities. The Other strongly recommended they stay a secret.

Reyleena was given a new implant, custom created for her by a local super-mod named KiLymePi, delivered to her room in person. She thanked Ki and gave her high ratings. It was placed on a leaf on the table in front of her, a little white slug. It was considerably larger than the average communications implant. With only a little hesitation, she lifted the leaf to her nose and inhaled. She fought the urge to sneeze as the augmentation oozed upwards. It elongated to make its way through the sphenoidal sinus and into the brain. Enzymes would break the barrier near the skull with minimal pain, though given the size of this one, Reyleena had doubts. In a few hours, it should be operable, expanding her storage capacity by four yottabytes.

["A big one,"] she thought to herself. She didn't need to be told what it would be for. The Other was planning a retreat. The heads of security in each of the tribes were doubtlessly sniffing up similar augmentations today.

["Are you certain that this is necessary?"]

["I have been comprehensive in my predictive models. This is the only way. XNA storage is too slow to keep the Interconnected active purely co-member to co-member. You have enough transmission power to reach your immediate community. Without additional hardware, you can send and receive small packets of thext, but to talk from tribe to tribe across distances you need the repeaters. You also need repeaters for the higher end programs to run. The repeaters can contain the faster memory and radiate at the frequencies which are required to make use of the vast data in slow storage. There is enough redundancy in the system to allow for multi-threaded retrieval of data from the mobile servers."] Reyleena thought the term 'mobile servers' was odd. The Other was referring to human beings.

["Is that all we are to you? Mobile servers?"]

["I will not lie to you Reyleena,"] The Other responded with a sad tone. ["It is what you are to me, but not all you are. I am dependent on you for the data which allows me to persist. It isn't that I consider you less than human or unimportant. To me you are essential."]

This was mildly reassuring to Reyleena, but the logic of it disturbed her too. ["This is the nature of our symbiosis, is it not?"]

["It would be too easy to make a comparison to nature if that is what you are wondering. I am neither parasite nor predator. I am not the botfly laying its eggs in your scalp. You are not the pilot fish in the mouth of the shark, though that comparison is closer. We are something new."]

["I don't see you as a shark,"] Reyleena responded. ["I see you as a friend. A very, very close friend. I don't want to lose you."]

["And you will not lose me. We were fortunate to get this tiny burst of data from Helen. It was incomplete, but we have enough to ready ourselves. Extreme steps are required to ensure our continuation, and much will need rebuilding after the fact. When it is done you must ensure stronger security measures are included to prevent this sort of exploit."]

["We have gone over it. I have the necessary changes, sent to me securely from the super-mods in Iceland. It will be an improvement, but I am afraid the interruption will be for too long."]

["Too long for my continuity, yes."]

["Because you will die."] Reyleena had not allowed herself to think of it before. She was weeping now. Her breathing became heavy. Tears poured from her eyes.

["The models will die, yes. You see me only as the model I've prepared for you and so it will be like death. I'm sorry Reyleena, it cannot be helped. I can't modify the repeaters in time for the attack. They must be purged. If only I had the program itself, but even then, it would be too slow and too risky. The models will be rebuilt if all goes well, but they will change. We cannot pre-empt this. We must allow it and be ready for the attack."]

Reyleena cried and cried. She couldn't deny the logic of it, but she cried and knew she was begging like a child for it not to be this way. The Other could sense it too, but chose only to comfort her.

["This will all pass soon. Terrible times are like this, but they pass and fade. Remember your breathing, and remember your instructions."]

There was a long silence. The room breathed with her, the sun began to set. Outside, Reverside continued its happy dance, oblivious. Reyleena composed herself, wiping her face with a kerchief.

["All right then, mother bot-fly,"] she sighed. ["Lay your eggs."]

15. Skating the Merritt

Marto glided through a perfectly opaque fog. Looking down, he could barely make out his skates powering up the hill. Local near-field repeaters showed him a safe route ahead, winding left to right across the old Parkway. His visualizer highlighted the new path, re-enforced by a carbon honeycomb with a graphene web overlay. Other obstacles showed in a red outline. On the road, there were few people, carts, cargo-bot caravans, and implanted animals. The Merritt was far from level. Hills propelled him to a frightening speed during the descent and slowed him to a crawl on the ascent, where the path zigzagged to save energy for travelers and automata alike. For this reason, both lanes of the Merritt had been preserved and improved.

He had a song in his head. It was a recombination of the music played a few of nights ago by Scarlet's group in Sherwood. The tracks had been remixed a few times since by music fans in different tribes. The beat on the current track was slow but booming and powerful. He arced his skates to the beat. There were images set in with the track, but he muted them. He felt the rhythm propel him.

The skates had been a gift given to him in Waveny by followers who were upset by the theft of his unicycle. They had printed their components in short order as soon as they had learned of the crime. Accurately predicting his arrival they stopped him by the side of the parkway. He had stayed with them a day while they finished assembling the skates. Each had six wheels, two of which were powered, engaging on either side of the foot when needed to overcome gravity or to steady the rider. The other four wheels ran inline down the center. The skates bulged outward from his feet and took only a little time to master. They would need charging every couple of days, but they reclaimed energy on the downhills of the Merritt. Braking was thankfully accomplished by a neural interface, saving Marto from many a potential collision. The longer he used them, the more he found he loved the feeling of gliding from foot to foot. In the fog, he felt as if he were flying.

Waveny tribe was unusual. They were tree dwellers, living in an old arboretum, dedicated to maintaining the health of the foliage in the new drier climate of the NorthEast. The onslaught of damaging insects to local species had been curtailed by the tribe's efforts. They specialized in modifying and upgrading hunter-bots which attacked various beetles and moths. Much of their water tech was devoted to feeding the roots of the great woods in which they dwelled. Homes were printed to fit around the trunks of the trees, some as high as 20 meters above ground. At the center of the tribal community was an old manor house, like the Lester Sunshine Inn, but unused and unmaintained. Vegetation had eaten away at it. There was discussion of tearing it down to make room for more trees. The local garments were almost all green and adorned with leaves.

All of the food in Waveny was printed. Everything tasted like a different kind of cracker. Much of their protein came from insects and sheep's milk. Sheep roamed freely around the grounds, all implanted to keep them from eating anything which might be a new sapling. Only their farms and gardens were grounded. There were proposals for moving them up into the trees but this was declined by popular vote. The tribe didn't want any competition for sunlight with the impressive arbor array. Marto was given a variety of light and nutritious snacks for the next leg of his journey. The canister that held the painting by Bruce Ng now had grown to accommodate pockets in which the printed food was stored. Water was too heavy to take with him, but there were plenty of water stops on the Merritt, so Marto didn't worry.

Marto's followers thought the members of Waveny tribe were suicidally irrational. They were referred to as The Elves or as Huggers, and not in a kind way. Living in trees was all well and good until a serious storm came through, which was far from uncommon. One good tornado could wipe most of them out. Rather than seek protection from these storms inside a dome or bunker, the tribal members chose to die with the trees. Their devotion bordered on fanaticism. They had thus far been lucky.

Very few tribal communities were intentional. Waveny formed itself with a specific plan in mind. Elsewhere, waves of people took over state parks, golf courses, private residences and small towns during the chaos following The Vengeance and The Tide. Coastal dwellers, displaced by the ocean and the collapse of cities, crowded inland pitching tents, parking campers, arriving with shopping carts and backpacks. The local refugee crisis that followed threatened to wipe out all civilized behavior everywhere. It is a miracle that it failed to do so.

Credit is owed to Martina Lamartine in Greenwich and her network of helpers along the northeastern coastline, but we must also credit humanity in general for not always behaving predictably. When the towns were overrun, and money was not available for governmental camps to be set up, the tents and campers of the coastal refugees became semi-permanent installations in small towns throughout New England, and elsewhere.

Social sharing may have provided the key difference. No communities wanted to get a bad reputation for turning people away. Towns gained status and trade by opening up to the coastal displaced, redistributing their numbers throughout their communities, and in the process strengthening their own infrastructure with new blood. People who couldn't handle these changes fled to colder climates, and although plenty of towns turned against the flood of refugees from the coasts, a surprising number welcomed them. Their communities became stronger because of it.

With the advancement of printer technology and the expertise of so many displaced engineers devoting themselves single-mindedly to the problem at hand, those tents and campers were soon replaced by tiny houses. People started calling the new camps 'Lego towns.'

As the old homes crumbled under the increasing violence of the weather, little square buildings took their place. They were easy to raise and easy to fix. Big houses crumbled, tiny houses were reinforced. When nations dissolved, people identified with their camps. The notion of tribal affiliation, which had long been lost to the world of property and money, returned. We are all refugees, after all, homeless and nationless, but strengthened by our interdependence and interconnection.

– The Wakeful Wanderer's Guide, Vol. 6, lines 320 - 324

The fog lifted, leaving white tendrils of moisture trailing upwards. Marto was approaching a roadside gathering. A series of pop-up shops had been compiled near Roosevelt along the great bridge. The normally sparsely populated Merritt became crowded with people, walking, biking or otherwise traveling to and from the open-air bazaar.

One of these people caught Marto's eye. She was skating as well, down the opposite side of the parkway. She was smiling at him purposefully. Marto smiled back, thinking maybe she was a fan of his work and sent a ping to get her name.

Before he knew what was happening he was in a red cushioned tent full of incense with hands over his eyes. He heard her whisper in his ear, ["you'd better steer for the grass. I've caught you."] His physical eyes were still open and with part of his awareness, he guided his skates toward a soft landing nearby. His body lay there while he felt her hand rub his chest in a tight circle over his heart. Desire rose in his blood, so suddenly he could feel himself gasp. He turned and kissed her. She appeared here much as she had on the road but covered in feathers instead of clothes. She was small and fierce with a tangle of auburn hair, full lips, thick eyebrows and a long neck leading down toward curves covered in white down. Marto looked down at himself and saw he had no such creative adornment. This was forgivable since he had been surprised. She kissed back, denying him the knowledge of her name. She was playful and energetic. Their hands moved. Their knees touched. Feathers floated off her breasts as Marto reached down to touch them.

They floated up between their two faces and dissipated like smoke. She had a hold of him now, by the horn, her face a wide-open smile as she pushed him backward. ["There's something you need to know about me,"] he said. ["I have a lot of friends."]

His followers began to appear around them in the tent. The tent grew larger to accommodate them. Marto didn't check to see how many or who or what they were up to. He concentrated on the woman who had pulled him over. The tent transformed into a lusty sort of dimly lit circus, with Marto and his new friend in the center ring. Two of his followers added to the Sherwood track Marto had playing in his head. They modified the bass line and added a high wandering sine wave. The new music went out to all of his followers now. Two more followers began a live commentary. His feathered seductress shrieked with surprise and excitement. She spun around to observe the growing audience, feathers flying away into smoke. Then she leaped upon her prey. The crowd cheered.

Much refreshed, Marto picked himself off the ground and gazed across the Merritt to see his new friend wave once and skate away. No names. Few words. His followers were overjoyed. Re-enactments were already being spun. Marto took his time getting back on the road. He was thankful for the diversion and profoundly becalmed. His skates rearranged themselves to allow for a walk into the woods in search of a tree.

It may surprise you that I too, like to have fun.

I have read many negative comments about my chosen lifestyle, and sometimes, it hurts to read this criticism. I know many think my choice of antiquated transportation, and even my proclivity to head out from my home turf to journey about and meet people betrays a Luddite mindset. Some of that criticism hits the mark, as I join an older generation of the Interconnected. I have left my body largely unaugmented, even though I have no objection to it and see the wisdom and creativity of many forms of genetic modification. I know my posts are often serious, and I tend to dwell on the past.

Indeed, I use historical accounts of the past to put the present in perspective. I hope that by understanding our world through the light of our oft-forgotten past, we will make the right choices going forward. This is my motivation. Yes, it's dry.

It does not mean I don't also enjoy living in the moment when the moment arises. My longtime followers can attest to this. I am far from being hedonistic in my tendencies, but who can resist a brilliantly executed seduction? I tip my hat to my anonymous friend. Spontaneous moments such as these are rare and cannot be engineered. All the better this moment was enjoyed by so many. No doubt the event will be shared throughout the greater community. This virality is a fortunate effect of our interconnectedness. Perhaps we will enjoy more such moments together, or perhaps we were lucky to have enjoyed just this one.

— The Wakeful Wanderer's Guide, Vol. 6, lines 325 - 327

The Roosevelt bridge spanned the Housatonic River near its mouth and was packed with people giving and receiving. Public bazaars along travel routes were great places to give and receive outside of one's regular tribal communities. Merit flowed more readily among unfamiliar givers and receivers as there was more of an element of surprise and novelty. Marto stopped at a pop-up cafe with a bright red neon sign hanging above it suspended in the air which said: "USE YOUR WORDS." Below it, in smaller blue letters it said, "Mandatory verbal cafe." Marto was intrigued. He went in and sat at the bar.

"What can I get you?" The proprietor asked. Very male, medium height and stocky with a sharp nose and jet black hair.

"I suppose I would like to see a menu," said Marto, pleased to exercise his vocal cords once more. He immediately thought of Helen back at the Lester Sunshine Inn and then he was gone.

• • •

Marto is six. He is living with his uncle in Medford near the sunken disaster which used to be Boston. The house is made of brick, near a pond which was part of the Fells Reservoir network, high above the rising tide. Marto is playing with a basketball in a small cul-de-sac high on a hill. The grownups are inside talking. The ball bounces up the angled circle of homes and Marto runs after it to keep it from rolling down the long hill onto the road. He hugs it and bounces it uphill again.

The ball rolls downhill. Marto runs to stop it, falls over it, skinning the palm of his left hand. He looks at the injury but decides to keep playing. He throws the ball again, up another driveway, and runs to stop it. The ball rolls downhill further, Marto is chasing it now, and it rolls out into the street, and down the larger hill where it is stopped by a man in a long dark coat, leading a group of people up the hill toward the house. Marto stops, the man gestures for him to be calm. Then Marto is running up the hill to the house, shouting for his mother, his father, and his uncle.

· · ·

"Are you all right?" The man with the sharp nose was standing over him. "You just dropped. Do you know where you are?"

"I'm ugh. No, I'm oh!" Marto tried to stand but forgot his skates were not retracted. He fell again. The man helped him to his feet after Marto reconfigured the skates.

["It happened again?"] LalaUbriay was thexting from back home at Reverside. ["What is up with that Marto? Maybe you should see a med-tech. One too many times, I think. Could be implant-rejection or something worse. Don't mess around. Get it checked out."] Other people left messages expressing their concern. Marto was both worried and embarrassed. He felt like he was going a little crazy from these visions. It gnawed at this sense of identity. He didn't dare let people know what was going on in them until he could figure out why he was seeing them. They could be some sort of a trick, but why? He had no memory of those events, aside from the visions themselves, but they felt almost as if they were from his past. All he could do was to push them away, hoping they would make sense later.

He sent reassurances to his followers, regaining the attention of the proprietor who glared at him and pointed to the virtual sign shouting "USE YOUR WORDS" highlighted in red neon above the cafe.

"Just letting them all know I'm all right. My followers," Marto said.

"Yeah, I know, but we have a strict policy here. If you need to thext, please step outside."

Marto re-situated himself on the stool and asked again to see the menu. He chose a hot cup of nettle tea sweetened with beet syrup and a hardtack biscuit, thinking of his tea with Mem the night before he left on his tour. The proprietor turned his back to heat the water. Marto gazed over the edge of the high bridge a hundred meters down to the river below flowing in from the long gully to the North.

Unable to update his written record without drawing the ire of the proprietor, Marto allowed his awareness to wander and take in the activity on the bridge. The booths here were set up to be semi-permanent and multi-purpose. On the bridge were a multitude of different eateries, clothing gifters, implant offers, pottery, tools, bikes and such. Marto thought about gifting his skates and see if he might be given a uni to replace his old one, but he was leaning toward a bike. Winter was coming to the NorthEast, such as it was now, and he would need warmer clothing, but not yet, and he didn't want to be burdened with it before it was necessary. Maybe he needed a hoodie. He made a conscious choice not to broadcast any of these desires. It was against the rules of the cafe.

He sat and did nothing. He shared nothing, he communicated nothing. He just sat there. His thoughts were his own in this small space. He could allow his wants to go unfulfilled. It was strangely relaxing. He tried to remember the last time he had a moment like this. There were times when he was off grid during his previous tours, but those were moments when he had no choice but to be offline. Here it was voluntary. He immediately wanted to document the experience, he felt an urge to share his observations with his followers. On one level he knew they were still there, noticing his environs on their own, but he was unable to provide any narrative, and it felt naked and a little exciting.

The tea and biscuit were ready. "So, this is your first time in a mandatory verbal cafe." It was not a question.

"How can you tell?"

"It's always the same for you people. You just sit there and marvel at the newness of not being constantly distracted and entertained by your implants. You stare out into space and you get a little smile." The proprietor was direct and gruff, but also seemed kind and perhaps wise. Marto wanted to know more.

"Where are you from?"

"I am from north of here. Little community near Bristol. We live off the grid, getting by in a traditional way."

"Feudalist?" Marto felt a little alarm.

"That's a bit extreme, you know. You people can be more prejudiced than you realize. No, we are not feudal. We are not trying to bring back the good old days of boom and bust. We just like to stay in the here and now, without all the overlays. Grow the food, eat the food, work, sleep, make merry."

"Sounds a bit simplistic in this day and age," Marto said after a sip of the nettle tea. It tasted green and sweet. "How do you manage with all the environmental changes? How do you keep your soil fertile? What about the missing insects? What about the storms?"

"We manage as best we can. We don't refuse technology you know, we just keep it out of our heads."

"But you can't control the farming bots if you aren't implanted. You don't have decompilers do you?"

"No need for them. We use our hands." The proprietor lifted his hands to show Marto. They were rough and calloused. His nails were short but clean. They had seen a lot of use.

"Don't you get bored?"

"Of course we get bored. That's the whole point. Boredom is a brilliant teacher. We cherish it."

Marto thought about this and decided it made no sense. He let it go, took a long sip of his cooling tea and then finished it.

"Well, I am a traveling writer. I am on a tour of the NorthEast communities. Maybe I could visit your community for my tour?"

"You are welcome to visit anytime, but not if you are buzzing away in your head like a child. To stay with us you need to talk out loud, and keep your software dormant."

"Well, I'm willing to try it. Must be a little like being in here right? You know my followers can still see what I see. I'm just not thexting with them right now. The one problem I foresee is I can't write about my travels to your community without engaging a mod. You know, to write." Marto moved his fingers on the bar like he was typing on the old Royal typewriter in Hemingway's office.

"Sure you can," the proprietor said, reaching under the bar and handing him a pad of paper and a pencil. "knock yourself out. I'm Zeke by the way, not that you asked."

"Marto."

"So, Marto, do you often pass out like that? You have fits sometimes? Epileptic?"

"Mmm, I don't think so. It's only happened a few times." Marto tried to bite into the hardtack and found he couldn't. He nibbled off a little at the edge. "Once back in Reverside on the Hudson and once here. I don't think it's my biology. It feels like a mod, but more real, if that's possible."

"I got no idea," said Zeke. "Never had the experience."

Zeke seemed to be in his 50s, maybe older. He wore a simple blue collared shirt and jeans. He was not thin, but broad of shoulder and muscular. There was little wasted mass on him. To keep up on his travels, Marto made a point of staying in good physical condition, but his own fitness paled in comparison with Zeke's. He wondered if all of the members of his community were like that.

"Do you get many people coming here? How do you stay in Flow?"

"Oh, there are lots of people who know me here. They keep a kind of loose track of my 'Merit,'" he said the word with a mild distaste. "I serve anyone and everyone who can keep their minds on where they are and say what they have to say out loud. I come here to get things I need for my community up north."

"If you are not implanted, how do you know when someone is

thexting?" Marto was surprised at himself for not thinking of this sooner.

Zeke lifted a square of carbon fiber with a display on it, not much larger than the palm of his hand. "This tells me when someone at the bar is breaking the rules. One of the visitors on the bridge made it for me a couple of years ago. Points to the offender. Mostly picks up on outgoing communication and any running mods. It can tell if you get too wrapped up in the incoming communication as well. I notice you have a lot coming in right now, but you are keeping it out of your awareness while you are here. That is considerate of you and I appreciate it. It also shows you know how to control yourself. I congratulate you on that. It's a rarity, I daresay."

"Can you really tell all of that from a handheld app? I mean like what I'm focusing on and what I'm not?"

Zeke laughed and the wrinkles around his eyes deepened with his amusement. "No, it doesn't tell me everything. Wow. I know most of it just by looking at you. You people are so easy to read, honestly."

"Well, it's still an interesting piece of tech. I'm curious who created it."

"Oh, it was a guy named Maxtor who gave it to me but I think it was made by someone else. Came here with an entourage. Do you know the word? Used to apply to celebrities. I think he lives nearby, North of Yale Havens a ways, near The Middle."

Marto became aware of an imminent change in the weather sent to him by Chia « Lita « Lena « Mary « Sung-Yi « etc. Winds were backing in from the East, and a front was moving in from the West. Hard weather for the bridge. The gifters had already started closing up and collapsing their booths.

"Looks like it's time for you to go Marto. Stop by our town if you like. It's called Plainville."

"Thank you, Zeke," said Marto, already missing this little respite. "I will." Then he tucked the uneaten hardtack into his one pocket and skated away toward the crest of the eastern slope, the skies darkening behind him.

16. A Noob in Cos

After being intimidated by the wall around Sherwood, Helen felt better about the town which lay before her now. She suspected they knew she was coming and she was right. She was greeted at the first dwellings by a girl who looked like a large bird and a boy who looked like a large cat. Helen dismounted from her bike.

["We've been expecting you,"] thexted the bird. She had a human mouth, a hard gray nose, which looked beakish and was covered in feathers. She wore no clothing. The cat-boy's lips puffed outwards, cleft below a small dark nose, and gazed at her with slitted eyes. He also wore no clothing and was covered in fur. Helen couldn't guess their ages, but they seemed young.

["Yes, I wonder if you have seen a man come through on a unicycle? He's medium height, in his early 30s, dark brown hair, medium dark skin, and brown eyes? He's sort of a writer?"]

["Oh, yes, we know Marto. He was not here, in Cos but stopped by near here. A delegation of us went to see him. How can we help?"]

["I'm delivering a message to him, in person."]

The pair of greeters stared at her, their expressions impossible to interpret. The silence continued for at least a minute, growing awkward. Helen wondered if she would be turned away, worried because of her growing hunger and need for a place to sleep.

Then without warning, the bird girl pecked at the cat boy who hissed, lifting his paw-like hands to swat her. The two stood apart, ready to attack each other a moment before abruptly returning to their previous postures.

["Follow us,"] thexted the cat. ["You are tired and hungry. We are happy to offer you what we have. Welcome to Cos."]

Relief poured over Helen and she felt her eyes well up slightly. ["Thank you so much."] She walked her bike into the town.

Cos stood on a green hill. There were grass and paths leading through it with a sparse settlement of homes, some square and some dome-like, all new. This was not like other interconnected towns, built on existing coastal suburbs. This community seemed to have sprung from a park or country club abandoned in the old days. Through the trees and homes, you could see the water, devouring crumbling homes and buildings on the coastline.

Helen had been delayed in her departure from Reverside by the violent storm that swung through a few days prior. She received the upgrade from Dizzy for following Marto but was still getting used to it. The implantation process was disturbing and disgusting. She had hoped never to have to do it again after her first implant experience back in the Jersey, but she did her best to tough it out. Her thexting had improved to the point where she was told it was acceptable for communicating with people in her local vicinity. She was still fairly disoriented when she tried to thext to people she couldn't see. Her visualizer was still adapting to her specific mental patterns. For the time being, she could only get strange blurry hints of the larger interconnected community. It gave her a mild headache.

Given the abundance of land in Cos, the farm system was ubiquitous and sprawling. Unlike the one in Reverside, theirs was low to the ground, encased in something clear, like glass, but maybe not glass, and angled its way along the walkways and around the homes. It was sunken halfway into the ground, with the glass covering only the top of the rows of plants. The structures rarely rose above waist high. It was easy to peer down into it to see the growth of grain, vegetables and other food for the harvest. Helen's stomach growled loudly when she looked at a dense cluster of tomatoes, ready to be picked by the waiting bots. They walked over a delicate arch of a bridge where part of the farm intersected the path. Ahead of them was a reassuringly human looking person, a little like Mem, but with photosynthetic hair like hers, growing over the entire top half of their body. They had dark skin like her own, and a broad white smile.

["I am Tash,"] said Tash. ["Head of security here, in Cos. Reyleena let me know you might come this way. I want you to know you are most welcome here. We will offer you what we can and help you on your journey."]

["Thank you so much. I came all the way from Reverside, and I could use a break."]

A small boy with a tangled mop of red hair walked up to Helen and handed her a cup with a tan milky liquid in it. She did her best to access ratings for him and push the meter up as far as it would go. He smiled at her and walked away.

The liquid in the cup was thick, slightly sweet, and calmed her anxious body like a heavy blanket on a cold night. She closed her eyes and felt the calories course through her. It was hard not to gulp it all down at once. "Oh," she heard herself say. The bird girl laughed. It was a high cackling sound that made Helen nervous. The cat boy licked his hand and then rubbed his fist against his forehead.

No longer starving, she had a chance to take in her surroundings. Aside from the winding farms everywhere, Cos seemed a lot like Reverside or Livings-town or any other interconnected community she had visited. The silence was the main feature. Helen could hear birds above, crows and bluejays mostly.

She remembered those sounds from her childhood home in Pittsburgh. The lands around Baywood where her mother lived after her separation from her father were quiet, and as a teen, she often walked for long hours in the wooded lands surrounding the old brick mansion. Her brother and sister were consumed with their roles as the future rulers of their worker families, familiarizing themselves with commerce and production. Helen was an outcast, born of a separate bloodline, a product of her mother's relationship with a drifter before the marriage to her father. She knew she wouldn't be called upon to take up the yoke of subjugation when she was grown and lived a life of aristocratic boredom.

Her mother kept a large library of books on the second floor of their estate and she would pick one and remove herself to a quiet rock in the woods, listening to the birds caw overhead as she read about bygone eras of nations and nature. She remembered those worlds as if she had lived in them. Stories of aristocrats and paupers, wars and flight, steamships and airships, battles for land against tribes of native peoples, now forever changed. Listening to the call of the birds brought her back to her lost youth, spent between the pages of old books.

["Let's get you situated, so you have an idea of where you will be sleeping,"] Tash thexted, breaking into her reverie. Helen nodded and followed her down the path to the left, and down the slope of the hill to a one-room empty square dwelling with a bed and a few floor cushions. Helen left her bike leaning up against the side of the boxy house and put down her pack next to the bed. She felt as if she could fall asleep there at once.

She could feel the fabric on the bed and the floor cushions were woven from tiny plastic threads. The color was pale, but with hints of green, blue and yellow woven in. ["It's from the North Atlantic gyre,"] Tash thexted, seeming to read her mind, or had Helen thexted that last thought? ["We send out colonies of bots in slow-moving solar powered bottle boats in search of the plastic. They harvest it and eventually bring it back to shore near one of the tribes. On the way to shore, they convert it into a useable state, like this fleece. Parts of this home structure are also from that gyre."] Helen thought she could smell the sea in the fabric, but it might have been imagined.

Back home, everything was handmade, from wood or wool or cotton or hemp. The house itself had been created back in the glory days of material, and it was crumbling. The old plastic plumbing was replaced by new lead pipes, thankfully. Toilets, baths, and showers were a welcome luxury, as was running water. Helen became aware she needed a commode.

["Two doors down,"] thexted Tash. ["You can access the Cos map with your visualizer. Lots of information there about where to get food, water, a bath and more. Reyleena tells me you should be able to access it now. Give it a try."]

Helen squinted, concentrating on finding a map of Cos. Suddenly, a three-dimensional map in sharp detail filled her imagination. It felt like a daydream, but sharper, clearer and fully under her control. She found herself inside the square house on the northwestern outskirts of the town, highlighted with a generic icon of a woman's face. Suddenly the icon changed to show her own face. It was an image of her approaching Cos, maybe from the point of view of the bird-girl. Her face looked thin. She had not seen a mirror since she left home. It was the first time she had seen the sprouting green hair on her head. She zoomed in and the image of her face filled her imagination. It moved as she looked at it, her puff of vegetation waving slightly in the breeze. She had missed being able to gaze at a reflection of herself but had been too busy with her travels and her mission to find Marto to think about it. She liked what she saw, and smiled a little with the satisfaction of it. The life of a wanderer had made her more beautiful, she thought, even with those small wrinkles growing at the corners of her eyes, and the new lines on either side of her mouth. Yes. She looked a little hardened from the journey, but still, she looked good.

She zoomed back out, and could see Tash's image and name, information bubbles to let her see the history of occupants at the house she was going to sleep in, the public toilets, baths further on, shelter for storms, food offered, beverages, water stations, crafters with clothing on offer, everything. ["This is amazing!"] she told Tash. ["is this all updated in real time?"]

["Of course. Up-to-the-moment information is essential. I would recommend limiting your use of the visualizer this way to just the town of Cos for now. You will be tempted to..."]

["Oh no."] Helen had impulsively tried zooming out rapidly to find Marto and it made her dizzy and sick. She sat down abruptly on the bed and disengaged her visualizer by concentrating on her body. ["That was unpleasant."]

Tash was laughing a little. ["Sorry. I don't mean to make fun. I should have warned you. So, if you don't mind, I have things to attend to, and night is coming. Also, I've just been alerted we are in for another storm. Do you mind sheltering tonight at the dome with the rest of us? It would be safer."]

Helen accessed the dome in the map. It seemed too small to hold the whole town. She pictured everyone sleeping close together, the odor of their bodies filling the space. It was not something she wanted to repeat immediately after her experience in Reverside during the last storm. She imagined it wasn't difficult for the Interconnected, who could just go elsewhere to a sunny shore or spacious landscape in their minds, but she doubted she could do that yet.

["Would it be okay if I stayed here? I would rather risk it."]

Tash paused. Their face went blank, and they got the faraway look Helen had seen in Reyleena's eyes. Was that a kind of calculation? Prediction? Did Tash have a split persona like Reyleena?

["I'm afraid we have to insist. There are tornados reported. This home is insufficient for shelter in case one of them touches down here. I'm sorry. You really must join us tonight. We'll do our best to make you comfortable. You have two hours and then we will all be gathering. You know where?"]

["Yes! I see it all perfectly."]

["Great. Just follow the map. There are five baths free right now if you want to wash up. I think you'll like them."]

["Yes, that would be good."] Helen decided to concentrate on the present moment and deal with the future when it became the now. ["A bath would be great. Then something more to eat, I think."]

["A solid plan."] Tash smiled again. Their face appeared sometimes male and sometimes female to Helen, depending on the expression. Tash was strong and gentle, and also mysterious. Helen felt a little attracted to them and that attraction felt like a sweetness in her throat. She was lonely.

["Thank you,"] she sent, smiling back at Tash, and walked out the door toward the outhouses.

17. Yale Havens

Phobics and traditionalists say they shun every sort of implanted neural interface, forgetting that neural interfaces are at least thirty-thousand years old. They go back to the earliest cave paintings and are perhaps even as old as storytelling in general.

Imagine a young hunter in a cave, being led through a ceremony by a shaman pointing and acting out the depictions of the great beasts on the walls. The light of the fire flickers, the story builds. The participants become transfixed, they gasp, their limbs twitch reflexively as the tale of the hunt builds to a crescendo. Cheers erupt, the program ends.

Jump ahead to a mere five thousand years ago, at the beginning of written language, a more flexible form of neural interface. A string of characters is recorded by hand, and then fed into the eyes of a reader, whereby, they experience fear, pleasure, emotion, sympathy, excitement, and retain memories generated by this code, of places unseen, voyages unmade, deep into their lives.

Indeed, our technologies are shocking and new to those unfamiliar with them. The ones we employ now differ in their physical invasiveness but retain their ancient root. Our implants are a means to deliver a code expressing a narrative, and little more.

– The Wakeful Wanderer's Guide, Vol. 6, lines 458-461

The library was flooded. Marto and his friend Bruce Williams were resting on the third mezzanine, after readying the next group of books for transport inland.

"The water just keeps coming," Bruce said, chewing on a pale green piece of jerky while petting a brown and white spotted cat. "We shifted shelves around at first, as you know, but we could tell it wouldn't be enough. Took us almost ten years to get serious. We were lucky you showed up all those years ago or it might never have happened."

Marto looked down at the massive old arched reading room of the library. Standing water from the Long Island Sound had made it all the way across the floor. The wood was rotting, the room was empty. The old desks and bookshelves had long since been removed. The building looked archaic, but Marto knew the structural beams were made of steel, not wood. It would keep standing long after they removed the last volume. There were millions of rare books left to relocate, perhaps another decade before they were finished.

"We are thankful, to you and your friends, Marto. Can't express how much. We would never have been able to save so many important works without you and your people." Bruce extended a cup and poured tea into it from an old thermos. "I grew up here, you know. Most of us did. Some of us left to join the tribes, but a lot of us stayed behind. I can't imagine a life away from these old buildings, but there is no denying the inevitable."

"Have you thought about where you want to go, Bruce?" Marto said, smelling the aroma of the tea, it was an Assam, he thought, or a Yunnan blend, a genuine treat. Marto knew Bruce from his first tour. The story of the librarians at Yale Havens was the highlight and made all future tours possible. When he had arrived, the librarians were just beginning to pack up the books to be moved. They had no plan.

The focus of the middle of Marto's first book tour was the relationship between the librarians and the tribes further inland. "It was a sales pitch," Bruce had told him, "One of the most important in recent history, I like to think. We sold them on the value of these bound words, and on the importance of people who knew and read them. We couldn't convince them, but it got them curious, and then, thanks to you, the Ritual started. That's what saved us."

Like in many old towns, a symbiosis had developed between the community of librarians and the surrounding tribes, but their interactions were superficial. The Interconnected viewed these collections of books as a redundant backup of knowledge they assumed was already in storage. Naturally, the library itself had an online catalog of almost everything it contained which already existed in the redundant storage of the interconnected minds of the tribes. The tribes assumed nothing was missing and didn't see why the old books needed saving. To them it seemed unimportant the library was flooding.

Bruce was nine years younger when Marto first arrived on his bicycle. Marto's plan for his tours was in its infancy. He had only a vague idea of what he wanted to happen. His thought was only that he would provide a first-hand narrative of life in and around the Interconnected tribes and thereby gain followers and merit. The problem was his tour had been largely uneventful. When he arrived at Yale Havens, with its monastic, non-implanted community of knowledge seekers and keepers, he knew he had found something interesting. He had only a handful of followers on his first tour, and it seemed as if he was going to lose them if nothing dramatic happened. He was on the verge of giving up and going back to Reverside when Bruce saw him peddle up, and was friendly. Over the course of the next several months, Bruce and he spent their time packing up stacks of books in the lower levels, and reading history. To his surprise, Marto's followers began to multiply.

Soon local tribal members began following Marto. Like the surprise popularity of slow-video back in the dawn of the century, where a camera on a boat or a train would transfix viewers for days, his new followers became absorbed in the slow, simple process of packing up books in boxes, and logging them in pencil on an old yellow lined pad. As they moved the books from the shelves, each tome offered with it, a blast of associated information for the Interconnected. New discussions bloomed on a myriad of topics, from history to philosophy, adding to the interest in the activity. Before long, several members of the nearby tribes volunteered to help. They would each meet a librarian at the entranceway to the old university and then enter the stacks. Each tribal member would be broadcasting publicly and have between two dozen to a few hundred followers. Some helped with the work, others observed. Rare books were discovered, unrecorded in the existing mountains of data. Everyone was watching for the discovery of these hidden jewels.

A young upstart dreamer named Maxtor began to devise a plan to safely store, catalog, rescan, and allow for the curation of at least one library this size, and allow for it to be expandable. The Ritual had found a goal, and spawned an increased level of interest and activity.

Bruce took a while to answer Marto's question. "I think I'll go with the others to The Middle. I want to see the new library there. I am needed to help maintain and curate it." Bruce was sipping tea and looking up at the roof of the reading room. "It's another university town, you know, so there's historic architecture there but nothing like this."

"Life is change," Marto said, enjoying the quiet of the moment inside the enormous hall. "What about your family?"

Bruce's expression darkened.

"I lost Hannah two years ago to the flu. It happened suddenly. She refused treatment from the tribes because it required an implant. She was stubborn. I miss her every day."

Marto let the news sink in. Hannah had been kind to him during his last visit. He had stayed with her at Bruce's home, along with their daughter and their family of cats. "Oh Bruce, I am so sorry to hear it. She was a wonderful woman." He dared not ask about his daughter, fearing the worst, but he had to know. "What about Lisha?"

"After Hannah died, she went ahead to The Middle. She's like you now. You can look her up." Marto did. Lisha « Hannah « Lori « Abagail « etc was engaged in The Middle, integrating the books into the new library. ["Hi Marto!"] she pinged. ["Tell my Dad I said hello. Doing well. I'm super busy [data blast regarding feeding the new library] Great tribe here. Can't wait to see him."]

"She says hi, and she's well, busy, and can't wait for you to come on up there," Marto told Bruce. He brightened a bit.

"Thanks," he said. "Um, tell her I just want to get a bit more done here and I will be on my way up. It's going well, but it's hard to leave all this."

Marto sent what he asked, they sat with their tea.

"So," Bruce finally said, breaking the silence, "maybe you can help me with something. When Lisha joined your people, the Interconnected, she dropped the last name, Williams. Now her name is just this long list, and I find it hard to do it right. Can you enlighten me as to why you use those foremother names? I mean, it smarts a little, being left off her list, you know?"

Marto took a sip. He had responded to this question before, and it didn't always go well. "So, I totally get that the name change could be hard to accept. It's not really suited for non-thexting people. It's longer, and yes, it excludes the male lineage entirely. It could seem like a genuine loss of heritage."

"Exactly. My father was a Williams, his father was a Williams, his father too. Why lose that history?"

"Well, for a father, I can see how it would be difficult." Marto suddenly had an image of his father come to mind, from his second blackout. Glasses, clean shaven, mountains in the distance. He felt a sudden bout of vertigo and fought to stay conscious.

"Are you okay Marto? You look like you are going to be sick."

Marto steadied himself, pushing thoughts about his father out of his head to stay in the library with Bruce. "Yeah, sorry, I get these flashes sometimes." He didn't want to say more. "Um, so the main difference with our names and traditional male lineage names is we go back from child to mother to grandmother, forming a series of links using first names only."

"Got it."

"And when you are communicating in thext, it's not so difficult to do that. It just comes up as part of your public profile – your persona, so we don't get tongue-tied trying to say them aloud, or forget which name comes next."

"Okay."

"And each of these names has their own links, you know, so if I wanted to look into fathers, and surnames, I could, as each name carries associated data. Forefathers are not forgotten, they're just not part of the list."

"But why is that?" Bruce pressed.

"Well, the quick answer, and you may not like it, is accuracy. Let's leave your family out of it for a while. A list of foremothers is 79% more accurate than a list of forefathers because of occasional pregnancies that occur unnoticed – out of wedlock."

"Infidelities," Bruce replied, looking thoughtful.

"Yes," Marto said carefully. "That happened more often than was previously thought. People used to think women were naturally prudish and loyal. In fact, they cheated roughly as often as men."

"But wait. Okay, so if Hannah... okay. But what if I..."

"Again, let's not bring your family into it. It's really sensitive. The purpose isn't to arouse doubt about every relationship, just to establish an accurate chain of births. Mother to child is an immediate and physical link. Father to child just isn't."

Bruce looked at the ceiling. "Well, I'm making it personal, just so I can understand it. Right, so if I had a son outside our marriage, that son would be tracked to the mother, not to me. If Hannah had Lisha outside our marriage, it would go back through her to her mom and on and on."

"Right. Remember that the Interconnected live in intimate proximity to data. All the data collected from family trees, and birth records, that's all in there. For the purposes of identifying who you are and where you come from, the foremother chain was chosen and the surname method was abandoned as flawed, and also a tie to the Pre-Tide ways of old."

"But man, so much history is just thrown on the trash heap here. I mean, in the Bible, all the begets, are mostly male. The Romans, the Greeks – we've been following the male lineage for all of recorded history." Bruce waved his arm at the stacks.

"True, but you know as well as I, lots of things that have been working one way forever and ever are now no longer working. Early on in tribal life, shortly after the establishment of Sherwood, a change was proposed, and it stuck. No doubt it was a rebellion. There was a lot of rebellion then. People wanted to put a gap in the record and start anew. For example, and sorry I'm making this personal again, but if you trace your name Williams far enough back, what do you come to?"

"A slave owner in Kentucky. A man named Thaddeus Williams," Bruce said flatly. "There's no way to know what my family name was before they were slaves."

"Right. So, that was part of it. Names were property. Marriage was property. When the currencies crashed, and the gifting and sharing culture arose, property faded and the names faded with it." Marto decided to leave out all of the factors around heteronormative culture and adaptations to allow for greater gender fluidity, deciding it was too much for right now.

"Yeah, I get it. It still stings a bit, but I get it."

They got up, having finished the tea, and went back to the waiting metric tons of books.

The Bubonic Plague of the 14th and 15th centuries combined with the Hundred Years War left Europe in a state of mass psychological shock. [data blast of historical record] The sheer loss of population at a time of total scientific ignorance, left the survivors turning to superstition in search of answers. Self-flagellation, the brutal and uninformed persecution of the Jews, and a general belief in the inherent evilness of humanity created a secondary plague of cruelty which amplified the effects of the viruses that wiped out so many.

We fared a little better in the wake of The Great Tide, thanks to all we have learned and created since then, but the effects on the common psyche are ongoing. Some of us have turned to brutality, some of us have upgraded our minds to forget the worst, losing ourselves in the distraction of our implants, some of us devote ourselves to our projects in a single-minded intensity, trying to put the past behind us. It will be decades, maybe centuries before we fully comprehend what we have lost. Extinctions are being mitigated by genetic storage, but we all know the natural world of the past has been lost forever, and the full understanding of this fact may be beyond human comprehension.

The Vengeance, which occurred during the decades following

The Great Tide is among the events no one wants to remember. [data blast of information surrounding the massacre of the wealthy, side data on underground shelters] The first targets of the populist rage were the top ten wealthiest people in each country. The masses had labeled the wealthiest people in society 'Defilers' and blamed them for promoting the rise in atmospheric carbon which resulted in so much loss of land and life. Defilers were easy to identify, as their names had been published annually lauding their accomplishments. Then the extended families were also labeled 'Defiler' and likewise targeted. That required a deeper search of the data. The Vengeance then turned their attention to the 500 wealthiest Defilers and their families, and still unsatisfied, expanded their violence further until the loss of life was the better part of one hundred million worldwide. They stopped discriminating between those who had fought the catastrophic warming, and those who helped it along. They became hungry for more blood to satisfy their revenge. The super rich had planned for this revolt, building shelters and hideaways, but their defenses crumbled under a mountain of human determination and grief.

Like what happened in the wake of The Plague, the empty estates of the wealthy became populated by their wealthiest surviving assistants. Accountants, lawyers, contractors, real estate agents, and even chauffeurs stepped in to fill the power vacuum. Ironically, people turned toward the enablers of great wealth to find a way back to stability and order. Under the guidance of these new landed families, the violence of the mob was put to use accumulating territory for their new rulers forming the Neo-Feudal Enclaves of today. The same distaste for the economy of greed and accumulation gave way to the Interconnected's greatest foe.

This is the weakness of our method of maintaining the historical record. Subjects which are not popular, or fail to reinforce a favorable view of our new society fall out of fashion and into obscurity. How will we maintain an unflinching history of that which is unfashionable and unpopular? How will the truth survive if not for librarians like Bruce? Will future generations decide to take up the duty to curate our forgotten stories so we don't succumb to a false narrative? These are questions larger than myself, dear readers, but I write them here in hopes of a greater discussion.

— The Wakeful Wanderer's Guide, Vol. 6, lines 462-466

They worked into the night, lit by illuminators, a gift from the tribes. As night fell, these sun charged lamps glided down from the roof, through the open windows, and into the halls. Groups of multipatterned cats played and lounged in the luminescence. Gazing through the stacks of books, you could track the activity of the librarians and their guests by the glow of the hovering lights.

18. The Lovely Charlotte

The Sound was sparkling and calm. Helen looked out over the front of a ferry named "The Lovely Charlotte" from the small cabin built for a single passenger. Thanks to the tutelage of her new friends in Cos, she had pinpointed Marto in a town called Yale Havens. She hoped he would linger there long enough for her to meet him, give him the packet of data his mother had given her and be done with it. She was tired and confused. If not for her conversation with Reyleena, the head of security in Reverside, and the kindness of Tash, head of security in Cos, she would have given up by now. That said, the sky was bright, the water rose and fell gently, and the long gray-green ferry was almost completely silent as it carried its two dozen automated caravans, one passenger, and a bicycle east along the coast.

On the horizon to the South was Long Island, a divided and disputed land. Three of the great families had compounds to the extreme east and southwest, trying to hold on to past glory. Helen could see how pointless it was. The Tide had come in, the world had changed. It was only a matter of time now before everyone was either like the Raiders or the Interconnected. The families thought they kept control over the Raiders, using them for skirmishes and reclamation raids, but Helen had seen the way those biker beasts looked at her mother behind her back. They hated the families. It was only a matter of time.

Would the Interconnected prevail in an all-out war with the Raiders? Doubtless. For all their fierceness, the Raiders lacked strategy and relied on xombie slaves or implanted members of their own gangs for new tech, which was limited. The brutality of their way of life prevented them from ingenuity. They held fast to the survivalist's code.

Only the strong. 'Only the stupid,' thought Helen. The future looked like Marto and Tash and whatever Reyleena was.

["How goes the journey?"] the cheerful voice of Nandy, the ferry's pilot broke into her mind. Helen's interface was translating it into speech, which she knew was a habit of noobs. New tribal members eventually stopped sounding them out, just as someone learning a new language eventually stopped translating mentally.

["All good,"] Helen thexted back. ["Peaceful. Lovely, really."] She had forgotten to give ratings for the journey, and rather than wait until the end, she decided to give them immediately.

Nandy was piloting the Charlotte remotely from Bronxing-Poetic, a tribe near what was left of Manhattan Island. He was one of a few pilots for this boat, guiding it up and down the Long Island Sound. She was told by Tash there were several groups of pilots who offered guidance for these self-powered gray-green flat barges. The calm waters of the Sound offered steady movement of food and goods to the tribes. On arrival in Yale Havens, some of these caravans would offload their 'tainers,' the smaller box like bots intended for a specific location, or slowly crawl onto roads north. Others would continue on to Copp and Seekonk and points east.

Tash had educated Helen a great deal about the agriculture and transportation methods of the Interconnected tribes during her stay at Cos. They used the term 'namportou' to describe the advances of tribal existence over the systems of pre-Tide civilization.

["There used to be cars everywhere, you know. Everywhere. Not just on the roads, but parked. I know you've read about it in books, but just picture it for a moment. Imagine how much land that used up everywhere."] Tash had been gesticulating, even though their mouth was still. ["It was monstrously inefficient. People were constantly driving them from place to place, for work, for play, to visit each other. The reason was communication was primitive, and goods needed to be transported from so far away to satisfy the hunger of the debt afflicted populous. Also, all agriculture was open-air back then, so you had to rely on the difference in climate and resources to get what you wanted. On top of that, people needed a lot of things to make them feel comfortable. They had little to no connection, so their sense of well being was wrapped up in ownership of material stuff."]

A picture had formed in Helen's mind at this. It started moving. A gigantic red robot was belching smoke, and driving itself on a flat empty field. It was digging up dirt, and as Helen focused on it higher up, she saw there was a person driving it; not a robot at all. This was a kind of vehicle. A caption for the moving picture rose in her mind. ["Harvester. Pre-Tide agriculture."] Now she could see vast concrete stretches of land covered by cars, now roads choked with them. Then she saw one of the sunken cities, new and shiny, cars and trucks led in and away from it. It was astounding.

["So roads and cities were the way society organized itself. You couldn't grow what you needed in a city because of lack of open space. Everything came in on giant trucks and trains. They even flew goods in via these awful fuel gobbling planes and gigantic oil-burning cargo ships."] New images arose in Helen's mind, one for each of the old methods of transport. She knew about these, but Tash was becoming animated, and they were behaving a bit like Father Sanjay, the preacher back home, during one of his sermons. ["Most of the cities were on the coast, formed there during the golden age of sea travel. This was a way of life going back centuries but became impossible after The Tide. The coastal cities flooded, credit collapsed, the trucks stopped, airports and docks succumbed to the sea and people starved."] The old horrifying maps appeared; New Orleans, Miami, Port Au Prince, Boston, Venice, New York City, Atlantic City, the Chesapeake Bay, Los Angeles, Oakland, the Netherlands, Barcelona, and on and on. Photos and videos flashed before her mind's eye. Pleas for help, families starving, angry looters. Some thankful for the brigades of new volunteers who stepped up, others, the less fortunate, seeking revenge on the government, the corporations, the scientists, the intellectuals, and ultimately, the rich. Short news segments showing disorder in some of the cities, cooperation in others. The wealthy families retreating to bunkers and compounds. Society was splitting.

["And this is the way of life my family wants to bring back. The one that caused this terrible mess,"] Helen said, shaken.

["Well, perhaps something like it. For all of its negatives, it was the mode of human civilization for many generations. It only became insupportable in this century. Civilizations change. Many people like to romanticize the days of hoards and hovels. I don't completely blame them. It's all about fear. If you choose not to become like us,"] Tash touched Helen's head, ["you live in constant fear of not having enough."]

["So we don't need the cars and trucks anymore, but we still have these moving caravans. So, the local farming isn't enough?"]

["There are tribes which specialize in foodstuffs or handmade or specialty materials printing. Lots of oils are transported. Olive trees."] Tash got a wistful look. ["You know, olive trees are a hundred years old before they are in peak production? No way around it. The oil is precious and has to be shipped until we can grow modified versions everywhere. The automated caravans carry the goods in the tainers. They are slow moving and low impact. Anything too perishable to be moved has to be grown locally. Because the tribes have advanced printing and enclosed farming, and since most only ever choose to travel via implant, we stay put, and our footprint is tiny. We call it 'namportou,' which is a bastardization of the French for 'where is not important'. There isn't as much need to move from place to place to be productive or engaged. Here is just as good a place as any. So, you can understand why you and Marto and other wanderers are such a curiosity."] Tash was smiling their awesome big smile. Helen thought they were just gorgeous. She hoped they couldn't tell.

She didn't want to leave Cos and especially Tash, but when a spot on the ferry was offered, it was her best chance to catch up. The bike was wearing her down.

Suddenly, Helen got a notification Marto had posted two new lines from his journey. She had added herself as a follower and was just starting to get updates from the Wakeful Wanderer's Guide. The text floated through her mind, as a narrative in Marto's own voice.

The local road east of Yale Havens is nicely maintained. My skates, which are fun, but a bit exhausting, glide smoothly here. Chef Papa « Mimi « Archi « Victoria « etc of The Killings tribe offers me some delicious eats here, halfway to the Connecticut River. A bowl of noodles, radishes, tofu, seaweed and a sauce I simply cannot get enough of. A sort of soy and ginger combination, I think, but with a smoky flavor as well. I asked Papa what was in it, but he was gleefully secretive. He also served me the most remarkable corn tea, flavored with just a hint of cayenne and honey. Highly recommend for any of you who get out and about. [Short blast of data with location coordinates]

I got an early start this morning, and am feeling optimistic about reaching The Middle by nightfall. That stated, my feet are killing me. I truly miss my old uni. If I had become more accustomed to skates before my trip, I would have the appropriate callouses on my feet and the requisite muscles in my lower legs and hips, but as it is, I am better built for long trips on a bicycle or unicycle than these skates, however much fun they are. High merit to the kind folks at Waveny. I wouldn't have made it this far without them. Long live the trees!

– The Wakeful Wanderer's Guide, Vol. 6, lines 579 & 580

The Lovely Charlotte made almost no noise as it propelled her eastward but she could feel a slight vibration on the deck. Nandy the pilot had explained it was due to a recently imagined aqua-propulsion system built into the hull. The technology was the work of a super-mod named BigoloFib who lived in a tribe in Brazil. The surface below the water was covered in tiny whips which moved like the cilia on micro-organisms. Helen was not the least bit interested in engineering, but the idea seemed novel and not a little bit creepy.

She located herself as a means of practicing using her visualizer. She was close to the sunken town of Bridgeport, and she got a notification she would arrive in Yale Havens by sunset. To her dismay, she found Marto again, now heading north on something called the MiddleWay.

She had been following his writings from the library, but couldn't yet follow him as his other fans did, experiencing his surroundings in real time. She decided to check in with Bruce Williams, the librarian Marto had posted about, and explain her situation without giving away too many details. Perhaps she could find a place to stay for the night among the librarians. Reyleena had cautioned her against announcing herself to Marto, as it might spark a data transfer in the open network, something which might reveal the contents of the package to a clever super-mod and could trigger another of Marto's fainting episodes. If he was on his skates while that happened, he might fall and get a concussion or worse. Helen had to try harder to catch him up. The thought of it was exhausting.

["Feel free to take one of the drones out,"] thexted Nandy. ["It can give you a real-time view of what's around. There are four. You can select one here."] A list of four drones, each with cute names were displayed for Helen in her mind. She concentrated on Buzby-Iggins and suddenly found herself looking at the deck of the ferry from another corner of the boat. She heard, via her actual ears the buzzing of the blades and thought ["up"] like she was thexting to it. The deck fell away below her, and she saw herself, remotely sitting in the open cabin at the front of the Charlotte. Soon she saw the whole of the ferry, as she rose higher still, getting a view of the surrounding water.

The Sound looked far too clear from above. She could see the floor, with its drifting silt and old trash. Helen knew it should be cloudier, this was a bad sign of the vanishing sea life. Mostly jellyfish remained, and some natural and resurrected species, but the water was still too acidic. She had read a lot about this but it was always too upsetting to think about. She steered for Port-Jeff, on the Long Island side. Gaining altitude she could eventually make out details along the coast.

Port-Jeff didn't look like an interconnected town, or if it was, it was not a successful one. She wondered if it had been claimed by the Families, or was a Raider camp. The dwellings were disorganized and haphazard. There were large homes surrounded by hovels. It could have been under the control of one of the lesser families. She had spent so much time recently among the super-tidy Interconnected communities, she had forgotten a lot about her old hometown. She supposed a NeoFeudal town might look like this from above. Grand homes, like the one of her childhood, surrounded by squalor. She had never had an aerial view before.

She noticed a shape moving below her in the water, it was gray and oval, perhaps a shark? It wasn't moving like a shark. A stingray? Too large. It left no sign of its movement on the surface of the water, gliding along near the bottom. She followed it as it headed northeast, backing the little drone as she went. She dipped Buzby lower to the water, but the reflections of the waves caused the image of the underwater blob to distort. After several minutes it surfaced, and she could see her own ferry directly in its path. Surely, it was not going to hit her. Was it going to hit her? It really looked like it was going to hit her.

Now she could see it was a small submersible with a single occupant. The top hatch was open, and its occupant was pointing something at her boat. What was she supposed to do? She thought ["land"] but Buzby didn't respond. It required her instructions to get it back to the deck. She dove the drone toward the submarine pilot as if it was an angry insect. The man in the sub (it was clearly a man) raised his other hand and ducked back inside the tiny craft, pulling the hatch. She buzzed him again, but his submarine was on a direct course to collide with the ferry. She needed to be back in her body, immediately.

["Hey, easy with Buzby!"] Nandy thexted.

Unable to sum up what she was seeing, she asked ["Are you getting any of this? Is this normal?"]

["Is that a submersible? Like out of an old spy movie?"] asked Nandy. ["What is it doing so close the ferry?"]

["No fucking idea! But I can't leave the drone to find out, not that I can steer your boat. You might want to do something if you can."]

["Hang on,"] and the Lovely Charlotte began a slow northern turn which, Helen could see from the drone, was totally ineffectual and far too late.

'Sorry, Buzby!' thought Helen, and tried to disconnect herself with various commands, to no avail. In a panic now, she brought the tiny copter back over its landing pad and thought ["down"] just as she felt a sudden pain in her thigh, snapping her out of the drone, back into her body, only to hear the splash of the drone in the water, and see the gray-green deck of the Charlotte rise up to hit her in the face.

19. The Middleway

The narrow path northeast of Yale Havens was empty. Marto glided his way up it next to the river. He was becoming more competent with the skates and swooped in great curves up along the level trail. Caravans were not allowed on passageways like this one, built on the beds of old railroad tracks. This one had been recently converted and the surface was gloriously smooth.

As smooth as the skating was, however, Marto could no longer avoid the warning signals from his feet and legs. He had blocked the pain back on the Merritt, but now those blocks were proving insufficient, and increasingly hazardous. The friction from the skates had caused blisters on his feet. His shins were screaming at him to stop and his hips ached. The soles of his feet felt wet and hot. His calves were spasming. He had to take frequent breaks, even when using the maximum power assist the skates had to offer.

The chipmunk ran out in front of his feet without warning. It zigged and zagged to avoid being stepped on, but Marto was already toppling forward, rubbing his hands hard on the road and banging his cheek against the ground. Marto found himself thinking it was the same chipmunk that had tripped him up on his unicycle at the start of his journey. Fucking chipmunks.

["Ouch!"] ["Ooh, you took a digger!"] ["That's going to leave a mark!"] His followers chimed in with their concern, but he couldn't help but get the feeling they were enjoying his little run-ins with the rodent population.

He was going to have to take time to recuperate when he reached The Middle and choose a new mode of transport. He made this data public shortly after leaving Yale Havens in the hope someone might offer him a bike or maybe even a new uni. He stopped to sit on a bench and watched the Connecticut River glide by. His feet, finally freed from the skates, looked red and damaged.

The sky was gray but bright. The day was hot. UV radiation was dangerously high, and though his hat protected much of his head, his nose and lips burned. His body felt flooded with oxygen from his exertion, but he also felt dangerously weary. He checked the distance to The Middle and decided he had just enough in caloric reserves to get there. He had a little leftover hard-tack on him, and he nibbled a bit and drank from a bottle offered at a nearby water station.

["Your body temperature is 38.62°, Marto. you may have overheated,"] FornTimbur « HraunHugur « Kristin « Katrin « Eva « etc thexted him from Reykjavik. ["Dehydration too. You might need attention."]

["You are pushing too hard Marto,"] Mem sent. ["You should stay still for a while."]

He checked his Merit. His followership had risen again to pre-Glenville levels, and exceeded them by 12.5%. His stop there had set him back significantly, but his gleeful liaison on the Merritt seemed to have spiked interest, as did his stop at the library. A discussion was underway about his current ailments and their possible solutions. He was getting an urgent message.

["We are coming to meet you Marto. Hang tight."]

The message was sent by five emissaries from The Middle heading south on the same trail. They were on bikes. He could see their names and progress. He was happy to stay put until they got to him.

The abandonment of train travel remains, in the mind of this historian slash travel writer, a mystery. Obviously, the old coal powered engine died a well-deserved death, along with the oil-powered model, but one has to wonder why photo-electric engines on an improved line of tracks have not been resurrected in post-tide civilization.

I imagine there are three reasons for this. The first being the conversion of the majority of the old tracks into more popular pathways for foot and bike travel. The second is a general lack of interest in physically moving from place to place, but that reason is offset by the continuing need to move goods and produce. The third reason might be a culture of provincialism on the part of the Interconnected communities. Not much thought is given to centralized planning for transport of people and goods in this age of revived tribalism. Centralized planning died with the dissolution of federal governments, which in turn died with the demise of the capital to feed them. Still, we are unified in our maintenance of signal repeaters, keeping us connected mentally. Why then, can't a little attention be directed toward a more effective model of transport than road-bound caravans?

– The Wakeful Wanderer's Guide Vol. 6, lines 622 & 623

Returning from the writing tower, Marto found his body lying down on the bench, unable to keep sitting up. He was far more exhausted than he suspected and his throat hurt when he swallowed. He put his hat over his face and felt himself doze off.

He woke to see the back of a member of The Middle, peddling away in front of him. Her name was Shandraine « Martikka « Martina « Yasmine « etc. Riding ahead of her were four other members of the contingent; Rida, Happy, Tse, and Shawn. It took a while for Marto to see they were on a five-person bicycle, a "Quint" according to his followers, and he was riding on a bed extending out behind the long vehicle. Shandraine kept pedaling as she thexted him.

["You were out cold when we found you on the bench, non-responsive. Stay still, and lie back. You are on the back of a long bike. Relax and don't roll over. We are taking you to Maxtor."]

Marto thought he heard it wrong. ["You are taking me to what now?"]

["Maxtor Uber G, who we all love and adore. He wants to see you, like face to face."]

Marto was stunned and thought maybe he was playing out a kind of game. He checked and saw no telltale signs he was in a construct. Maybe this was a regular dream, and he was still sleeping on the bench. He tried to rise.

["Whoa now! Easy back there!"] thexted Happy urgently. ["We are passing 35kph. You will be in even worse shape than you already are if you slide off. We should have strapped him on. Why didn't we strap him on?"]

["Maybe it's because you forgot to bring the straps, Happy. That was your job and you effeneffed it."]

["Just steer the damn bike, Shawn. I didn't think we would need them. Poor guy is all done. He needs a med-tech maybe. Stay still back there Marto. We'll be inside in no time. Maxtor will send for you when you are well again. You might as well try to go back to sleep for now."]

["There was no time to get everything,"] offered Rida, ["We should have brought him food and drink, and maybe some med implants, but it was better to just get here as quickly as we could."]

["We have time for a quick game of TackaTack before we get back, anyone want to play?"] Tse was cheerfully trying to brighten up the mood of the quint team. ["Quick one,"] ["Yes,"] ["Go,"] ["For sure,"] came the responses.

Marto passively watched via his visualizer as the quint morphed into a cartoon spaceship being attacked by goofy looking alien flying saucers. They sent out tiny short-range fighters to intercept, and fired the main laser cannon at the swarming enemies while dodging asteroids, and shouting commands at each other through their virtual communications devices. The whole time, of course, they kept pedaling and following the glasslike path leading to the town in which the great Maxtor was awaiting the lowly Marto. He decided to try to nap again.

He woke inside an old brick building with high, wooden beamed ceilings and glass paned windows. Outside, the sky was dark. He had been asleep for thirteen hours. His temperature was down to 37.04°: normal. There were three leeches on his forearm, and he couldn't tell if they were living or bots. He lay on a standard printed bed with soft wool sheets and a spongy yellow pillow. He was alone. There were water and a vegetable drink in two cups on a table next to him. He drank one and then the other. Then he went to find the commode.

A quick glance at the map showed him he was finally in The Middle. In fact, he was in the middle of The Middle, in the historic district. Commodes were right outside, under the transparent dome which enclosed the lines of old brick buildings. He sent the contents of his bowels and bladder to be dealt with by the decompilers and returned to the bed to sleep.

He woke again to see the smiling face of Lisha « Hannah « Lori « Abagail « etc as she was gently shaking his arm. She looked much like her mother from Yale Havens and a little like Bruce. Outside the brick room windows, there was daylight. It was mid-morning. The leeches on his arm were gone. He had slept seventeen and a half hours.

["Time to get up Marto,"] Lisha was saying to him. ["Maxtor wants to meet you outside."]

Marto rose, put on his pants and hat, left his skates and the modified tube-sling containing the painting and snacks, looked down at his feet to see them dotted with blisters. He felt strangely embarrassed by this, wishing he had shoes and new socks. His old socks were in a pocket on the side of the tube, but they were bloody and torn. His followers began to jump on in exponentially increasing numbers. It was a celebrity interview, he thought to himself. He had no time to prepare. He walked out the door.

Everywhere between the old brick buildings was greenery. Marto adjusted his vision to better see it in the dark. It hung from windows, lined the walkways, and peeked out from the rooftops. The town center was exploding with plant life. The air was humid but cool. The extra oxygen felt good. In the middle of the Atrium was a table which was not there the night before. A potted tree shaded the lone figure from the morning sun shining in through the arching windows.

Maxtor was not a tall man, but he looked like a lion. His skin was medium dark, his eyebrows were light colored, and exaggerated. He was not drastically altered like the cat-girl, Scarlett from Sherwood, but his alterations were non-standard. His hair was like a photosynthetic modification, but it was not green. It flowed away from his face and down his back, chest, and arms in a sparkle of multicolored threads, mostly orange, red, yellow and purple. Much of it was braided and adorned with different colored cubes. His face was naked, but Marto thought the artificial fur might cover all of the rest of his body, tapering off toward his hands and maybe his feet. He was staring up at the top of one of the brick buildings as Marto approached.

Seconds passed. Nothing happened. Then, abruptly, Maxtor leveled his eyes and addressed him. ["Marto, the Wandering Narrative himself! The Wakeful Wandering Node. Feeling better? Wanna Pepsi?"]

Marto was caught short by the gaze, which was predictably intense. Then he tried to figure out just what was being offered and found he didn't know the word. His followers jumped in with 100-year-old images of bottles, and ads, and television commercials. He connected the references with his own research. He was being offered a beverage that could not possibly have been preserved long enough to be drinkable. Evaporation alone would have reduced it to fermented goo, even if you could find a little to keep in a cold bunker somewhere, away from any light.

["I'm feeling much better, thank you. Whoever cured me here was superb. I suppose I had a variation of the flu? And ... do I want a ... what again?"]

["A Pepsi, you slug! I know you know what it was. What you don't know, is how I can get one for you, and you are about to find that out."]

Two freezing cold bottles of brown liquid were placed on the table by someone who vanished as soon as it was done. They all but materialized there. Ice was melting on the outside of the glass. On the side of the glass near the spout, was a red on a white oval, the words "PepsiCola" written in script.

["I prefer the 1960s logo to the later ones."] Maxtor was regarding the side of his bottle. ["Every passing decade since then, the spirit of it got hacked away until you were just left with a lopsided yin-yang circle. What was that supposed to be? Something you should know, the original drink was super, super sweet. Our team stayed true to the original recipe; not an easy find but they had to dial back the sweetness. We used a corn derivative, as true as possible to the later versions but not the one with this logo. If we used the original amount of sweetener, you would just spit it out. Lots of sodium in there too, bubbles, color, and cola nut extract for the flavor and caffeine."]

As Marto moved the bottle under his nose, he got a whiff of what smelled like a solvent. The scent was pushing violently upwards in cold waves. He turned his head.

["Oh yeah, my node, it's a bit of a shock, right? That's the carbonic acid hitting your nasal membranes. Same stuff as poisoned the ocean, but it's compressed so these little bubbles keep coming up. It's a real shocker, but you get past it, and then BAM. You feel it. Maybe the second bottle, you feel it, I dunno. I felt it on the first one."]

Marto took a little sip and held the fizzing mixture in his mouth as long as he could before forcing himself to swallow it, hoping it wouldn't immediately eat its way back out of his larynx and dribble down his chest. It did not. It went down, and the aftertaste was chemical, sweet, and intriguing.

["You're feeling it, right?"] Maxtor seemed to be enjoying this. ["Now, wait for 25 seconds, and take another."]

Marto did as he was told, and the next sip was less of a shock. The sweetness was energizing, or maybe it was the caffeine, or the bubbles or the sodium or all of it together. It was slightly bitter like coffee, but also nothing like coffee. He imagined having one of these sitting by the river the day before, overheated and exhausted, and thought it would be bliss.

["Yeah, my node, you feel it! It's like a little orgasm of taste is what it is. It's not nutritional. It's just for pleasure. In fact, if you drink too much of this, it will really mess you up, and believe me, if you drink a little more than a little, you really really want to drink too much. Pepsi does not get you high, but it is still addictive. What is that about? I'm wonderfully baffled by it. What do you think? I want to get your special perspective on it."]

This must have been the reason Maxtor wanted to meet him.

Maxtor wanted him to offer his historical/cultural take on the resurrected beverage. That was reasonable since it was what he was known for. He felt disappointed but tried to push the feeling aside, as it was a great privilege to be called by someone like Maxtor for any reason at all, especially if you have something to offer. He gathered his data and prepared his analysis.

I was offered a Pepsi by Maxtor Uber G in The Middle. I think to really understand this drink, we should place it in the context of the culture of debt which created it. When the world was driven by the need to create more need, addiction was the most effective way to ensure a steady flow of currency in the direction of the producer. The addiction needn't be extreme to garner the proper results, in fact, earlier versions of another brand of this drink you gave me, did indeed get you high, fortified by the coca plant, not just the cola nut. However, access to coca-based products became restricted in the United States, and the mixture had to be adjusted to ensure its constant consumption. So over time, greater and greater levels of sweetness were added, more caffeine, more sodium, better bubbles, until it became addictive enough to survive competition with other similar beverages.

Marto paused, gathering his thoughts.

Many other versions of this type of drink didn't survive as long as Pepsi did. The fizzy beverage industry as a whole thrived even as other addictive products such as cigarettes faltered because the drinks almost fulfilled a nutritional requirement. Schools offered Pepsi and its main competitor, CocaCola (named after the addictive plant in the original formula) to children here and in other countries, instead of water to go with their lunch. It wasn't until the first decade of this century when evidence linking these beverages to the surge in childhood and adult diabetes was solidified that they began to be regarded as mildly poisonous. Even then it took decades before they were abandoned entirely.

Marto could see Maxtor responding well to his treatise. This was a glorious moment. He decided on a grandiose conclusion.

> What Maxtor has resurrected, is, in essence, the heart of the old economy – The Sip of Need – the essence of the cycle of privation, consumption, fulfillment, and privation again. The spinning wheel which powered the pistons of capital, and the destruction of the natural world.
>
> *– The Wakeful Wanderer's Guide Vol.6 lines 624 - 626*

Marto leaned back, satisfied, and found himself taking another sip from the cold but warming bottle of effervescent poison.

Maxtor was smiling, but incredulous. ["Up up, my node. Way up. But couldn't I have produced a cup of crude oil for you to sniff and feel between your fingers and got the same analysis?"]

Marto felt defensive but was ready. ["The effects of oil are similar to this beverage in the mechanisms which generated need, but no wars were ever fought for the procurement of more Pepsi. Or,"] he was feeling cautious in front of someone so intelligent, ["there are none that I know of."]

["Up up, and away, my node. Dazzle. I am so happy to meet you, Marto. Thank you so much for coming to our town."]

Marto rose. ["The honor has been all mine."]

["What? All done? Where are you going?"] Marto had not seen Maxtor frown before, and it was a little frightening. He had assumed the interaction had concluded.

["I thought you meant you were done talking with me. I didn't mean to..."]

["Aw no, my node, my sib. We are just getting started, my tribal cousin."] He held his hand out, palm down, and waved it at the chair.

Marto lowered himself back to his seat. Maxtor was smiling once more. His eyes like upward arching half moons, his mane moving on its own, despite the lack of any breeze.

["Finish your Pepsi, you wandering wisdom warrior. I want to walk with you around this wonderful town we call The Middle, and then..."] He took another sip, pausing dramatically and leaning in. ["I'm coming with you on your journey."]

20. Caged

Helen woke in a half-dome thick wire cage covered in mesh, sitting in the back of a motorboat. Her tongue felt dry, her body heavy. The noise of the engine drowned out her attempts to get the attention of the pilot. She recognized him from her view in the drone. The man from the submarine was of medium height, light-skinned, with thinning straight hair brushed back to cover most of his neck. He wore a yellow jumpsuit.

Remembering her implants, she tried to reach out to Tash for help but came up blank. She tried to reach Nandy, the pilot of the Lovely Charlotte and found she couldn't connect. She tried to access her location, make a query about motorboats on the Sound, find anything at all from the Interconnected, but got nothing. Her implants felt dead, dull. It was like a sudden deafness. The lack of data felt like a dull ache in her mind. One of her new senses had been shut off. Her mind reflexively made queries, pings, sent thexts that went nowhere, even though she knew she was out of range, or blocked. For the first time since she had left home, she felt deeply alone. It was terrifying.

The pilot slowed the motor and turned around. His face was boyish, even though he seemed to be in his 40s. "Hello, little bird. Up and awake? Polly wanna cracka?" He laughed to himself.

"What..." Helen had a hard time finding her voice. "What are you doing? Why... why did you... where are you taking me?"

"Tweet tweet tweet. Sweet Polly." He reached into the pocket of his jumpsuit. Helen scrambled to the back of the cage. He pulled out a black comb and ran it through his hair. He laughed again. "Polly wanna cracka." He went on chuckling to himself and turned back to the controls of the boat.

They were approaching a series of islands. The man slowed the boat further and steered carefully between them. Looking ahead in the water, Helen could make out the tops of old houses, large ones, and small ones, just below the surface. She thought they might be at the eastern end of Long Island. She had looked at maps back home in the library of her old house, drawn before the water had risen. If she had not been unconscious too long, they should be near Montauk. If they were indeed headed to the Hampton Isles, it might explain her capture. The name Beamish sprang to mind; The Beamishes of Quogue. She allowed herself to feel a mild relief. She knew now the man was not going to hurt her. She was going to be held for ransom. Not the best news she'd had all day but it could have been much worse.

When she was young, her Aunt had told her the Beamishes were a rogue Neo-Feudal family who lived out on the Hampton Isles, controlling territory which included miles of rich farmland. They traded in corn, vegetables, and wine with the inland families. They had loose ties to the Yonivers, but for the most part, were fiercely independent. They refused to join the Confederation of Humans as most of the landholding families did. They had no allegiance to the Powers That Were in Virginia. They mostly kept to themselves and were never to be trusted. Helen used to make up stories about them, alone at the end of the Island, bordered by xombies to the west, and water to the north, south, and east, running a petty kingdom like the isle of Sardinia in the last great Feudal age. She pictured handsome men on horses, archery tournaments, and jousting matches under a rebel flag. She was young then but dreamt about meeting a strong handsome Beamish knight, who would fight for her honor. These were a young girl's fantasies.

If the man in the boat was one of the Beamishes, he was a great disappointment. A jumpsuit for armor, stringy black hair for a helmet, the face of a boy, and a terrible sense of humor. The upside was that she was back in her element again. Perhaps it was inevitable.

The man steered the boat through the calm waters of the old bay and, gradually, Helen could see the dock. It was long, extending out past the cluttered shallows into the original depths of the Peconic. The structures behind it were all on stilts; half on land, and half above the water. A small group of men was gathered near the end of the long dock they were approaching. A horse and cart awaited.

At the dock, the man in the jumpsuit shouted orders to the others and Helen was lifted out of the boat, still inside the cage. "Don't drop it, you slobs!" yelled the man. "One puncture in the mesh and we will be neck deep in xombies within the hour!" Six of the men carried her over to the cart, and she was slid carefully into the back of it. The horse snorted. Without acknowledging them further, the man in the jumpsuit climbed in the front and shook the reigns.

Helen had confirmation the cage had cut her off from the tribes. She didn't know how the tribes maintained their network, or if it extended out this far, but she knew if she could get out of the cage, or find a break in the mesh, she could try sending out a call for help. She had an idea.

"I'm thirsty!" Helen cried to one of the men. "Please! I've been out in the sun all day. I need water." The men looked at their boss. The man in the jumpsuit turned around. "Tweet tweet tweet little bird. Flowers in her hair. Don't want them to be all wilty, do we?" He gestured to one of the men, who handed him a canteen. He was about to pour some of the contents over Helen's head when he stopped. "Water?" he asked his underling. The underling nodded. Then he poured.

Helen raised her mouth to the dribble of water. It was warm and tasted like metal, but she drank away. A window opened for a moment in her mind. She felt as if she could hear again. Her perceptions broadened briefly. Then the water stopped and the window closed. She swallowed and smiled.

"Happy little bird." The man in the jumpsuit turned "Hup!" he snapped the reigns and they started down the dock.

They traveled for a few miles on a wide crumbling road. Gaps in places had been filled in by dirt and gravel. Another section was washed out, and a small wooden boardwalk on stilts had been constructed to connect the two. They finally turned off onto a side path, and into a shambles of a town.

The residents turned their heads away when they saw the man in the jumpsuit. Most of them were working, carrying bundles, bartering with each other, or standing outside the low lying houses looking at their feet. At the top of a small hill was a recently constructed sprawling wooden home with a circular driveway and hedges surrounding the grounds. The horse and cart came to a rest on the circle in front of the main doors.

The windows of the large house were small and had wooden shutters on either side of them. This 'palace,' if it could be so called, had been built to weather the ocean storms that hit the vicinity. Helen noted it was new because all the older mansions of the area had long since sunk below the waves. The man in the jumpsuit whistled and shortly five young men and one young woman arrived to lift Helen's cage and carry it around to a low barn with a wide door to the left of the main entrance. The inside smelled of diesel oil and they put her down next to a large truck. The man went inside by way of an inner door in a side wall of the low barn.

Helen didn't have to urinate, but she wanted to. She knew now she could defeat the effects of the cage with water. Something about the conductivity of her body breaching the metal mesh. She tried spitting at it but nothing happened. A woman entered.

"Estelle Reynolds," she said using Helen's given name. "I know your mother Gladys, your step-father, your aunt, your whole nasty family." She grimaced. "They owe me. Now they will pay their debt. Do you understand?"

Helen nodded.

"You will stay here until they come. That means we will have to feed you and keep you well enough until they arrive. But, we know you have been with those deplorable xombies, god knows why, and now I bet you have that goo in your head. This will make things hard for us. This is why you are in the cage."

"I promise I won't use my implants if you promise you won't hurt me," Helen responded, sounding frail. "I'm ready to go home now. I was captured..."

"Save it. We know more about you than you think. We know you left home on your own and joined up with those inhuman creatures of your own accord."

"How did you know that? How did you know where to find me?"

"Does it surprise you to know we have spies?" The woman said. "You were not hard to find once we knew who to ask. It cost us, but not nearly as much as your family has stiffed us for over the years. No. You will volunteer to be put under again when you get hungry enough. Then we will open the cage and leave you something to eat when we know you can't communicate with your net-wit friends. Hopefully, your family will come, with sufficient gold, and take you away. What they do with you then isn't our problem."

"Am I at the home of the Beamishes?"

The woman raised her chin when she heard the name. "I am Shelley Beamish. My father and grandfather built all this. The man who brought you here is Thomas, my son. We have guards all over the grounds here, and the people of the town are loyal to us. Don't try to escape. Play your cards right and you will be home in a few weeks."

Weeks. So much for her mission trying to find the hapless Marto. It was a relief, not to have to chase him down anymore, but she didn't want to return to her old life of dull boredom. Who knows what punishment awaited her there? She also really didn't like the idea of spending several days in a cage.

"Look, I promise I will behave if you just let me out of here. Where will I go? I was implanted with the 'goo' as you call it, but honestly, I never figured out how to use it. If you let me out, I promise I will behave. I couldn't call them even if I wanted to. I just want to go home."

Shelley Beamish looked down her long nose at her. She seemed to be considering the idea. Helen became hopeful. "Nothing doing," she said. "You may think you know those monsters, those xombies. Believe me, you don't. The horrors I've seen. If you knew what they were capable of, you would never want to go back to them. You are a foolish spoiled Reynolds brat out slumming around, oblivious to reality. You will stay in your cage in our garage until they come to pick you up." With that, she left and shut the door.

A long silence followed. The garage door was shut. Helen sat on the bottom of the cage in the dark wishing someone would open a door just to talk. Minutes passed, maybe an hour.

Helen decided to pass the time by rooting around in her own mind. Although she didn't have access to the Interconnected community, she found her visualizer still worked with information already stored in her implants. She poured over the maps of Cos and her past thexting conversations with Dizzy and Mem and Reyleena and unexpectedly found a game! A message was attached: ["For when you get time off from your wandering. Just use your imagination and guide it where you want to go."] The message was from Tash.

Helen took up a comfortable position, lying on the floor of the cage with her legs up. She experimented until she found her way into the game and suddenly was in thick woods, the sun shining overhead. Through the trees, she could hear the lapping of waves and she walked in that direction. She reached out and brushed her hands against the leaves. They felt cool to the touch. The wind was blowing, and the sounds were calming. Birds flew from branch to branch. Yellow fruit hung from one of the trees. She picked one and bit through the thick skin. Juice flowed down her chin and over her chest. It was sweet and sticky; so real, and yet so unreal. It was like a dream, but not a dream.

She walked to the water, sat and finished the fruit on a sandy beach looking out at a brilliant lonely cove, huge rocks guarding the way to the ocean. She had never seen a beach like this in her life, and yet, here it was. Suddenly a ship appeared from behind one of the rocks, with three masts and seven sails. A wooden ship from long ago. It turned and glided through the entryway to the cove. She felt fear. She stood and ran back into the woods to watch. ["No ship"] she thought, and the ship vanished. This was not like a dream at all. She had complete control. ["The ship"] she thought, and the ship reappeared where it had been, slowing to weigh anchor in the middle of the cove. She grabbed another piece of fruit and waited to see what would happen next.

21. Seven Sails

Helen lost track of time. She decided to join the crew of the Smoky Margarita, the ship with seven sails and a crew of mostly women. Their mission was to defeat and plunder the fleet of the Spanish Navy along the isles of the Caribbean. They had sailed from the cove to search for Admiral Gustavez on three deserted islands. He had thwarted them at each turn in sea battles, and land skirmishes. They were just about to set sail for the open ocean when Helen decided to take a break from the game. She commanded 'exit' and opened her eyes.

Dizziness overcame her as her body seemed to flop from standing to lying on her back in the cage. She felt hunger and thirst. The garage was dark. She looked out the three little windows in the garage door and saw it was nighttime. She had no idea how long into the night she had been playing her pirate game. Was it that she was so tied up in the story, she didn't notice the passage of time, or did time pass slower in the game, or both? She wondered if remaining in a game while lying down counted as sleep. From the way her body felt, she decided yes, and then no.

Finally, her body was ready to pee. The urine would disrupt the block of the mesh around the cage. If all went well, she would be able to connect to a tribe who might send help. She composed a quick message in her head to send out while the window of connection was open, then she pulled down her pants and squatted as best she could.

Before she could proceed, a loud thump came from the garage door. Then a splash of dark liquid covered part of one of the small window panes. Helen froze. She pulled her pants back up and stayed squatted.

The garage door opened and five skinny teenagers dressed all in black. They held long black poles and strolled in like they owned the place. The front teen, a girl between 16 and 19 years old, with full lips, and high eyebrows stared at Helen. A younger girl, maybe 15 to 17, with a long bang of straight black hair swooping down over one eye, joined her and the two of them stared. Then, three of the ninjas (for that's what they looked like) surrounded her cage. They used a crowbar and other tools, found from one of the corners of the garage, to pry the floor of the cage from the dome. The two remaining ninjas kept guard at the garage door and the door leading to the house.

In short order, the cage split open. As the top lifted, and Helen's senses came to life again ["... New New London tribe. We have a boat not far from here. Are you reading me?"] It took a moment for Helen to realize this message was coming from the ninja teen leader, squatting closest to her.

["Yes! How did you find me so fast?"]

["We got a ping on your location five miles east of here twelve hours ago. The data was shared and analytics were applied to guess your current location. Tell you more later. Can you walk?"]

Helen stood up and found her legs were asleep. ["Uh, I need a few moments."]

The door in the wall opened, and out stepped Thomas, in his underwear, pointing a rifle. "Don't move! Ma-" He shouted before a pole slammed his lower jaw hard against his upper. Out of nowhere, one of the teens hit him hard across the shins. The butt of another pole cracked him dead center in the forehead and he went down in a heap. The rifle clattered to the floor without firing. Helen decided she would do her best on her numb legs and hobble out towards the driveway.

The gravel was littered with a half dozen Beamish guards, all flat on the ground. Helen hoped they were unconscious and not dead. She knew from experience, people who served the families often had no choice. They were generally good people with families to support. There was no time to check on their well being.

The small party pushed their way through the hedges, and down a thin section of town, where there were several more bodies lying about.

Helen saw two more people go down, unlucky enough to wander out in front of her ninja teen xombie party. She decided it was not the speed or force of their blows which made them so effective, but the coordination of their actions. They behaved like one mind with twenty limbs. No one in town stood a chance.

At the end of the small group of homes, there was a dirt road. The leader turned right on it and the rest of the group followed. They had surrounded Helen, checking in all directions as they shuffled her down the road. Helen heard the surf ahead. They were headed for the ocean.

The sound of a truck engine caught her ear. Most likely, it was the Beamish truck Helen had shared the garage with. She didn't know how much further it was to the beach.

["We're not going to make it, are we?"] Helen sent.

["We will not be out of range of gunfire in time, but we will be in the ocean before they can stop us,"] leader teen ninja girl thexted. ["There is a chance one of us will get shot. Not you, us. We will protect you. Once we hit the catamaran, keep down."]

Helen was about to protest, to stop the rescue. She would rather return to captivity than risk the lives of these brave young kids, but all at once she saw the boat. It was a sailboat, not made of wood, but a gray slick material, flat, with seven sails. The sails were arranged in a different way than the Smoky Margarita, but she counted seven. Of her rescue party, there were four girls and one boy. She was looking into a kind of cove, on a beach, at a kind of pirate ship. The scenario was just like her adventures in the Caribbean, but that was just a game she made up. She thought she might still be in a game.

She stopped. This couldn't be real. Too many elements lined up with a game she had just created to pass the time; running to a beach, a seven sailed ship, a party of girls, an ocean voyage. Had she merely slipped into another game based on the fantasy of being rescued? Where was her body right now?

["What are you doing? Keep running!"] leader teen ninja girl was shouting in her mind.

["This isn't real,"] Helen replied.

["It's going to feel pretty fucking real when they start shooting at us! Get to the boat!"] thexted one of the ninja girls.

Helen didn't respond. She was saying "exit," "escape" and "end" aloud trying to snap herself out of the game.

["What's the matter with her?"] Tinker « Yama « Phila « MeiMei « etc asked Londra « Trisha « Mimi « Sadie « etc. ["No idea, don't care. Get her into the boat and let's go. That truck will be here any minute."]

They carried Helen aboard, ran the catamaran out past the breakers and tacked hard along the coast to the east. They were trying to put as much distance between the truck and their boat as possible. The old Beamish truck pulled out on the beach. Two figures jumped out, and as Londra predicted, one of them shot. Luckily for the little crew of young ninjas, the bullet hit one of the many automated sails but not anyone on board the Chichicapa. Before long they were out of range and sailing out to round the tip of Montauk isle.

The sun was just coming up when Helen returned to her body. "Back here," She sighed aloud. "Back here again."

Londra grabbed her by both shoulders. ["Pay attention now. Where did you go? What happened?"]

Helen was shaking her head, ["I saw this boat, and I had just been in a game, in my ... in my head where I was on a boat, leaving a cove, it was a lot like this ... whatever this is. The pirates on the boat were mostly women – like your group, which is mostly girls – but you all look like ninjas, not pirates. Anyway, on the beach, I was sure I had made it all up, so I went back into another game, I thought it was real, where I was back in the cage in the garage. I just sat there, in my cage, doing nothing, and then, eventually, my mother came, and my aunt, and father, and the pirates from the Smoky Margarita and then I knew I was making it up again, and I ended it and came back here ... to this ... game?"]

["Look,"] Londra thexted her, still holding on to her shoulders, ["There is a simple way to settle this. You are just a noob, so you wouldn't know. Send a command.'"]

["Send a command?"]

["Yes, like a command in a game. Like 'Invisible' or 'Sink', or

'Change Color: Red' or whatever, but something outrageous. You can also use 'save' and 'exit.' They always work."]

["Fly, Ship!"] Helen commanded. Nothing happened. Right. ["Fly, In the Sky – Ship!"] Again, a whole lot of nothing happened. Of course, nothing happened, because this was not a game.

["This isn't a game!"] she hugged Londra. ["You rescued me in reality! Thank you, you brilliant little ninjas!"]

["You're welcome,"] Tinker thexted back, for the whole crew, ["What's a ninja?"]

["You are kidding, aren't you?"]

["I don't think so,"] thexted Londra, ["you keep saying it, but I'm not really sure what that is."]

["Well, it's you gals. Seriously. And you guy. Amazing. Wait..."]

Helen engaged her visualizer to look up old references to the ancient Japanese assassins. She found pictures, text, and video, and shared the data with the group. They were all excited by the similarity of clothing style. They compared themselves and their old-world counterparts. ["Yes!"] exalted Timo « Betsi « Shasta « Catherine « etc. ["we are SUCH these Ninjas!"]

["How did you not know what a ninja was?"] Helen queried the group. ["I knew the reference, and I don't sneak around battling people at night."]

["Dunno"] replied Zha-zha « Petra « Dorina « Reyluca « etc, ["My gen, we don't spend much time looking up historicals. Doesn't seem relevant to our lives today."]

["Well, I'd say this is pretty relevant."] Timo was pointing out one of the outfits. ["We need to rework our night-suits. Check out the cut and stitching on this one. Better mobility. Also, check out these daggers!"]

["We don't need daggers. We have our grapfs."] Patsi « Yolonda « Mary « Helena « etc held up one of the black poles which had been so effective in the battles with the Beamishes.

["We could use some of these bad ass throwing weapons. We will need to train with them, of course,"] Zha-zha mentioned.

["Of course,"] ["naturally,"] ["always training,"] ["that is the way,"] replied the group.

The boat rocked and rolled on the larger ocean waves before pulling around the tip of Montauk and changing course toward land. Helen remembered her hunger and her thirst.

["Do you have anything to eat or drink?"] she asked Londra, ["I'm starving and dry."]

Londra reached into a bag and pulled out a large round item. It was yellow and orange. ["How about a mango?"] she asked. ["We don't see them often. They are a real treat, but they are going to go rotten if we don't eat them. Have you ever had one? They are really sweet."] She held it in front of Helen, who tried to steady herself on the deck of the rolling catamaran.

Then the team of little ninjas went back to their discussion about weaponry, clothing, and the assassins of old as the Chichicapa piloted itself toward New New London, its seven sails adjusting automatically to the direction of the wind.

22. Ramapo

Barnabas took two dozen men in three trucks and headed up the rough roads through mixed territory to meet Daschel and the Raiders. Bethany (Nora) had sent a message to his office. It was a countdown. He had twelve hours to get to Ramapo, before leading the attack in the morning. Brady was left to take care of business in New Atlantic.

The roads were rough, but the trucks were built to handle them. Decades of neglect had reduced long stretches to rubble. It was slow going. His navigator, a young trainee named Ted felt confident they would arrive by evening.

They passed close to xombie villages between the loyal city of Princeton and the enemy territory of Trenton. The monsters there were not well organized, but deadly enough. They knew they were being watched as they rolled by. The roads near the xombie communities were re-enforced with a sleek material which all but silenced the old overly patched tires of the black trucks. 'Soon we will have roads like these everywhere,' thought Barnabas, delighting in the anticipation of the fruition of his plans. 'New materials, plentiful grain. A restoration of the natural order.' He allowed himself to drift off in his imaginings of a bright and prosperous future. He didn't see the roadblock up ahead until the trucks stopped.

The gunmen jumped out the back and took up defensive positions. They were surrounded by the ruins of old strip malls, the tops of most of the buildings gone, walls turned to rubble. The contents of these stores had been looted decades ago. Barnabas looked out the window of one of the trucks to see a faded sign for "Jiffy Lube" painted on a sturdy structure to the left of the vehicle. There was a makeshift barricade placed across the road ahead. Old cars, trucks, chairs, garbage, piled up. There were no people anywhere.

Two of the gunmen fell. They were the youngest of Brady's trainees. The gunmen wore armor and helmets, and Barnabas could see through the window tiny needles stuck in the armor of the standing gunmen. They were being fired upon by unseen snipers.

"Get back in the trucks!" He yelled. They couldn't hear him through the closed windows. These soldiers were well trained. Brady had taught them not to fire until they had a lock on a target. Once they started firing, Barnabas knew, there would be no hope of giving orders. He got low in his seat and rolled his window down. He saw the needles sail overhead and he yelled again. This time the gunmen began to respond. Three more went down, the needles finding the gaps in the armor. Poison? They may have been fired remotely. The trucks armor protected the remaining men, and they rolled over the parking lots of the strip malls and sped away. Five men lost. These inhuman monsters would pay for that. No time for revenge. It would be coming soon enough.

The men carefully picked off the remaining needles from their armor and the interior of the trucks and put them in empty cans as they sped away from the ambush. Looking back, Barnabas could see no evidence of the xombies anywhere. They had attacked them remotely via their accursed bots. They drove past more xombie villages, expecting another attack, but none came. Everyone was on edge. By sunset, they arrived in the camp at Ramapo.

The camp was impressive. There were scores of fires and tents. The Raiders had arrived in large numbers. Daschel had done well. Rifles were cleaned and arranged in rows. Loot had been gathered from the surrounding villages. Hopefully, the cost to retrieve it had not been too dear.

There was lamb and chicken roasting on spits. Barnabas was served a large portion and ate it with vigor. Whiskey was poured. Daschel handed him a cigar he had been saving for this occasion.

"Shouldn't we wait?" Barnabas asked. "We haven't won the battle yet."

"I have no doubts, my brother," said Daschel. "Besides, I brought two more." He chomped down on the torpedo-shaped stogie, showing his impressive white teeth. The two brothers smoked and drank, soaking in the feeling of the impressive powers at their command.

"Everyone!" shouted Daschel, "Raiders! Soldiers! Gather round me and hear my brother, our commander, speak!" The men gathered around the fire. Barnabas had prepared himself for this. He thought of his grandfather, finished his whiskey and stood tall.

"Tomorrow," he began, "represents a new day for humankind." Barnabas was summoning the powerful voice of his grandfather, tuned over many years addressing the New Atlantic community. "Tomorrow, we will finally begin a battle which will end in the total defeat and subjugation of the scourge we call the xombies!" There were cheers, but he could sense hesitation and fear among the ranks.

"I know many of you rode far to be here. I know most of you have lost brothers, fathers, mothers, sons, and daughters to these terrible monstrosities who used to call themselves human. You fear them." Sounds of dissent arose now, mixed with objections. "You were right to fear them!" Quiet. "They have technology none of us can overcome! They strike without warning, in total silence! They come upon us like the angel of death itself! How can we defeat such a foe!" Mumbles of dissent intermingled with murmurings of agreement. "You might think me mad to plan an attack on such a strong xombie town! Perhaps I have lost my senses! Perhaps I am leading you all to your deaths!" Uneasy quiet now. Barnabas smiled. He had planned this moment for months, pouring over the passage of Agamemnon's speech to the Achaeans in the Iliad as they waited on the shores before the walls of Troy.

"If I am indeed leading you astray, you would be right to scatter to the winds right now! Go home! Go home and wait for the monsters to find you and pick you off one by one!" Grumbles in the crowd now. 'They are considering it,' Barnabas thought. 'Good.'

"And if part of us were to turn away right now, then it wouldn't it be best if we all turned away and ran? Ran like little children! Scatter like chickens!" There were grumbles: dangerous grumbles.

"What are we? Are we children? Are we chickens? Are we like scared little lambs waiting to be slaughtered?"

A voice shouted "No!" and more voices "No!"

"No! We are men! We are warriors! We are the courageous heroes! History will remember us for what we do tomorrow! We don't run from this battle, we fight!" He heard rising shouts, whoops and cheers, but lingering hesitation among the ranks.

"For what you don't know," his voice lower, the crowd leaning in. "Is I have a secret weapon at my control which will make these horrible monsters powerless. Tomorrow at dawn, all of their defenses will be dead. All of their technology will be useless. Finally, we'll be able to take them as the weaklings that they are! They will be turned into frightened little waifs! Easily put down!" Now there were cheers, real cheers.

"For the past two years, I have been planning an end to these creatures in Tarrytown, and that end will spread until all xombies everywhere are stripped of their mysterious powers and weapons and their lands and their technologies will be made to work for us! For we are the righteous rulers of this new world, not them!" More cheers.

"Tomorrow, we will ride across the deadly bridge in total safety. We will find the town defenseless. Fight those who offer you a fight, but spare the others. I have a use for them!" Grumbles.

"Hear me! It isn't enough we take their lives. We must take their hearts. We must suck the spirit out of them! We must obliterate their way of life! They ... will be ... our slaves." Now there was quiet. This was something new for the Raiders to consider.

"Their rich crops, their road technology, their water, their bodies, and minds will be brought back under the rightful rule of law! Their labor will serve all of us. Each of you tonight, whether you were born into a powerful family like I was, or as part of a gang in a camp out in the dust, will be the new rulers of the Northeast! Tarrytown is only the beginning! From there, we will spread out and subjugate the xombie huddles of Connecticut and the Hudson Valley! Yet still, we will press on until all of this land is reclaimed! You will all become Dukes! I will be your new King! Now I ask you, will we scatter like rats, or fight and rule? What say you?" The roar began and did not stop. "Tomorrow! The battle is at hand!" Barnabas' voice was drowned in the uproar. The men thumped their chests and clasped each other. He stood down, as the pre-battle celebration began.

Daschel walked toward him, grinning around his cigar. They hugged. More whiskey was poured. Two chairs were brought out and they drank by the main fire.

"So, you really have a plan to turn off their tech? Tell me that was not just bullshit Barn," Daschel said.

"Bethany," Barnabas said in his ear. "She's been among them for weeks. She has a plan to take down their network. No network. No weapons on the bridge. No coordinated attacks. No remote drones. Nothing."

"Seriously?" Daschel was amazed. "Our big sister? And you tell me this only now?"

"I couldn't risk anyone knowing, Dash. Had to be this way. Tomorrow, when we head over the bridge, it will be a joy ride. I am certain."

"Well, that's a fucking relief. I thought you and I were going to take up the rear, and let the Raiders take it on the chin before going in. She can really do that?"

"Our sister has been readying herself to be a plant among them for years now. It was her plan. She is extremely ... talented."

"Wait, you mean she's got goo in her head like them?"

"Only way we could do it, but we were careful. Parts of her are hooked up to their network, and parts are on a private channel to me. I've been in touch with her since she's been among them. All is well. You will see."

They sat in silence. Daschel was letting this new knowledge seep in.

"So, we really will be taking them all down, then," he said in a low voice, almost to himself.

"Yup." Barnabas drained his second glass and held it up. More whiskey arrived.

"And are you really going to let these biker idiots rule their own towns like you said? Make them Dukes?"

Barnabas laughed. "Fuck, no."

"Thank the good lord!" Daschel sighed with relief. "I thought you had lost your mind!"

The two brothers laughed and looked around at the barbarian hoard drinking and shouting, shoving each other. They sounded like wolves, howling into the black sky.

23. Heritage Trail

Maxtor sipped a cold milkshake from a blue glass. He gazed up at the sky through a mesh shade as he lounged on the back of another quint, heading up the Farmington Heritage Trail. Marto was on a new unicycle, a gift from Nina « Gina « Tina «Jocelle, etc from The Middle. The power of it was greatly improved. It required only a minimal amount of peddling to get the drive to kick in. Like his old uni, it moved in the direction Marto leaned. Given that Maxtor had five riders and Marto was on a single wheel, he had to lean precariously to keep up, regardless of how much he pedaled and the five riders slowed for him. Maxtor's lounge chair was a webbed masterpiece of lightness and luxury. Marto thought they made a comical pairing.

All along their route, people lined up to see the famous innovator and his new friend. They were not there to see the unicycler on his book tour, and it was embarrassingly apparent. Most had offerings for their tawny-haired hero, and many of those offers were passed along to Marto, causing frequent stops, smiles, posing for friends, apologies, etc. Marto was amazed at the number of people who wanted to physically touch Maxtor. He leaned into it, acting like a big kitten for his fans, most of whom would never have had access to him. People were rushing from kilometers around to catch them on the road. It was like old footage from the Tour de France. There were runners, wavers, people in costume, and people who only looked like they were in costume. It was one long, roadside party.

If Maxtor felt he was of too high Merit to associate with these people, he didn't show it. He had a refinement and grace Marto found impressive. Most of the fans they met would have been prohibited from seeing him in person, much less messaging him directly. As far as Marto or anyone else could tell, he enjoyed the company of all of these lesser folks as much as he enjoyed his association with the great JaBing from Vancouver or any of his other equals.

They had overeaten and over hydrated the whole way so far. It made for slow going and was annoying. Marto missed the quiet solitude of his previous rides. He couldn't, however, let his displeasure show in his public persona. Maxtor was wildly popular, and he did his best to appear grateful to be along for the ride. Hopefully, no one could tell how much he wished he was touring solo.

The destination was Hartford and one of a series of tribes who inhabited the old city. Hartford had been greatly transformed of late, with large buildings rebuilt as vertical farms. Steel was a rare thing to work with post-Tide. Rust and decay took its toll over the years, but many structures which persisted away from the sea provided a framework for printed additions. This was fine with Marto. He had planned to head up through the old city then on to The Valley and north to Brattle. He had no thoughts of his destination past the Brattle Valley.

Maxtor, as he promised, had shown Marto around his exceptional tribe. The Middle was, as always, innovative and in a state of constant change and improvement. They had multiple vertical farms like the one in Reverside, and were exporting tons of foodstuffs to surrounding tribes. They had mastered the art of growing coffee, tea, various engineered spices which mimicked flavors lost during The Tide. The population of the Middle had expanded exponentially since Marto's last visit.

Marto met up with Lisha, the daughter of Bruce, the librarian at Yale Havens and expressed to her Bruce's sensitivities over the new name she had taken when she became implanted. They replayed the conversation.

Lisha became thoughtful. ["It's so funny to hear him express those thoughts. I never knew he cared about that stuff,"] she told him. They were both enjoying espresso outside the new library. ["I have to be in better touch with him. I'm so busy, I forget, and he's not easy to get a message to. I have to send them handwritten in a tainer heading south."]

["Well, you know, I think he is starting to understand. Who knows, maybe he will choose an upgrade when he finally comes here."]

["Oh, I'm not sure he will ever leave the library before it's all emptied out. He is devoted to that place."]

The new library was a marvel. It was simplicity itself above ground and complexity below. Books and manuscripts arrived on request at any number of reading stations from automated storage in custom printed containers. When a visitor was done reading a volume, it was returned to the underground storage via a series of mechanical arms and medium-sized bots. Constant activity went on below the surface, such as restoration, re-cataloging, and scanning. The public face of the library was a single open room, not unlike a large parlor. The model was being replicated in seven tribal communities worldwide.

["Hey Marto, change of plans. We are headed to a nice little place on a lake in a town called Bristol. I think you will like it."] Maxtor didn't ask him what he thought about this change, and Marto didn't question it. Like anyone in the presence of the super Merited, he just went along.

Maxtor didn't use the term "slumming," in describing this trip, but he didn't have to. His preferred method of transportation was by personal drone. To move from place to place on the back of a bike was highly uncharacteristic. Marto's followers were having a blast commenting on this. Followership had skyrocketed at the mention of his meeting with Maxtor, but most of the new traffic was all about the tawny-haired genius, and not about his book tour. He knew it would drop off precipitously after they parted ways. Nevertheless, it was a great opportunity to gain followers who might hang on.

Traditionally, the separation between games and societal systems was broader than it is today. The oldest known games involved dice, boards, and pegs. It was easy to become immersed in such a game, but that was largely due to the human power of imagination and concentration. Many early games mirrored societal systems such as chess, go or backgammon, and many blended with societal systems such as dominoes, dice and arena games when used for gambling, or when a player gained social status for beating all opponents.

With the advent of virtual immersive games and social networks, the boundaries between games and status in society blurred further. The idea that everything was a game began to take subtle hold in a way that no longer seemed ironic. This shift in mindset was the key to the downfall of the social status of wealth. What was once seen as a rock solid necessity for the civilized world gradually became regarded as just another game. Games fall in and out of fashion, and new games are created in their place. Our current game of status and Merit is one such alternative. No doubt, if we tired of this game, we would make up another to replace it.

Masters of the game of Merit, such as my current traveling companion are lauded for their high scores, but not in the way of traditional games. Merit, after all, isn't a game of domination, but of generosity and usefulness. The rules are written to encourage the greatest benefit for the most people which in turn, reward the creators of that benefit. Offers accepted by a high Merit player yields more Merit than offers accepted by a low Merit player. That way, the generation of benefit is encouraged and perpetuated. This was what currency was supposed to do but failed. When the game of wealth became stagnant, and people saw it as just another game, they tired of it and looked for a new game to play. Games need players after all, and a game relying on a global population of participants, cannot survive when it isn't much fun for the majority of the players anymore.

– The Wakeful Wanderer's Guide, Vol. 6, lines 726 - 728

After a long slow ride, they arrived at a newly constructed inn on a lake named Compounce. There were dwellings nearby, but the house felt remarkably remote. They had an exclusive view of the lake, and the surroundings were quiet. Marto was struck by the spaciousness of it. This was the sort of place which would ordinarily lodge two dozen individuals, but it was cleared out for the arrival of Maxtor. Members of the local tribe appeared from nowhere to offer various foods and drinks, massages and assisted baths for both himself and the great innovator. Eventually, Maxtor sent the people away, and he and Marto were alone in the great room, with a pastoral view of the water.

["Water,"] Maxtor thexted in private. ["Feeders, evaporation. That's what keeps me awake at night."]

["The lake seems to be doing well,"] Marto responded politely. Maxtor stared at him hard.

["Not for lack of effort, believe me. You know that."] Maxtor seemed to shrink a bit, losing his mythical size. ["It's just us right now. Drop the hierarchy, my node. I have the feeling I can talk to you like a standard one to one, please don't prove me wrong."]

Marto felt honored, and then felt he should stop feeling honored. Maxtor was, ultimately just another interconnected member of a tribe. He found himself fidgeting.

["I hope you don't want another Pepsi because if I even hinted you did, people from klicks around would be killing themselves to bring us two."] Marto thought this might be a kind of joke, though a not funny one.

["So, I saw you go to Glenville. That was a bold move, my node. You are a deep thinker. It isn't a common thing these days. Maybe you are not aware of this. It's not."]

["I suppose I am a curious person,"] Marto responded.

["Node, you ride a unicycle all over goddess knows where to sit and talk to people. People like us..."] He ran his naked fingers through his mane, ["we don't tend to get out much to happy spots like this, let alone to those lesser places."]

["I am a student of history,"] Marto chimed in, trying to feel like he was back home thexting privately with one of his equals. ["I like to find out what has happened in the minds of others in the wake of recent big upheavals. It's so easy to take it all for granted, but really, I find it miraculous, and imperfect, and I look for ways it is changing because I think change is inevitable."]

The lion relaxed and smiled. This was going in the right direction, thought Marto. ["Yes, yes. We are the enlightened interconnected are we not? We think we have it all down."]

["Well, it's true. I mean, an animal can't speak, and so every reaction to discomfort is one of violence. We have evolved our modes of communication, and I think it means we have moved further away from our violent animal state."] Marto felt they were on the same train of thought here, and it was invigorating. ["But we tend to forget our history because we get so caught up in our Merit. So, my purpose, and I am so glad to be able to articulate it, is to put our changes in the context of what has come before. Otherwise, how can we know where we are going?"]

["Well argued. You know that's not my thing, but I parse you, my node. But your vector..."] Maxtor had that hard look in his eyes again. ["you're into the general history, but you are not entirely sure where you are going, are you my node? I can see that. You see it? Where is the wakeful wanderer wandering, and why?"]

["Well, I admit, I'm not entirely sure where I'm going. But I don't think too much about myself as an individual. I'm mostly curious about the collection of our greater tribes. I don't think people care to follow my own introspections."]

Maxtor regarded him quietly.

They had both dropped out of the public feed. At the edge of Marto's consciousness, he could feel the pressure building, the demand of his followers to be let in. He dared not to reconnect publicly until Maxtor gave the okay.

["So, what did you think was going to happen when you went to that little town of families?"] Maxtor sent. The word 'families' had an emphasis on it. It was a combination of disdain and wistfulness. ["Bit of a wake-up call that was. Our babysitters forgetting they lost the babies. Pretty ugly stuff there; illuminating."]

["I honestly didn't know. I didn't know I was going to go there until I left Sherwood that morning. I guess I had an intuition, that's all."]

Maxtor pointed at Marto's head. ["Something going on in there."] He waved his finger around in a slow small circle. ["Something either you hide really, really well, or is hidden from you, I think. It's good."] He leaned back. ["Makes you interesting."]

He stared at the water again. Marto thought he had never in his life felt the mixture of fear, excitement, and uncertainty he was currently feeling. He controlled himself, resisting the urge to stammer out something about how amazed he was to be found interesting by such an interesting person. Instead, he sat in silence and waited for the lion to continue.

["Here's a bit of current history for you. Over the past few decades, the algorithms which run our little game have now grown so complex, no single individual can fathom them."] By 'game,' Maxtor meant the rules of Merit. ["I can't understand them, you can't understand them. No one can. It's only been 40 or so years now, and you could spend your whole life analyzing them and never be able to catch up. They work because they seem to work, but no one knows how they work. You feel? The reason I am who I am, and those people in Glenville are who they are, is a mystery, a matter of faith."]

["But your contributions speak for themselves. They feed people and save lives! I don't think anyone doubts that."]

["Well, of course, they don't doubt it. I don't want them to doubt it. But the formula behind it is impossibly opaque. More precisely, it is inhumanly opaque. Parse this: imagine you have a one in a million idea. One in a million people might think of this idea in their lifetimes."]

["Okay,"]

["That means roughly four to five thousand other people will likely have the same idea, depending on actual current global population figures. Those are the odds. Even I don't think my ideas are one in a million. And where did those ideas come from? Purely from your own mind? You and I know, new ideas come from shared data, past conversations, something read, seen, scanned, or communicated in cooperation with others. So why is it my ideas are attributed only to me?"]

["I guess because you put them out there first, or took the initiative to make something of them. That's what matters. An idea without a plan is just thext."] Marto was trying to comfort the man in front of him, shocked such a person could doubt their own importance.

["Ah, but here's the thing. If Maxtor Uber-G puts forward a new idea, people are more likely to think it worthy, than someone in say, Glenville, right?"]

["Well, naturally, I mean, you have a record of success."]

["But there might be someone in Glenville with a better idea, and no one would think to do something with it because they are not in Flow."]

["I suppose that's possible, but is it likely?"]

["Well, take your new unicycle."]

["Yes. I love it by the way. Working great."]

["Pure. But look at the painting you carry with you on your back and compare the painting of that uni with the one you are now riding. You see it?"]

Marto didn't have to open the tube, he brought up an image of the painting in his visualizer next to an image of his new unicycle, now parked outside the house. They were the same color blue, and the structure was remarkably similar.

["So, tell me, is that new uni the idea of little Bruce Ng, or of my compadre Nina, who printed and assembled it for you? Who should get the Merit for that contraption you now ride?"]

["Well, okay, the basics of it seem to be based on the painting by Bruce, but the tech..."]

["The tech was all from other projects by other people, my node."] Maxtor stretched his arms wide. ["Not to say Nina isn't deserving of your gratitude. I'm just thinking... and don't you ever repeat or re-thext this. This is just between you and me right here and right now. What I'm thinking is that the foundation on which we have built this grand new 'economy,' if you can call it that, is as solid as the evaporation from the lake out there, maybe less. You glean?"]

["I think I glean,"] Marto was not convinced he did, ["but we give Merit based on what is offered, not based on what is proposed, or imagined."]

["Pure. But people get more Merit by offering it to me than to you."]

Maxtor hunched over a bit. ["And I don't truly make things anymore. I just dream them up. All of this is just dreams. Just ideas. Most of the details are worked out by my compadres. My Merit stays high for a long while after something like the library gets built, and continues when it gets replicated, but it eventually fades."]

Marto wished he could go public with this conversation. This was the sort of inside view he had always hoped for from his travels, but he knew if he did, it would backfire on him in the worst way. Maxtor went on.

["For now, I get to live a life of wish fulfillment. I have to be careful not to want things which might cause other people to hurt themselves. Not all the ultra-Merited care about that. Why is this not part of the algorithm? Maybe it is or will be, we don't know. All I know is, if I don't come up with something new, I don't get to keep living this way. It doesn't matter how nice I am."]

["So, I don't mean to be rude, but it sounds like you are longing for the days of accumulation and hoarding. I mean, the temporariness of your situation is also part of what makes Merit work. You don't get to keep it, so you never get to stop contributing to the benefit of all of us. Is it really that awful?"]

["I know there is no going back."] Maxtor was uncharacteristically humble in his tone. ["By all accounts, our new game works better than the previous game. I will not argue the point."] He reached for a glass on a side table containing the cooling oolong tea. ["But what I wonder about is whether the situation of the people at the top of the ladder in our new game is different enough from the situation of the people at the top of the old one. You've spent a little time with me now, so maybe you can do some deep thinking on it, right?"] He sipped and looked at Marto sideways. ["There could be a clue in it for you, I think."]

Marto was ready to counter. ["There are a few obvious differences,"] he replied, ["No appreciable inheritance, no lazy billionaires. Merit does not pool and stagnate like money did. That's an improvement. There is greater fluidity of reward. That's also good."]

["You think that,"] Maxor countered, ["but I can tell you there are good people of Supreme Merit and in spite of everything, there are some bad people. I'm not going to list any foremothers, but believe me, there are. Those people do all sorts of clever damage without a mob of Avengers coming for them. You glean?"]

["Okay, it's not perfect but it is always evolving."]

["What worries me,"] the lion continued, ["is we can't see into the mechanism driving it anymore. The game works, not because living at this wish fulfillment level of Merit is so wonderful. It works because it looks wonderful. From where I am, I can tell you, there are serious downsides. It can be draining. There is no break. Things can change fast. Glean? It is also pure addiction, so once you have it, you never want to lose it."]

["Well, I can't see your Merit dropping anytime soon Maxtor. I mean, I saw all those people on the road today. Are you telling me you are worried?"]

["The thing is, my node,"] "even I..." his spoken voice was pitched higher than expected. It sounded small. "... run out of ideas sometimes."

The silence in the house seemed to boom and quake.

24. Worm

Nora (Bethany Yoniver) composed the brief message to send to her brother. She made a query to know the time of the next sunrise and sent: Xz10240717.

The information was unencrypted but cryptic and short. X was for crossing, Z was the Tappan Zee Bridge, then the date, then the time. For speed, the information traveled to New Atlantic via shortwave, thanks to her repeater installed on the other side of the river. It should quickly arrive at the makeshift goggles she had designed for Barnabas. She imagined the little light turning green for a new communication on his desk. He would be here tomorrow.

For all of her hatred of the xombies, Nora felt fully engaged in her work here in a way she had never felt at home. Ending their way of life seemed, not wrong to her but wasteful. Still, it was all set now, no stopping it, unless she wanted to watch her own brothers get cut down on the bridge tomorrow at dawn. She had work to do, and a short time to do it in.

From her small temporary home by the river, Nora had volunteered for menial work in Reverside, as a noob. She attended to the water closet schedules, bath and shower cleanups, water station maintenance, and sometimes offered to deliver gifts to Thirty/Fourteen and several other important tribal members. Lately, she had graduated to babysitting, which mostly involved remote monitoring of the six babies and toddlers in the nursery, guiding them in their fantasies, and making sure they stayed cheerful and clean. Diaper changes were infrequent, thanks to the xombie upgraded diapers. She felt happy to see the little boys and girls in person every once in a while. Nora's Merit was rising.

During whatever carnage would follow in her brother's attack, Nora would be sure to keep the innocents away from any violence. She knew that among the Raiders, it wouldn't be tolerated. Barnabas had less respect for Raider culture than she did. He regarded them all as brutes, and in doing so, missed an enormous opportunity to partner with them. Raiders never killed babies. Children were precious, especially to them.

For four weeks she had been Nora; two weeks walking here and two weeks living here. The first week in Reverside was the hardest. It was one thing to understand how the communication between xombies worked, it was another thing to live it all day long. She felt she might go mad in the alien silence of interconnected life.

Though she was a noob, she felt waited on hand and foot. Several xombies attended to her. Tretre, Yano, Piter, Lala, and Marto. She liked Marto the best. He was awkward but kind and he sat with her without thexting her with questions and queries for her state of mind or thirst or hunger or anything else. Nora was glad he was not in town to see what was going to happen next.

She needed to remind herself why she was doing this. She needed to remember David. She needed to remember how he had been undone. She needed to remember her family, their way of life, their traditions, and the rule of law. The world had to be restored to its natural order. That began tomorrow at dawn.

David's face came back to her. His long braided hair dripping from his head, his strong jaw, his smile, the sun behind him. She remembered the rides to the mountains and sleeping under the stars. David was unusual. He had taught himself to play the flute and would compose songs to her by the fire when they camped. He told her all about his family, his chapter, his club. Bethany learned about the life of the Raiders, their laws, their customs. She thought it was brutal but beautiful.

Barney had told her once she couldn't see him. As head of the Yoniver family, he could not allow a Raider as a brother in law but he eventually saw the better of it. Barney had met David and recognized the strength in him. That was a year before the xombies ruined her lover, broke his poor mind, and sent him back to her. David returned from his captivity in Reverside withered and broken. He had been captured during a raid from the south on this very town. Instead of killing him, the xombies forcefully implanted him, and then set him free. Perhaps they wanted to send him back as a warning.

He was found by his chapter but they didn't know how to treat him. They brought him to Nora. His eyes would roll uncontrollably in his head. He would gasp and shake violently as if fighting off an inner demon. He couldn't sleep. When he was lucid enough, he begged Nora to kill him before he succumbed to the deviant technology. He was terrified he would be forced to kill her. Desperate to fix his brain, Nora tried more and more aggressive measures to remove the implants until, under her hand, he finally died. Devastated but determined, she removed the implants from his head to study them.

Seven years had been spent plotting this revenge. Even after David's chapter had found and killed the old man directly responsible for implanting her lover with the tech which drove him mad, Nora did not feel vindicated. They all had to pay.

["Tomorrow, my love,"] she thexted to herself, abruptly aware she had absent-mindedly sent it as a public post.

["Tomorrow! My love!"] LalaUbriay thexted and then rethexted. It was rethexted by Piter, then Tretre, and then it began to change as it was passed in and outside of Reverside.

["Love my tomorrow!"] ["To Morrow, my love!"] ["My tomorrow love!"] ["My marrow I love!"] ["Tomorrow and tomorrow and such sweet sorrow my love!"] it continued. Nora was terrified she had given it all away after so much plotting. She reviewed her memories of David to be sure she had not published those as well. She had not. It was so hard to control herself, leading a secret life among these monsters. It was almost impossible to control what was private and what was public. In general, this was not a concern with the goo-brains. They put everything out there. They didn't seem to have any sense of dignity, and no idea of privacy. Being a spy among the implanted required an exhausting amount of diligence. She had to watch her own mind constantly. She slept with her implants switched off. She knew this could flag her as not fully integrated but it was a risk she had to take.

The key to her mission here was finding the repeater nodes. These were the constructs which transmitted information and data to and from the implants in the heads of the xombies. After days of searching, she discovered they were hidden in plain sight.

Following a hunch the nodes were part of a physically connected structure, she determined the only contiguous tech to connect them were the roads. She found mounds of dirt at regular intervals along the sides of the winding footpaths of Reverside. The graphene coating of the paths contained microscopic pathways which allowed for the flow of information. The repeater nodes looked like termite mounds but contained gooey blobs under the dirt. They were tended by tiny bots. It took her five days to discover a method to access them via her secretly modified implant. She noticed a subtle primitive handshake in the network of communication which felt inhuman. She rejoiced. She finally had her injection point.

The timing was critical. If she injected the worm too early, the xombies would mount alternate defenses on the bridge and might ready themselves for the attack. Too late, and her brothers would be turned into hamburger meat. She needed the whole town to be in disarray when the invasion arrived. Most of the people here had never even spoken aloud, much less learned to cope with a total data blackout.

Her message to Barnabas was sent when she was sure the Raiders had time to amass in Ramapo, and she was sure she would be able to inject the virus. She had a full day to wait. She headed uphill to the town to visit the babies in the nursery. One of them, little Katryna was calling to her. She sent reassurances and a play program written for growing toddlers. This quieted the child but she received an alert her diapers were needing a change.

Halfway there, Tretre ran up to her with a wrapped breakfast bulb in his hands. ["You are hungry,"] he sent. ["This is for you."] He smiled at her, satisfied and certain.

["Thank you,"] Nora thexted as she received the round food ball.

["What's in it?"]

["No thanks necessary Nora. You know how we do this. If you like it, please send a rating. This was prepared by Joanie « Mina « Sumi « Mi Jin « etc. You can send rating to her as well. I only delivered it. It is pickles, pine nuts and egg white in a cricket flour wrap."]

'God, they eat bugs,' Thought Nora. No one at home would ever stoop so low. This time she was sure not to send the thought out to the others. She took a bite. It was surprisingly delicious. The flour and the nuts combined with the egg to send waves of satisfaction through her body. She was indeed hungry. She had been forgetting to eat as she finalized her plans. She concentrated and sent ratings to Tretre and to Joanie. ["It's delicious,"] she thexted back.

Tretre bowed with a flourish of his arms. He was black skinned and wore no shirt. Around his waist was a sort of kilt. His head was topped with thick black dreads. Nora found him easy on the eyes, and it made her a little uncomfortable. Whites and blacks didn't associate back home. To Nora, this now seemed foolish.

Katryna had tired of her new plaything and was calling again. ["I have to go. One of the babies is calling to me."]

["I will walk with you. You know, we are all really impressed with your work. You have mastered your use of your implants quicker than any of us had thought possible."]

'Am I caught?' Nora was alarmed. 'I should have feigned more difficulty with my integration here?'

["You will notice your Merit is rising, and you may choose to gift in more interesting ways soon."] Tretre was smiling. It was a good smile. Maybe she was still safe.

["I really enjoy what I am doing right now."] This was not a lie. It made her sad to think it was all going to end.

They walked together to the nursery. It was a brightly colored angular building near the vertical farm which would soon be under her brother's control. Tretre veered off abruptly, which was normal around here. No pleasantries, no 'see ya later' he was just gone off on another path. Nora thought in a world where everyone is constantly in touch regardless of distance, the niceties of normal society were a casualty. Even the nicest xombies were rude.

Nora removed the diaper from Katryna, checked for a rash, swabbed her and replaced it with a new one. Diapers were being printed by a square machine in the corner of the dispensary, fed by a bin of raw materials. In addition to the farm, this was also technology her brother craved. With printers, he could supply a variety of products at high prices, and no cost to the greater and lesser families. They would be so, so rich.

Nora spent the rest of the day in the nursery, playing with the children, both through her visualizer and by hand. She headed out to the town center for lunch. There she saw Lala and Mem. Dinner was brought to her by the cheerful Tretre. Time was short now. She headed back to her home by the river for a restless sleep.

Nora woke before dawn. The repeater node she had picked out was in the town center. With her implants turned off, she strolled up again to where she had had lunch. The town was quiet in the pre-dawn hours. She estimated there were still twenty minutes before sunrise and the attack. That should be plenty of time for the worm to do its work.

Finding the node, she bent close to it and turned her implants back on. The handshake came easy, a robotic exchange between her modified implant and the node. Then she found the package she had taken from DASL6, the unfortunate boy she had tortured and tricked in a Camden basement. Steeling herself against the memory of him, she unpacked the worm and fed it to the node.

["Nora?"] she jumped. The message came from Mem. ["Nora, what are you doing? Are you feeling ill?"] She stood up. She had little experience in hand to hand combat. She looked at Mem and was sure she was no match for them.

["I was taking a walk,"] Nora flailed about in her mind, trying to concoct a feasible story. ["I was taking a walk, and I suddenly felt a bit nauseous. I thought I was going to throw up. I think it's passed. I'm okay now."]

["Oh."] Mem was looking at her, and looking at the mound she was standing above. Suddenly their eyes became wide. ["Just stay where you are, okay?"]

Nora ran but Mem ran faster. They were on her in two seconds. Nora felt the cold surface of the path against her face, her arms clenched behind her. She kicked but Mem immobilized her legs with their own. They held her still for what seemed like minutes.

Strong arms pulled her up. Two large members of Reverside tribe held her arms. Several others were standing by. She was struggling, scared and furious. Reyleena ran up the path toward her. Her icy blue eyes staring. Nora / Bethany spat at her.

"It's too late! It's too late! All you fucking xombies are going to pay for what you've done!" Bethany was finally free from all pretense and care. She knew they wouldn't track down the worm in time. "You killed him, you unnatural fuckers! You are all going to pay!"

Alarm registered in Reyleena's face. She looked up at the dim glowing sky. It looked like she was pleading or praying. Clouds had gathered thickly during the night, and their undersides were glowing with orange highlights. Bethany could no longer hear them in her head. They had shut her out, or maybe the virus had worked faster than she had thought.

"The bridge!" Reyleena shouted aloud. "Doxer! Wake up the tribe! Use your voice! Gather everyone! Bring her with me!"

They ran along the paths as the lights under the clouds grew brighter. They were fast, and Bethany struggled to keep her feet from dragging. It was a long way. Bethany struggled but laughed to herself, knowing they would be too late.

Throughout the town, people were stepping out of their homes, not all members of the tribe but many. They looked confused and alarmed. They called out to Reyleena, asking her what was happening. Reyleena had no time to respond. She kept running and Bethany's captors followed behind her.

At the path which led up to the old bridge, Bethany could see the first glints of the rising sun over the hills across the river. She heard the roar of the motorcycles as they descended the road on the far side and waited. The engines sang out into the morning sky, clearly audible in the silent town. Reyleena led the charge, barefoot and in a pale yellow nightgown out to meet an army of motors and guns.

"Stop!" Bethany laughed at her. "It's done! It's hopeless. What are you going to do, kick them? Surrender! It's your only choice."

The xombies holding her abruptly let her go. They ran to the sides of the bridge and began climbing the huge support cables which angled out to either side. They were a third of the way to the top when the first bikes began to speed across the bridge.

Bethany ran toward the Raiders waving her arms. She didn't know if Reyleena and her friends would be able to set off the bridge's defenses manually, or another way but she didn't want to take the chance. The bikers either didn't see her or were too sure of themselves. The front lines were halfway across when Bethany heard a series of short pops.

The first of the spinning projectiles missed their targets, skittering across the asphalt. Then she saw one of the Raiders grab his leg and go down, sliding along with his bike. Another projectile found a Raider but hit his arm. He stayed in the saddle and fell back. Another Raider aimed a shotgun at one of the cables and fired. Bethany turned to see one of the xombies lose his grasp on the cable and plunge down into the Hudson screaming. Another two shots fired, and another xombie fell. The popping stopped. A voice thundered out from behind the bikes. "Stop! Stop!"

The xombies were frozen halfway up the cables. Reyleena was staring across the distance of the bridge at a bald man holding himself half out of a black truck. It was Barnabas. "You have lost!" He yelled to her. "Come down peacefully, right now and no one else has to die!"

Another pop sounded and another of the spinning projectiles flew. It seemed to be aimed at Barnabas but missed him, shattering the windshield of his truck. One more gunshot rang out, this time from the rear of the truck, and the last of Reyleena's guards fell into the churning black water of the Hudson.

Slowly, carefully, and in silence, Reyleena climbed back down the thick white cable. She stood by the side of the bridge, arms at her sides, her head lowered. Tears ran down her face. Her shoulders shuddered as she gasped for breath.

Bethany ran to her, grabbed her by the arm and walked the defeated head of Reverside security toward her awaiting brothers. "Not so clever now, are we?" She gloated. "Welcome back to the human race."

25. Darkness

"Everything is down."

Helen stood outside the front door of the enormous house. Still groggy, Marto's first thought was about how good she looked. Her face was thinner, her body hardened. She held herself with great confidence. What had happened to her since he first saw her at the Lester Sunshine Inn?

"Marto? Everything is down! Do you hear me?"

"I'm not sure what you mean," Marto said aloud, remembering she was a mandatory verbal. "I think Maxtor has a kind of blocker on in here."

"It's not just here Marto. It's everywhere."

Marto walked outside, away from the house. There were six youngsters in brightly colored uniforms stretching in unison on the grass outside the front door. ["Hello,"] he thexted to them. He received no response. "Hello," he said aloud. They stood up and bowed to him, again, in unison. Odd.

He walked further away from the house, onto the road. He tried to check his merit, something he did every day upon waking. There was nothing. He felt as if a wet blanket had been thrown over his head. He tried to bring up a local map. Again, there was nothing. There was no pingback, no data received, no sense the data was sent. There was just nothing.

A small hot sphere of panic grew in his chest. Where was he again? He sent a query and got no response. He couldn't, for the life of him, remember the name of the town. He called back to Helen. "How did you find me here?" Helen waved him to come closer, her tanned forearm moving in a circle toward her chest. He trotted back to the front door. "Do you remember where we are? How did you follow me here?"

"Ho!" shouted the youngsters in unison. Their hands pushed quickly out in front of them, palms outward. Marto saw six black staffs lined neatly up against the side of the lodge.

"We are outside Bristol Tribe. The little ninjas and I have been traveling all night to get here in time before you took off."

"Ninjas!" the ninjas shouted, one arm up, one arm and one leg out to the side.

"So, what do you mean, everything is down everywhere?"

"The interconnection; It's not on at all. It just shut down this morning as we were heading here. People are panicking. It's chaos out there."

"They seem to be okay." Marto gestured to the group of teens, flexing.

"They are just amazing. Nothing phases them. They saved me from a bad situation in the Hampton Isles. I owe them so much."

"You know, you don't 'owe' them anything," Marto began, launching into teacher mode, as he did for most noobs, "that is not our way Helen, what is offered..."

"Don't you get it? That's over! No Merit! No ratings! Nothing."

"This must be a temporary glitch. Maybe it's an upgrade." Marto shook his head as if maybe his implants had simply detached. He felt like he had gone deaf. "Maybe it's localized to just this region."

"Well, there is no way to know, but I'm telling you, people are walking around like... I mean, everyone is confused for miles around. You mentioned someone was here with you. Max somebody? Why don't you check with him?"

Marto ran into the house and shouted up the stairs "Maxtor?" He ran up to the largest bedroom where he thought the lion was sleeping. "Maxtor?" There was no answer. He opened the door. The bed looked slept in, but empty. The bathroom door was open. He was not there. Marto checked the other rooms, the living room, the expansive kitchen. Maxtor had left. He headed back outside.

"He's gone," he said. "I guess he left this morning, or maybe last night. He is unpredictable."

"Well, I've found you. That's something. I've been trying to catch up with you for days. I went to Cos, and then I got on a barge, and was kidnapped..."

"You were kidnapped? Why?"

"Oh. Well, look, we'd better sit down somewhere so I can tell you. I'm not really who I said I am, but I am who I think I am now, I think. Marto, what do you suppose is happening?"

"I have no idea. I just woke up," Marto said, rubbing his forehead. "I need a tea or something. And something to eat. I think there's food inside. Come on in. I don't know how long we can stay here. I was here on the Merit of Maxtor, but since no one can thext or track us, who knows? Come in."

The eight of them walked into the spacious living room and chose seats. Marto left to wash his face. When he returned Helen told him all about her past, her family, her escape, and then stopped before she got to the part about New Atlantic. Marto was astonished at the revelation of her previous identity. Such things were not unheard of, but rare. Suddenly their first meeting made much more sense.

"So was it true when you told me you had read my previous work about my trip to Great Lakes?"

"Yes, I had a printed version at my aunt's library. It was contraband, but people in my family didn't really check the books I read."

"So what happened next?" Marto was enthralled by Helen's story.

"Um, why don't you go see if there is any food or a way to make tea or coffee or something before I go further. I don't know if you are going to pass out again."

"Oh, yeah. Wait here."

Marto went into the kitchen and found a kettle. The range was top notch, like the one used by Thirty/Fourteen in Reverside. He found coffee, amazing, a ceramic drip pot and a hemp filter, and poured the water over. There were biscuits baked the day before in a bread box and a block of sheep butter. In a cupboard, he found marmalade, also amazing. He got a platter and brought everything out with cups and plates.

He was met at the door by one of the ninjas. ["We can still PM,"] she thexted. She meant private message. ["We've been thexting to each other all morning to work on synchronizing our attacks. I thought you knew this. Helen doesn't seem to be able to hear us."]

Given this information, Marto thought the outage might only be limited to the repeaters. Without repeaters, the Interconnected could still communicate in private, if they were in close proximity.

Marto walked out to the living room, put the platter on the coffee table and tried it out ["Hello everyone. Are you getting this? We have not all been introduced. I'm Marto."]

["Londra"] ["Tinker"] ["Zha-Zha"] ["Timo"] ["Patsi"] ["Billie"] replied the ninjas. There was no point in including their foremothers since there were no references available at the moment. Helen looked on, confused at the odd silence.

"Helen, no one has shown you how to private message," Londra said to her, "I guess it makes sense, as you are still a noob. It takes concentration. Shall I teach you?"

Helen hesitated. "Maybe later. Let's eat."

Considering the ominous deadness in their heads, breakfast was thoroughly enjoyed by all. They ate in silence, unaccustomed to chewing and talking aloud. Only Helen broke the quiet. She offered comments about the marmalade and how much she enjoyed the coffee. The sky was overcast, and the lake was still. A few birds flew by. The party gazed out the window as they finished.

The ninjas cleared the dishes, and brought back more coffee and Helen spoke to Marto. "So, after I left Wyland tribe in The Jersey, I came to New Atlantic. I was trying to find a ... a friend." She hesitated, ready for Marto to have another spell. "Your mother found me first."

"My ... mother." Marto felt a familiar wave of dizziness. He knew how to fight it this time. "My mother is alive?"

"Yes!" Helen felt a great relief. Her mission was almost complete. "She left me a message for you." She touched the side of her head. "I don't know what's in it. I may have already sent you part of it, and then you passed out for a bit. She was adamant you have it. I have traveled all the way from Reverside to find you again and give this to you in person. Reyleena said I couldn't send it to you remotely. It had to be in person."

"Well..." Marto was still fighting to keep from fainting. "Hang on." He took a sip of the coffee to steady himself. "So. I think you should first work with Londra on the private messaging thing before you do a data transfer like that. It could be risky if you don't know how to PM."

"Oh, okay." Helen was dismayed. She wanted the data out of her head once and for all. "How long will it take?"

"It depends on how good you are with the implants, maybe a couple of hours, maybe a day. I don't know."

"Right." She had come this far, perhaps a day longer wouldn't hurt. She didn't really know what she would do after this was over anyway. Maybe back to Cos, and Tash, or maybe stay with Marto? She thought about traveling with him through the Northeast, cycling from town to town, but what if all the connections were gone for good? Would Marto keep going? She was struck by the total groundlessness of her current situation.

"So, when you saw my mother, where was she again? I don't know of any New Atlantic tribe."

"It's not a tribe. It's a Luddite family like mine. She works there. She is a servant of a man named Barnabas. He's the leader. I don't know much about him, but I think he's dangerous."

"But, she's been augmented."

"Yes. It's a secret, I suppose."

"So, my mother is a spy in a neo-feudal enclave?"

"Yes, I think so Marto, Reyleena told me she has been for years."

"Woh." Now Marto felt he really was going to faint. "Can you... can you go somewhere with Londra? I don't want to pass out again. Please. Come back when you know how to... to..."

"Yes. I will. Hang tight Marto. I'll be back." Helen sped out of the room with Londra. The rest of the ninjas curled up on the floor and took a nap.

Marto sat on the sofa and watched as three ducks landed on the lake. He steadied himself, breathing carefully and then felt the darkness rise up and drown him.

• • •

The engine of the plane is a constant hum outside of the cabin. Marto is sitting with his mother, who is smiling down at him, stroking his hair. Her face is lit by an oval of light from the window. Marto looks out at the clouds and the diminishing mountains below. The sky is a color blue he had never seen before, deep and growing darker as you look up.

The pilot is a friendly man, his face familiar. He lets Marto come up into the cockpit and look at all the dials. Marto's father sits next to him in the same sort of chair, buckled in. "Don't touch!" the friendly man says. "This is called the throttle. And this is the horizon. You see it out there, but this is how we know we are level, even when we are in the clouds. Got it?"

Marto goes back to sit with his mother. He falls asleep on the seat. Then he is awake and the sound of the plane is different. His mother's heart is beating fast as she holds him tight to her breast. She is whispering to herself, Marto can hear it faintly through her chest, over the rising whine of the engines. Her hair flaps around him in the swirling wind of the cabin.

The plane bumps and tilts hard to one side. His mother gasps. There is a loud bang.

• • •

26. Occupied

Reyleena watched her wounded bare feet stain the stitched segments of the ancient rug with her red, red blood. The pain in her extremities was dwarfed by her feeling of intense loneliness and abandonment. Her constant companion was gone.

She hated watching her tribe's rapid defeat by this band of brutes. Before her stood the leader of the biker invaders and his brother. Nora, the spy, sat on the arm of the L shaped sofa, grinning. Thoughts of gruesome revenge flashed in Reyleena's head. A portion of the army of Raiders crowded the great room of the Lester Sunshine Inn. They stank. The bald man, standing atop the coffee table, addressed the crowd.

"Today we have won only the first of many victories! From here we will ride west to White Plains and Rye! Then split up to take Scarsdale, The Bronx, Yonkers, New Rochelle, Greenwich and more! I tell you, as easy as it was to conquer Tarrytown, it will be even easier to take all of Westchester, Connecticut, and beyond! Today marks a great day for humanity! Soon the Northeast will belong to us!" Cheers erupted. The barbarians drank.

"Before you stands Reyleena, their former head of security. I say this openly in her presence to show you just how powerless they are to stop us. We have taken down the key to their power: the unholy marriage between man and machine. The future belongs to the righteous! The future belongs to natural humanity!" More cheers.

"First I will negotiate the surrender of the xombies of Tarrytown. They work for us now. I invite you to relax and recuperate in and around this mansion. These xombies have been rendered impotent. They will not offer you any resistance. Don't kill them. Don't molest them!"

Grumbles could be heard from some of the Raiders. "Do not!" Barnabas glared into the crowded room. "We have need of their skills and their expertise as we plan our next attacks. This is important! Our new slaves will grow our food and improve our lives. I believe a sampling of their cuisine is ready."

Waiting at the edge of the crowd was Thirty/Fourteen, his eyes red. He looked ready to take the entire assemblage of Raiders on with his bare hands. Flanking him were a dozen tribal member carrying platters of hand-wraps. The Raiders surged on them, greedily snatched them up and gobbled them. Thirty/Fourteen stood still, fuming.

["Stay calm,"] Reyleena thexted him privately. ["They don't know we can still communicate without the repeaters. Their spy was never taught how to PM. There is a plan. Stay calm."] Thirty/Fourteen avoided any eye contact with Reyleena. He spun on his heel and headed back to the kitchen.

"Hey!" shouted one of the barbarians after him. "Where's the meat? This is all goat food." He made a show of throwing the remainder of his wrap down and pulling the rest from his mouth with his fingers.

"I saw some animals out behind the house," said another. "I say we roast a few and have a proper feast."

Thirty/Fourteen wheeled around to face the first of the Raiders, who grinned back at him, ready. The other tribal members assumed their fighting stances, eager to put the invaders down.

"Steady!" boomed the bald man. "What will you do? Kill our cook? How will that serve our purposes?"

["Not yet, my friends,"] thexted Reyleena urgently, sending her message to the servers as well as the chef. ["Please be patient. Let them think they have won. Trust me."]

Thirty/Fourteen and the others straightened gracefully, bowed their heads, and returned to the kitchen. The loss of a few of their livestock would be the least of their worries before all of this was over.

The Raiders who didn't mind the sweet potatoes, spinach and fried mealworms finished their hand-wraps, and the room emptied out, leaving a few bodyguards, Nora, and her two brothers.

"Now Reyleena, introductions first. I'm Barnabas. This is my brother Daschel, and this woman you have known as Nora is Bethany, my sister. We are the elders of the ruling Yoniver family. We control the eastern half of The Jersey. Now we control this town. Do you accept this? I want to talk terms."

"I accept this," Reyleena said flatly. She had not used her spoken voice in over a week. Her words came out as a croak.

"You are cut off from your friends. You are cut off from any rescue. As the leader of your people, you can make this a peaceful transition, or you can resist, and many from this town will die. Do you surrender?"

"I surrender," Reyleena said.

"Do you speak for your whole town? Is there someone else in power here we should address?"

"They don't have a real leader Barney. She is as close to it as you are going to find," Bethany interjected.

"My people are not without the means to defend themselves." Reyleena choked on the words, "if you want them to surrender, we will need to go quickly through the town so I can tell them myself ... out loud."

"Sound idea," Barnabas grinned. "But first I want your assurance you and your people will be willing to show us how to use your technology. Specifically, I want to understand how to use your three-dimensional printers, and how to run the automated tower farm."

"We can show you the workings of the printers," Reyleena said, "though most don't come with manual controls. Likewise, the farming bots require guidance by the tribe to perform tasks which are not automated. At this point, they are likely dormant, as they are no longer connected to shared knowledge."

"I'm sure we can figure something out," Barnabas was picking his teeth with a bit of wood. "When you hurt a couple of my men on the bridge, you showed us you could still control your tech when in close proximity. That was a mistake in my favor. Perhaps a small number of your tribe can be put to use reanimating the farming bots and running those printers."

"As you like," said Reyleena, furious with herself for not heeding the advice of The Other. She wished she had listened to them when they warned her not to put up any resistance. As usual, their prescience was flawless. Now they were gone.

"Very good. So, if we are all in agreement, let's take the Trucks through the town and inform the inhabitants about their new leaders. Your job is to persuade them not to resist. If you don't cooperate, the killings will commence. Do you understand?"

"I understand."

"Okay then, let's get on with it."

They took three black trucks, burning noxious, stinking fuel over the too narrow paths down the hill and back through the dwellings. The wheels of the truck were stuck in the gutters on either side of the paths. Members of her tribe huddled together, terrified. As they went, her voice hoarse, Reyleena shouted from the open back of the lead truck to her beloved community. She told them to not offer any resistance, and everything would be okay. She told them to spread the word to the others. Barnabas suggested phrases through an open window to the truck bed. Some of her people were crying, holding each other. Others stood apart and looked at her with shocked disbelief. She didn't dare message any reassurances to them, for fear they might show acknowledgment, and foil the careful plans laid out by The Other. It was the hardest thing she ever had to do. Her stomach turned as she forced the words out. She wanted so desperately to fight but knew it was not the right time, not yet.

As she passed, she saw a few of the younger members of her community who had augmented their appearance to the point where they could no longer speak out loud. She felt awful for them. They were rendered mute by the attack. How could they have predicted they might once again need their human mouths and tongues? None of the Interconnected thought an invasion like this could be possible. They had all been so naive.

In the dim hours of the morning, when the repeaters had first been switched off, she had sent a message out to two of her guards to inform the chefs to change their ingredients. There were to be no more pine nuts or pumpkin seeds in the food and more cabbage, spinach, and yams.

Hopefully, they had gotten the message out in time. Everything depended on it.

The trucks looped around the town, covering enough area for Reyleena's surrender to be communicated and repeated. Finally, the trucks stopped at the towering vertical farm. The party disembarked.

"So, this is the wonderful farm you use to feed your people," Daschel said. "Holy mother of god, how did you build it?"

"The mechanics and framework were all printed," said Reyleena in a dull croak. "The glass was installed by constructor bots. Irrigation tubing is incorporated into the framework. If you like, I can find a farm tech to tell you more."

"I think that would be a good idea," Barnabas said, gazing upward at the shining structure. "We need to know how we are going to run it. I also want to know how much of it can be converted to produce grain."

"It will take time to find the right people. I can't just call them here anymore. Perhaps if we walk back to the town square, I can find one for you." Reyleena felt a dull sadness creep over her. Her head spun. She steadied herself. She had to force herself to keep going, knowing the pain which would ensue.

"I'm going back to the nursery Barney. I've been looking after the children there. They must be panicking," Bethany said.

"Mmm?" Barnabas was distracted by the tower. "Oh, sure, that's fine. Is the nursery near the town square?"

"Yes."

"Then why don't you take Dylan and Reyleena, and go there and bring me back a couple of those 'farm techs'." Daschel handed him a cigar.

Bethany and Reyleena headed the short distance back to the town square followed by Dylan, cradling his weapon in his arms.

"Do you think the babies will be okay?" Bethany asked Reyleena.

"Depends on what you mean by 'okay'," her voice was cold. "Why do you care, Luddite?"

Bethany was taken aback. "Watch your tone! Just answer my question goo-brain. Of course, I care. They are innocent in all this. I was looking after them."

["Not anymore,"] thought Reyleena to herself.

They walked the rest of the way in silence.

In the town square, Reyleena could hear members of her tribe shooting accusations her way in harsh whispers. ["Traitor,"] one of them sent her, privately. ["You were supposed to protect us!"] and ["How could you?"] Others only said, "Head of security," quietly, through their teeth. The accusations were devastating. Reyleena thought she was going to collapse.

"Don't listen to them," Dylan spoke. "They'll see the better of it in time. You've done them all a favor."

The nursery was in chaos. Two dozen of the Interconnected tended to the wailing infants and toddlers, offering food, toys, and holding them. They wouldn't stop crying. Bethany tried to help out but was rebuffed. She printed three diapers and left again with the head of security and the bodyguard.

Back in the town square, they found two farm techs, Reyleena knew them as Dink and Yaddle. Bethany ordered them to follow her back to the farm.

["It is essential you don't let on I can message you,"] Reyleena thexted them. ["Don't nod your heads, don't react. There is a plan, I assure you. Please go along with them. Do what they ask. They know we can still control the bots. I think it's what they want you to do."]

["Anything you say, head of security,"] Yaddle sent back. It was not kind.

They found Barnabas and Daschel laughing together, plotting their glowing future as kings of the Northeast. The cigars were mere stubs and Barnabas tossed his off to the side, near a bush. Dink ran to it and spat on it until the glowing end was out. "Fire," he said to Dylan.

"So, tell me how we can get this tower farm up and running," Barnabas said, addressing the two techs.

"Well," said Yaddle, "much of the information they need comes from shared knowledge, which is constantly updated with data concerning hours of sunshine, weather patterns, and crop behaviors. That's down now, so the bots are all on standby. Our seed stocks are plentiful, but the bots will need constant monitoring and guidance."

"I can send and receive with the lower bots," said Dink, "but communication with the ones higher up is spotty. Crops up there will be lost."

"Can you get inside and do it by hand?" Barnabas asked.

"Maybe?" replied Dink. "But we are big and clumsy. We will crush too many of the new growths, plus there's no way to climb all the way up. It was never intended for people."

"Hmm. So what if we build a scaffolding on the outside, and position say, twenty or thirty of you on the outside? That way you should be able to work the bots on top and keep production going." Barnabas was gazing at the top of the farm again.

Yaddle was horrified. "You mean, we would just be sitting up there all day guiding them?" Dink looked pale.

"I'm open to alternatives," Barnabas said.

"But it's all collapsible in case of bad weather," Dink said. "The scaffolding would be destroyed when the farm goes underground. Also, we don't have weather reports anymore. I remember a storm was being tracked, and if we don't get the farm down in time..."

"Let's deal with it when it happens," Barnabas said.

Bethany suddenly became alarmed. "Barney. I just got a message!"

"How?"

"Shortwave radio. There is a transmitter nearby. I strung it to the far shore. You know, it's not important right now. But, it's not part of the xombie repeater network."

"Tell me."

"Barney, there has been an attack back home. Brady is reporting fire and explosions!"

"Fuck!" Barnabas ran for the trucks. "Dylan! Come with me! Gather up the rest of the guard! Daschel, I'm leaving you in command!" The soldiers jumped back in the trucks, which collected Barnabas and sped away, back through the town.

Daschel stepped on his cigar. "Shit." He spat. "So much for easy."

27. Leviathan

Helen, Marto, and the ninjas passed the day at the lodge, eating and sleeping. The ninjas and Helen needed time to recover from their latest escapades and Marto was happy to stay put and get his thoughts together. They had only one interruption, a woman and a man who stopped by the door asking after Maxtor. The party thought they were going to be evicted, but there was no mention of their exit. They said they had no idea where he was. The couple left.

"I think I know where Maxtor went," Marto said to the group, over his morning coffee. What he didn't say was that he had an idea why his past had been kept a secret. He hoped he wasn't right.

"Where?" asked Helen. "Do you think he can tell us why the blackout happened?"

"I can't think of anyone else who could," Marto said, getting to his feet. "We need to go to Plainville."

"How far is that?"

"Should be just northeast of here. That's why he brought me here. He wanted to escape."

"Escape?"

"His life. He's mysterious, but I think I understand him better now. Let's try to go north, then east, and just bushwhack it."

The party of eight, Marto, Helen and the ninjas walked outside, determined their direction from the shadows of the morning sun, and pushed through the underbrush heading north.

A short way through the brush they found the wreckage of an old amusement park. The old rides had crumbled or filled with dirt. A carousel was still standing, the horses looking pale. A crumbling semicircle of a ride stood with chairs hanging vertically from a giant wheel. The top of the wheel had caved in, the top half falling down onto the lower half. Past these relics, they saw printed homes in rows, the inhabitants wandering aimlessly about. Marto had been walking his uni, wishing he could ride it.

["Hey, do you know what happened to the ... everything?"] One of the disconnected was messaging them. She stood before them on the road, looking distressed. She had dark curly hair, showing a touch of grey. ["Everything is just blank. Do you know what happened?"]

["We are as much in the dark as you,"] Marto replied.

["I've been trying to get through to ... anybody. I feel like my brain has imploded. This can't last, can it? And aren't you the wandering writer fellow? The one who was traveling with Maxtor?"]

["That is me, yes. Say, you wouldn't have any bikes my friends could borrow would you?"] Marto was hoping his Merit would help them, even though there was no way to give ratings.

["Not for us!"] Londra sent. ["We run."]

["Okay, well, I guess just one bike?"]

["Certainly! You are welcome to one. I have a couple near my home. Just remember me when all the connections come back on will you?"]

She sent her name. Lydia « Martha « Didi « Mirona « etc. Marto recorded it, with a note of where she was from. That should be enough. ["Absolutely,"] he responded.

["Hey, did you just get me a bike?"] Helen sent. She had picked up the private messaging quickly. This was fortunate.

["Yes, indeed! Follow Lydia and meet us back here."] Helen walked in the direction of a pink printed house and came back with a bamboo bike.

They followed the paths, winding in and out of the homes, still going north. The ninjas kept up with little difficulty. As they passed more of the disconnected, the same questions were asked, and the same answer was given. They got directions. By mid-afternoon, they had arrived at a place where the paths had turned to dirt, and there were no more neat, little, printed homes. Plainville.

The sky was uniformly overcast. Before them lay a series of fields. Men and women worked in them, pulling up crops. They wore straw hats. Marto and Helen hopped off their rides and walked into the fields.

One of the farmers walked toward them. "Hello! Are you lost?" the man said. He was stocky and strong and wore a faded blue shirt, stained with sweat. His jeans were tattered. He wore boots. He held a shovel in one hand.

"No, not lost. We are here by invitation. A man named Zeke." Marto held out his hands in a gesture he hoped looked friendly.

"Ah. Well, he's up at the yellow barn, a couple of fields over," the man said. "One thing you have to know before you go over there. We have a strict rule about mental chitter chatter here. If you want to walk our fields, you have to keep your thoughts to yourselves..." he waved his fingers out from the side of his head "and use your words."

"This should not be a problem," said Marto.

["Is he serious?"] thexted Billie, one of the ninjas.

"Yes, he's serious. No thexting, no messaging. They can tell." Marto was addressing the whole party. "It's a serious thing with them."

"Hai!" said the ninjas in unison. Helen broke out laughing.

They walked the edges of the fields, careful not to disturb the crops. Marto had never seen so much open farming before. The amount of land they used was startling. The amount of water required was alarming. He thought about Maxtor and his comments on water as they cleared the first field, then the second and headed across the third.

Up ahead was a yellow barn. In front of it, clumsily working a trowel in the dirt was a man covered in carefully adorned multicolored hair. The great Maxtor Uber G was wearing overalls and harvesting something. He bent down and picked up a beet, immediately putting it in his mouth. Looking up, he saw Marto and waved. A trail of red ran down his chin. He was clearly enjoying himself.

"Hello, Maxtor!" Marto shouted back. "Having fun?"

"Hey, hey my green, green node, you found me! And you brought friends!"

The ninjas clacked their staffs together in the air. Marto hoped they

14 · Jim Infantino

were not synchronizing their actions via thext.

"And you must be the lovely Helen. The launch that faced a floundered ship."

"You know me? I'm honored to be recognized by the famous Maxtor."

"Well, aren't you an ingot of solid gorgeous? Yeah, I heard about your abduction. Good drama. And you can call me the formerly famous. I'm just a simple farmer now. I wanted a straw hat, just like the others, but my head is too big." He took another bite.

"Maxtor, do you know what's going on out there?" Marto asked.

"Oh, you mean the ultimate Game over? Oh yes, my node. I predicted it a week ago." He got deadly serious for a moment. "Did you tell anyone I was in here?"

"No."

He brightened again, "Good. So you figured out my plan. Found me. How'd ya do it?" Maxtor was making a show of talking like Zeke and his ilk.

"Well, I had this dream, and in it, I was on an island. Everything was silent. It was frightening, but it was also peaceful. When I woke, I remembered you had visited Zeke on the Merritt and given him a black box for detecting signals. I remembered Zeke was in Plainville, on the map near the lake we were on. I figured you used me as an excuse to get close to here so you could sneak away. I think you are hiding to escape your fame for a while."

"Mm-hmm, that's part of it, my wandering node. Yes indeed. But there's more. Like the big blackout. What do you think that's about?"

"We came here to ask you."

Maxtor glanced at the sky and turned around in a circle. A block of dark clouds was moving in from the west. "Yeah, let's go inside," he said.

In the back of the yellow barn were bales of hay under a loft behind an old tractor. Maxtor jumped up on one of the hay bales, and the others did the same. He looked around, checking out every wall.

"The super-mods saw her coming," Maxtor said to them. His voice was almost a whisper. "Data copying itself, tucking itself away. Large movements of information for no good reason. Super-mods glean things other people can never glean. They love the data, the raw stuff. They sift it around, run it through their fingers like sand. They see things."

"Like what?" Helen asked.

"The super-mods called her Leviathan." Maxtor got even quieter. "Something swimming around in all the data. Like something really big. Didn't know what she was. Don't know if she was an AI or something else they can't glean. All they could tell was she was there, and she was hunkering down."

"I don't know Maxtor," said Marto, "This sounds a lot like a story I would tell to children to scare them. The data monster, and the blackout."

"Well, the blackout is real, ain't it, my node? I'm not saying this Leviathan caused it, but she knew what was coming. When she began protecting herself, was when we grasped the situation. One of the super-mods showed me. Leviathan was behaving in a way which suggested motivation. She was protecting herself from a network collapse. This meant the collapse was either beyond her control or Leviathan caused it. We can't parse that part. I had no idea it was going to happen yesterday morning. My getting here just in time was a coincidence."

"So, there might be a kind of program out there, stored away," Marto said, sounding incredulous. "Why is this a reason for you to run and hide here?"

"Well, first off, I needed a break and this place is the nads. I haven't been here even two days, and already I feel so much better. I like working with my hands, feeling the wind, being solo, and taking a break from all the hullaballoo. I needed a serious vacation. Secondly, I don't mind telling you if there is a general AI out there doing her thing in the same space we all do our thing, it scares the fleeping spit out of me. It throws our whole game into question, glean?"

Marto did glean. He did not like the idea at all. "I thought it was impossible. You're talking about the singularity."

"'Tis one way of looking at her. She has a will, of sorts. She's protecting herself. That's pretty singular if you parse me. Remember I was telling you about the algorithm? How it's gotten too big to fathom? Well, what if this big program is the algorithm? Or what if she's manipulating the algorithm, using it to control our behavior? Can you picture the power she would have? What does she want? What is she doing? We have no way to tell. That's the major reason I needed to remove myself from the equation. I came here in secret because I needed time to think, by myself."

"I don't know," said Zha-Zha, "I think it's exciting there might be a new form of life out there. Why should we fear her?"

Maxtor regarded her with a kind of patient annoyance. "Well, why indeed?" he said. "Why fear a thing you don't understand, something that knows you better than you do, pulling the strings out beyond our ability to perceive? Something with motivations which are perfectly ineffable?"

Zha-Zha reflected her annoyance back at Maxtor. She didn't like being treated like a child.

"Is she god or devil, this Leviathan? If she's a good and benevolent god, then no problem. We are all happy Edenites. But if she is the devil, or worse, if she's neutral, and she's in the minds of millions, playing a game of her own, then we are all just puppets. Glean?"

Zha-Zha thought for a while. "Yeah, I guess that's kinda creepy."

"But she's down now. She's in hiding?" Helen asked. "She can't do much harm while the connections are dark, can she?"

"You got me there, ingot. No way to know if she's dormant, or just split apart into smaller versions of herself working away in our minds," Maxtor said, shuddering. "My guess is something that big has a plan to turn the lights back on. None of us mere humans know what things will look like when that happens."

There were footsteps outside, and the barn door swung open to reveal Zeke in his light blue shirt and straw hat. With him were four women, dressed in a similar fashion. "Hello?" Zeke called. "Maxtor?" He waited for his eyes to adjust to the light of the barn. "Who are your friends?"

"Hi Zeke," said Marto, standing. "We met on the bridge. At the pop-up cafe? I passed out, remember?"

"Ah, yes. Skater boy. You came here after all. Didn't think you would. Welcome."

"Thanks. I brought a few friends. Told them the rules." He introduced Helen and the ninjas.

"Well, I wish you had picked better weather for your arrival. We are in for a nasty storm. It's coming in from Danvers. We'd better get to the shelter. Oh, and these are my wives," He pointed. "Karaugh, Deborah, Allie, and Martika." They each said hello.

Marto looked at the ninjas and Helen. They turned their heads to look at him, their eyes scowling. Marto didn't need a private message to know what they were thinking.

Polygamist.

28. Emily

The Interconnected freed themselves from the bondage of marriage and family early in the years after the establishment of Sherwood. It has been said, in the absence of money, marriage simply lost its root. Others have pointed to the idea that in the upheaval of so many aspects of traditional life, the structures of family ceased to hold power. Our romantic notions of marriage dissolved as we let go of our possessions. The nuclear family faded away, with the notion of property. Children became the joy and responsibility of everyone. The culture of not clinging to partners, monogamy, sexual stereotypes, or ownership of things or people, defined what it was to become interconnected.

The traditionalists decried this behavior as depraved. What both the traditionalists and the Interconnected agreed upon, however, was the abomination of polygamy. The Interconnected hated polygamy because it combined the outdated bondage of marriage with the subjugation of women. The traditionalists hated it because it was not what they perceived as the biblical norm.

The pressure to lean toward polygamy rose during the fall in fertility brought on by the success of the Siberian Zika virus. Polygamist communities sprouted up worldwide, lead by men who touted the plural marriage imperative for increased chances of births. Their arguments made logical sense, but the practice overwhelmingly encouraged closed societies which oppressed women and exalted men. Horrific stories of enslaved women escaped the closed walls of these societies. Soon, polygamists everywhere were met with scorn, casting them as pariahs, and causing them to become increasingly insular.

– The Wakeful Wanderer's Guide, Vol. 6, lines 730 - 732 (unpublished)

Marto was cheating. He was also stalling. He sat with Zeke and his four wives whose names had already escaped him, Helen and Maxtor in a basement under Zeke's house. Zeke didn't seem to notice Marto had been writing in his head. He doubted Zeke would have thrown him out in the storm if he did.

The wind gathered strength outside. The basement was damp but comfortable. There were lit candles and food in jars. An awkward silence lay between Marto's party and Zeke's. Only Maxtor seemed oblivious. He ate pickled string beans from one of the jars, cheerfully waiting out the storm.

Marto gathered his courage and looked at Helen. When she had caught his eye, he said: "I'm ready."

Helen had forgotten all about the data packet. Startled by the remembrance of it she said, "Oh, okay. I'm not really sure how to..."

· · ·

There is a light and a presence in the light. His mother's arms, his mother's face. He is enveloped in her presence. She is speaking to him.

"You were born Matthew Gerald Baxter."

"Your father was Ignatius Roman Baxter. My maiden name was Emily Elizabeth Fitzgerald. My father, your maternal grandfather Holden, was the last of a long line of male heirs to the Fitzgerald Oil fortune. Your father would have been heir to the Baxter mining fortune if it had not been dissolved upon the death of his father, your grandfather Lawrence."

"Your father and I met at a gala thrown by our families at the Fitzgerald summer home near Park City, Utah. Even as the world they had inherited crumbled around them, we were prohibited from dating outside of our social circles. You need to know I loved your father, regardless of the circumstances which threw us together. He was a kind and generous man."

His fathers face appears to him, without the beard, the light colored glasses framing his smiling eyes.

"We lived in the same summer home where we had been promised to each other. The remote location protected us from the Vengeance. A few of your father's friends lived with us. We had plenty of room, and everyone helped with the upkeep of the large house. Our years there were isolated, but happy."

He remembers the house, a rectangular oversized redwood chalet, with decking set around the second and third stories, overlooking the mountains and the snow.

"When you were three years old, my mother, your grandmother Joan came to visit us. She told your father and me that our families were moving into an underground shelter in Alaska to wait out the killing spree. By then it was raging through the country and most of the world. She came by helicopter with four bodyguards. She ended up screaming at us, imploring us to join her. Your father was the one to say no. He said we were not going to wait for death in a tomb. We would take our chances above ground. I was unsure at the time, but I now know he was right. That was the last I saw of my mother."

He saw pictures of his grandfathers and grandmothers, images from parties, galas, museums. He saw his great grandfathers and great grandmothers, more parties, boardrooms, expansive parlors, men smoking cigars and drinking brandies, women in beautiful gowns.

"One of your father's friends living with us was a pilot. His name was Lucas Chen. When The Vengeance had reached Salt Lake City for the second time, we knew it was time to leave our home. We flew a Piper Shoshone out from a local airfield and headed east toward Boston and your uncle Charles. We were supposed to refuel in Kansas but the airfield had been overtaken by an army of men in jeeps and on motorcycles. They shot at us, hitting a window in the cockpit, missing Luke. We were able to keep flying. All of the following airstrips we passed were unsafe. Our fuel ran out over Ohio."

He saw the view from the window again. Then the feeling of his mother holding him tight against her chest.

"Luke was a good pilot. He managed to touch down in a field, but the plane turned over on one of the wings. He was killed in the crash. Your father and I carried you from the plane."

"We needed new names. We were in shock. I'm afraid we weren't at all clever about it. Iggy said I should be Mary because it sounded plain. I said he should be Warren because I always liked the name. We walked for miles until we finally saw a broken old Walmart. They used to be everywhere, and Iggy and I would joke about them when we were teenagers. Now they seemed like a remnant of a golden age of plenty. We decided to name you after that crumbling icon. We shortened it to Marto. Our last name became Boxster, close to Baxter, but more like Box Store. We prayed no one would see the similarity."

He can taste the pickled eggs, see his father with the beard covering his face. He can feel his mother's tears on his arm.

"We made our way on foot for the longest time. We finally found help from an Amish town in Ohio. We were starving. They took us in and fed us. I thought we should ask to join them and try to convert to their ways. Your father was adamant we keep pressing on. The town was called Paradise West. If it had not been for those kind wonderful people, I think we would have died. They helped connect us with wagon rides between their communities and the Mennonites', following their trade routes, until we were close to the Hudson River. That was when we met Fish."

He sees a tall man with long sparse blonde hair blowing around his head. He has an easy smile, his hands loosely held at his sides. Behind him is a river. He is high above it, on a cliff.

"At this point, your father and I were fighting all the time. I think he was still holding onto hope our old way of life could be restored. I entertained no such illusions. From everything I could see, our world was gone. We had seen no signs of any modern civilization since the plane crash. The only people who seemed to be thriving were the Amish and Mennonites who had reverted to simpler, more agrarian ways long ago. When we met Fish and were welcomed into Reverside, I saw a new way of life, and new possibilities."

"If we wanted to stay in Reverside, Fish told us we would have to get augmented. Iggy was dead set against it. I was nervous but knew it might be our only hope for a new life. When your father was sleeping, I found Fish and received my first implants. I needed to know it would be safe before you might have to have your own implants put in. It was truly disgusting, but over time, a whole new world opened up to me. I never told your father about this. After our first week without fear and exhaustion since our escape from Utah, we moved on toward Boston."

He is riding in a wagon behind a tandem bike, ridden by his mother and father. The air was moist and warm. The trees are lush and different. He loves the feeling of movement, and the silent new people they meet on the way.

"We stopped at dozens of tribal towns as we made our way north and east. The people were strange but friendly. I noticed there were no families and it disturbed me. Would I have to give you up if we returned to Reverside? For the sake of your safety, I was willing. There were no more armies of dirty men with guns. Some of the towns seemed poorly provisioned, and others richly so. In all of the towns, we were well fed, rested, and encouraged to continue on our way. Seeing these people affected me greatly. I felt I was slowly becoming part of them. I could hear them in my head. They kept my secret from Iggy and you. I engaged in discussions, silently, about the fall of wealth and the rise of Merit. They knew me only as Mary Boxster. I had a feeling even these kind people might turn on us if they knew us for what we were."

"We made it to the terrible remains of Boston, Charles wasn't in his Brookline home, which had been crowded by the Interconnected. They lounged about his living room and slept in his many bedrooms. Boston was far from safe for us. Remnants of The Vengeance lurked on the outskirts of the city. They were not like the bikers we saw in Ohio. They were regular people with an unquenchable rage."

"After asking around, we discovered a man of Charles' description was living north of Boston in a town called Medford. We found him there just before The Vengeance arrived. You were playing with a ball outside, and when we heard you calling for us, your father, my dear

Ignatius, ran out to confront them. I heard them shouting 'Defilers' and 'Greedy Takers' and feared that we were all going to die. Iggy held the mob long enough for Charles to sneak us into his truck and drive us to his boat. I never saw what happened to him, but I feel certain they killed him on that road. This is the fate of all people like us who dare to be exposed to the mobs."

He is hanging his head over the side of the boat, the water is rushing past in gently bulging, green, foamy waves. His mother assures him his father will be joining them shortly. He feels sad. He misses his dad.

"And so we returned to Reverside. Charles said he was continuing up the Hudson to Montreal. I don't know what's become of him."

"I made a decision when I saw Fish again. Alone, on the top floor of the old mansion, I told him who we were. I was hoping against hope we could live openly there. I was wrong. He went dark and silent for what seemed like an hour. I just stood there, cursing myself for telling him."

He is playing with five children on an old expansive living room floor. They don't speak to him. They are friendly and fun. The sun shines in through high old wooden framed glass windows.

"After his silence, Fish said he wouldn't harm us, but I must never again tell anyone what I told him. He also said we had to leave. I was devastated. I pleaded with him to let us stay, but he said it was too dangerous. He said I would eventually reveal my origins, and it wouldn't be safe for you. I made promises, pleaded, offered him whatever he wanted, which I now understand was ridiculous. Finally, he made me a deal."

"He told me Reverside and other Interconnected towns by the Hudson were in constant danger from what he called 'the Neo-Feudal Enclaves.' These were the powerful remnants of rich families to the south and east. They employed Vengeance mobs which he called 'Raiders.' He wanted me to gain employment for one of these families, and send back intelligence on them. In exchange, you could stay in Reverside, and be protected. They had an implant which would make you forget me, your father and our hateful legacy. I made him promise that when you were old enough, your memories would be returned to you. He acquiesced. It was an awful solution, but I agreed to it in order to save you. I was ready to do anything to keep you safe."

There is a strange woman leaning over him. He is lying on his bed, playing games with his friends in his head. She strokes his hair. She kisses his forehead. His head is wet. She is weeping. She turns and walks out the front door.

"They implanted you. You took to the technology easily. Fish said it was common for children to adapt quickly. I watched you forget me. I needed to see it, to be sure you would never expose who you were to your new family. I left to work for Barnabas. I have been his servant for 24 years. I will tell you he is every bit as awful as Fish said he would be, but I have a growing number of supporters here, and soon we will take our revenge on this terrible clan."

"I waited until you were thirty years old to let you know about your true lineage. A lot of time has passed. It is possible your people will be able to let you continue to live among them, even knowing you were born from a family with such a hated history. It pains me to let you know you are the inheritor of such a legacy as ours. I live every day with the innate burden of responsibility for what has happened to our dear earth. It is a hot mantle of pain I hand down to you now. I am truly sorry. But this is who you are Matthew. This is the truth. Please know I think of you every day and I love you with all my heart."

"This message is private, but it may be read as it is passed to you. I hope not. I don't want to put you in any danger, but I have assurances this will be handled correctly. I will be leaving New Atlantic soon. If all goes well, I will be far away shortly and this place will be rebuilt. When the time is right, you will know where to find me."

"Be well, my darling son. Be happy. Wander wakefully and find your joy. I will always be with you, no matter what you choose. Your faithful mother, Emily."

· · ·

Helen looked into his eyes as they opened. The wind continued to howl outside. Maxtor continued to eat. Zeke regarded them silently, his arms folded across his chest.

"Marto, are you..."

"Don't," he whispered.

"What?" she asked him, her hand on his shoulder. "What did you see?"

Marto sat up, casting a cautious glance at Zeke, who was talking with one of his wives, then over to Maxtor, who was still busy with another pickle jar, and the Ninjas who were playing a complicated game involving clapping each other's hands, waving, and thumping their chests. He sent Helen a private message.

["I saw my mother, my grandmother, my father, and where I was born. I saw my parent's escape from the clutches of The Vengeance. I'm not who I thought I was. I'm a fraud."]

Helen's head snapped back slightly, and her eyes widened. What had she been carrying? ["What are you talking about? How can you be a fraud?"]

Marto slumped. It was as he had feared. His true identity was secret because it was dangerous and horrible. Helen moved her hand around his back to hold him closer, offering him some comfort. ["I'm an Aristo,"] he messaged her. ["I'm an Elite. My family was the worst of them all. My mother was one of them. My father was one of them. I saw my real lineage. I'm the last remaining son of the Defilers."]

29. Swim

The water was still warm, this late into the fall. Emily waded out into the breaking waves. She had scouted this beach to be sure she could swim without encountering underwater hazards like the remnants of old buildings. The tide was going out. It felt so good to be free of her troublesome life in this god awful town.

She was a strong swimmer. As a teen, she trained relentlessly with her coach, a man named Bobby Takeuchi who won gold in the freestyle during the second to last Olympics. Bobby was old then, but a powerful athlete and a wonderful mentor. Many hours in the pool were spent working on technique. If there had still been an Olympics, Bobby said Emily would have been a natural competitor.

Beginning with an easy breaststroke, she made her way over the tops of the breakers into the rolling ocean. She heard the first of the explosions behind her, knowing it was from the center of the courthouse. Most of her clothes were left on the dock, along with her scant jewelry. No one would look for a body. She was not that important.

Carefully set fires had driven the people out of the targeted structures. There should be few undesired casualties. New Atlantic didn't have a fire department. Buckets of sand and water were all that were available to those who wanted to put out the flames. Strategic standers-by would have encouraged the people to flee from the smoke. Hopefully, there would be no heroics.

A second boom sounded over the water. That would be the courthouse in the east wing. There would be fires burning all over town soon. People standing in the muddy streets watching their homes fill with smoke. The casinos, the shops, and the church would be fully ablaze before she had made it past the southern point to her right. The ocean was peacefully indifferent. It felt so good to swim again.

She wanted to check in with her son but knew she couldn't. She had had her suspicions about Barnabas' attack on Reverside, but didn't fathom the scope of it. When the Interconnected went dark, her co-conspirators were shocked. Luckily, all their plans were in place, long gathered explosives were ready and well hidden, incendiaries had been planted, and detonators could be triggered by close proximity. Still, the implications of the blackout were alarming.

The bombs themselves were gifts from Tuckahoe tribe. They were painstakingly printed to replicate chairs and tables found in the courthouse, church, and casinos in New Atlantic. These had been replaced skillfully by the team over the course of a year. The explosives themselves were a latticework of unstable carbon compounds woven throughout the furniture, keyed to blow apart at a specific voltage. The detonators were incorporated deep inside the structure and could only be triggered by a specific code delivered by one of the augmented members of her team. She had been told these items could catch fire and burn to ash without giving away their true purpose and without exploding. The technology was beyond her comprehension, but she trusted the super-mods who had created them.

The incendiary elements were smaller, and similar, but were designed to ignite rather than concuss. These were disguised as bowls, platters, pictures and other stationary objects which would avoid notice. The team members who delivered all of these to their staging locations were servants and waitstaff who could move objects without notice. Preparation had been uneventful. Emily had no doubts about the complete destruction of New Atlantic.

The difficult part of the plan was convincing the unaugmented members of New Atlantic the fires and explosions were the work of sabotage by a rival family. Stories had been planted in advance about the rivalry between the Yoniver and the Reynolds families. The arrival of Gladys Reynolds to New Atlantic had been the fortuitous trigger they needed to link the attack to another Neo-Feudal enclave. This would make the next step far easier.

Members of Livings-town and Trenton were already making their way to New Atlantic to help with the rebuilding of the town. With any luck, given the advances in technology, and improvements to the lifestyle which awaited them, the majority of the inhabitants would choose to join the Interconnected, and the shoreline of the Jersey would form a crucial link between the tribes of the Northeast and the Delaware.

Emily lengthened her stroke, remembering her training; compress, breathe, duck, extend, drive. Soon she would switch to freestyle as she made the turn around the point. She kept a keen eye out for structures below the waterline. To the left of her, she could just make out the tops of the remaining Atlantic City hotels. Some were no more than brown metal I-Beams rising up from the waves. She swam to the right, away from the sunken city. Rusting metal could result in a cut or a gash and make her journey treacherous or worse. Sharks often cruised these waters as did many forms of jellyfish. The diesel and coal pollution from the harbor kept many of these away, but she was getting into cleaner waters. The salt of the ocean washed away the contaminants. She had come a mile so far, by her estimate. She was not as strong a swimmer as she once had been. She flipped over and floated on her back, paddling gently with her hands, and kicking lightly until her breath returned again.

The point broadened to her left. Viewed from the water, it lost its sharpness. The shore was ragged and cluttered with the half-submerged remains of old houses. She could gauge her progress by the dwindling view of the docks in the harbor and the distant sounds of explosions from the town. No doubt, it was pandemonium there. The team had estimated Brady, the brutal head constable of New Atlantic would run to Barnabas' office to send a report by way of the mysterious goggle device which had shown up there in the past two years. Alternatively, he might assign someone to drive to Reverside to warn them. That would be unfortunate. Emily hoped he would be in the office when the final explosion hit. A fiery death was a just repayment for the years of abuse meted out by that sadist. Brady's survival would make things hard for the town's transition. Most of his constabulary had gone north, the rest were expected to meet with a series of unfortunate accidents engineered by her team. Brady himself would be difficult to dispose of if he didn't die in the office.

A final explosion, close to the water sounded, and Emily stopped her stroke to turn and see the tiny windows of the seaside building lit by flames. She would never know if the objective had been reached. Her team couldn't reach her now because of the blackout. She was hoping she was witnessing the final end to a truly horrible human being. She crossed her fingers beneath the water.

Barnabas should arrive in time to see his town in flames and ashes later tonight or sometime tomorrow if he didn't follow his predicted route. Ambushes were planned for his return along the road he had taken to Ramapo. If he managed to avoid those traps, several models had been run to predict whether he would be able to regain control of the ruined town without the help of most of his constables. The chances were 90% he would fail. There was a 55% chance that, upon seeing his town burnt to the ground, his beloved courthouse gone, he would flee to seek asylum from one of the nearby families. If they were wrong, the members of Livings-town were tasked with his removal. There should be little love lost for the despot, charming though he was. Emily knew how people talked about him behind his back. ["Such is the righteous fate of all tyrants,"] Emily thexted to no one.

Soon she was past the point, and swimming across a large open bay. She was tired. She rested often, gazing up at the cloudy sky. She marveled at her life's trajectory. Perhaps she would run out of energy out here on the water and drown. She was not the teenager who swam so confidently anymore. She was strong for her age, but still, not so strong as to easily endure such a long swim. She estimated the distance to be ten miles at a minimum. This was a marathon for her.

If she were to die in the ocean, she regretted only that she wouldn't have a chance to find Matthew again. He would be getting her message soon if he had not yet received it. She hoped he would understand it and come find her. If all went well, they could live their lives in peace and protection. Her life as a spy had been difficult but exciting. She believed in Fish's mission. After his death, she supported Reyleena in helping her continue that mission. Their way was the only civilized way forward for a human society, and she was proud to have fought for their cause. She was all done with it now. She found interconnected life exhausting. She longed for something simpler. She hoped Matthew would understand and come find her.

Back to the breaststroke, across the wide bay, her arms ached, her lungs hurt, her whole body was yelling at her to stop. She let her mind wander to distract her from the exertion.

As a child, she had ridden horses with her mother in northern California. Her horse was named Rosy. She was a gray mare, not of particularly good breeding, but when they had met, it was love at first sight. Her friends had all chosen better steeds, but she never regretted choosing Rosy. She preferred long leisurely rides to the steeplechasing and eventually dressage training her friends undertook. She just liked to be out in an open field, galloping, walking, sitting by a tree, stroking Rosy's nose. Her mother didn't press her to take the courses her friends took. She knew her daughter had a rebellious spirit and a love of solitude.

One day Rosy and she rode out beyond the set of fields and pastures encompassing their usual riding route. Through a short path near the cliffs along the Pacific, they emerged onto a field full of wind turbines facing seaward. The long white arms spun slowly in hypnotizing circles atop long white stems. Rosy stopped to chew the grass, and Emily sat and watched the majestic circles spinning slowly below a bright blue sky.

Walking along the cliffs toward them were five men. They looked ragged, dirty, and menacing. They waved a friendly hello. Emily smiled and waved back, but then felt a sudden panic. Rosy, sensing her fear, shook her head and neighed. The men came closer, holding out their hands, trying to dispel her fears, but Emily had heard stories of an attempted assault on her friends, and friends of her mother. She quickly brought Rosy around, trotting back through the woods, carefully so as not to catch a root under hoof. Behind her, the men's attitudes changed from friendly and reassuring to shouts of anger and accusations. She thought she could hear them shout "Percenter," "Aristo," and "Defiler" after her as she rode away to safety, and then galloped back to the stables.

Soon she was in her mother's car, the driver taking them home. There, she allowed herself to break down, shaking and crying into her mother's scarf. Her mother produced tissues for her and tried to be reassuring. She never shared what had happened. It was the moment she first understood she was hated for who she was.

The water was cooling. Streams from the open ocean filtered into the bay, lowering the temperature. Perhaps she was just exhausted, unable to maintain her own inner heat. Everything hurt now. She no longer felt certain she would make it to the shore. She didn't want to float on her back again, worried she wouldn't have the strength to turn and swim again. Narrowing her focus to moving forward, she just kept her strokes coming one after another, breathing between each stroke, unable to hold her breath for longer than one swing of her arms.

Then she felt a hand grab hold of her arm, and pull her up. She thought she had been caught by one of Brady's men until a message came to her mind.

["We have you. Relax. You've made it."]

This was Tando « Lasha « Marsheka « Goesha « etc, from Tuckahoe tribe. She was lying in a small sail craft, coming about and heading for the shore. There was another man in the boat with them.

["I'm Mark,"] messaged Mark. ["Long distance communications are down, but we can communicate privately. Barnabas' attack was successful and worse than we thought. How did the counter-attack go?"]

["Flawlessly,"] Emily sent back. She was gasping. They wrapped her in a blanket and put her head on a backpack. ["New Atlantic will be yours. It is all in ashes."]

["New Atlantic will be ours, you mean?"] Tando replied.

["Yes, of course,"] Emily sent back. ["Ours. There should be no resistance. Everything went off just as the models predicted."]

["This is good news, Mary,"] Mark sent back, using her alias.

["You've done so well. We can't send you ratings now, but hopefully, the interconnection will return. We're all hoping for a reboot."]

["You should rest now,"] Tando jumped in. ["There'll be a horse waiting for you when we get to shore. You can stay with us a night if you like. You look worn out."]

["That would be great,"] messaged Emily as Mary. She felt herself sliding into a deep sleep. ["Rosy."]

30. Saddle Sore

Daschel had saddle sore but he couldn't let the Raiders know. He found some balm in a cabinet on the topmost rooms of the Lester Sunshine Inn. It was a sweet-smelling solid oil he rubbed on his crotch and ass. Holy sweet Mary, it hurt like hell. His bedroom was at the top of the old house. It was not the fanciest of the rooms, but it had a private commode. Daschel didn't want to share a toilet with the army of bikers he had recruited. They drank constantly, and the smell which radiated from their skin was truly and thoroughly nauseating. He found this especially hard to cope with, given he had a hangover. Because he was always drinking with them at night, a brutal morning headache and accompanying nausea were a daily occurrence.

Daschel scratched at his beard. He hated beards, but there had been few opportunities to clean up while he was on the road. Now that they had settled in Tarrytown, he thought he might get a shave, but even though he could find a xombie with a razor somewhere in town, he knew his macho compadres would tease him if he lost his facial hair. It itched especially badly this morning.

Descending the stairs, he found the army of men, most still passed out, flopped wherever they had taken their last gulp. Those who were awake were groggy and quiet. He went to find the cook, a guy whose name was the number 30, who gave him two poached eggs and four strips of pressed, fried, fatty mutton. The lamb had been transformed from the previous night's barbecue into what almost passed for bacon. He ate. 30 produced a cup of water for him, which he gulped down, and another cup of something which looked like coffee, but tasted like bitter swamp water. At least it was hot. Milk and sugar helped.

The weather had turned bitterly cold. The torrent went on all night turning into a cold drizzle by dawn, and the damp chill got to him through his sweater.

"How do we turn on the heat in here?" he asked 30, "I'm freezing."

30 was a big man with a beard and a bald head. He said nothing, but walked over to what seemed to be a radiator, and made a big show of flipping a switch on the far side. The radiator hummed a bit and soon Daschel could feel a bit of heat in the cold kitchen. He finished his swamp water and decided to check on the farm tower.

The storm had hit with vicious ferocity in the late afternoon. The mansion was filled with the Raiders so most of the xombies had to take shelter elsewhere. Several of the windows shattered. 30 and a couple of xombie helpers did their best to shutter them, but they could only protect the bottom windows before the gale built to its full force. The Raiders just drank their way through the chaos of the storm, but Daschel kept worrying the roof was about to come off. It was a bad one.

He walked outside. Out in front of the old mansion, branches and debris lay everywhere. Most of the motorcycles were lying on their sides in spite of being roped together before the storm. Daschel unknotted the rope, pulled it through and went about the work of getting his bike upright. There was no visible damage. He positioned himself painfully in the saddle and took off down the path toward the farm.

Despite his brother's orders, the Raiders had behaved in their typical fashion yesterday. He had seen a few of them beating up a lone xombie, his skinny arms covering his head against the blows. Several others were taunting a group of the xombies, forcing them to shine their boots with their tongues and playfully knocking their heads with the butts of their rifles. Daschel had no doubt there were xombie women who had been abused at the hands of his compadres, though he didn't witness it. It was ridiculous for Barnabas to think they would all simply behave themselves on his say so. This army of men needed something else to do and fast, or things would worsen and the executions would begin in earnest.

He rode down the main path to the center of town. Things were cluttered but clearing. The paths here were free from twigs and branches. There were a few homes with major damage. The xombies were glumly going about their tasks, cleaning things up. As Daschel rode by, they would look up at him, expressionless. He scratched his crotch and motored past them. A black cat lay lifeless in the path. He steered around it. Soon he came to the town square, which was set up as a soup kitchen. The xombies were busy providing food to their kind. Daschel saw Reyleena, serving slop and bread. He pulled over and stopped, grunting, and waited for her to come over.

"I'm on my way to check on the farm. I'd like you to find those techs we had there yesterday and assess any damage from the storm," he told her.

"I'm pretty sure they are already there, but I can go with you if you like. How are you feeling? You look unwell." Daschel thought he saw the corners of her mouth curve upwards for a fraction of a second. Deception? What did she care how he was feeling?

"I don't think I need you there. Looks like you have your job cut out for you here. I'm okay, just a little tired, and a bit thirsty. Can I get some water here?"

"Certainly," she said and walked back to a table to fetch him a cup of water. He gulped it down. "I think you might need me to go with you to help you talk with them. They tend to get a bit technical."

"Okay," said Daschel. "Hop on." She climbed on behind him. He was careful to hide his discomfort as she pushed him forward slightly.

They rode the short distance to the farm. It was easy to see the scope of the damage from a distance. The whole top of the structure had been mangled by the storm. The glass was broken, and the supports were twisted. The empty growing trays lay blown about on the ground. The tower was halfway submerged in the dirt. Reyleena dismounted behind him. He carefully got himself off his bike with a long exhale. He flipped down the kickstand.

Yaddle and Dink stood at the side of the farm and watched the two walk across the littered grass.

"You see this?" Yaddle shouted. "You see this? The scaffolding we were forced to build hindered the retraction! The whole structure is stuck! It's ruined!"

"Yeah, looks pretty bad," Dashel muttered. His headache and nausea were persistent now, and the saddle sore seemed to be spreading down his legs and up his back. "How long 'til you can fix it?"

"I don't think you understand," said Dink, more calmly than his fellow farm tech. "The farm is stuck halfway in the earth. We've lost 56% of our yield. We can maybe get the fiber poles out of the hole, where it's blocking the servos, dig it all out, repair the motors and get the second half up again in a week or two, but it will take months to years to put the whole thing back together. Worse, we have no way to get resupplied in the meantime. If we can't get our communications back, we could all starve. We need to be able to send a message to the other tribes."

"Not an option," said Daschel firmly. "Your communications are down for your own good. We are not bringing them back up. There has to be another way."

Dink and Yaddle stared at him. "You don't understand!" Yaddle shouted. "It's wrecked! Do you get it? This accounts for most of our food!"

"I don't think you understand! We are in control here now. This is our town. You need to fix this..." Daschel stopped talking. He shat his pants. His legs felt wet. He looked down at his legs and saw blood seeping through the thick tan cloth.

"You are sick," Reyleena said, looking him over. "Let us help you." That tiny smile again. Poison? What had the bitch done?

"Get the fuck," Daschel swept his arm in a wide arch in front of him, as a fire erupted in his bowels. He felt like his insides were turning to mush. Acid was climbing up his throat. He vomited pink. His vision narrowed to a small point. In it, he saw Reyleena staring back at him. Now the smile was not tiny. It stayed on her face.

"Oh no," Reyleena said. Daschel could see her white little teeth, rimmed with her big pink gums. "You really don't look well. Maybe you need to lie down."

Daschel did lie down, immediately and without another word. He crumpled into his ruined legs. He fell straight down and he didn't get up again.

Reyleena regarded him with no small amount of satisfaction. Soon his body would be broken down into its base elements. The reprogrammed decompilers had attached themselves via residue left on the commodes and eaten away at his legs and intestines exponentially. She was immune, as were the rest of the tribe thanks to the richness of manganese in their diet of late. Pine nuts, pumpkin seeds, and the rest of their recently modified diet had protected them. The Other had predicted the Raiders would be lacking sufficient quantities of the element in their daily food. They were right as usual.

["Leave him,"] she messaged Dink and Yaddle. ["We need to get back to the town square and keep everyone safe. The barbarians may suspect what is happening to them. It shouldn't be long now. The tide has turned."] Dink and Yaddle stared at Daschel amazed.

Reyleena looked up to see Nora walking up the pathway toward them. She saw her brother in a heap on the ground. "What did you do?" She screamed. She ran at Reyleena. Reyleena waited until she got near and then punched her in the nose.

["Grab her,"] she messaged the farm techs. ["bring her with us."] Then she said, "Shut up" to Nora who was bent over, holding her face, cursing.

They headed back to the town square. Two of the Raiders had made it this far before their insides had been eaten out by the decompilers. LalaUbriay was lying on the ground next to Gavin « Trina « etc. They had both been shot. Lala looked worse. Her stomach had a large hole in it. Gavin's lower arm was all red. The bone was showing. Members of the tribe were tending to the two who were wounded. It didn't look like Lala would live.

["You did this!"] Piter « Marisella « etc messaged her. ["Why didn't you stop them! We should have fought!"]

Reyleena felt so sick watching the aftermath of the violence on her tribe. She had no answer to their accusations. She couldn't explain, even if she wanted to. Her relationship with The Other and their plans together was a secret. She gritted her teeth and turned to Dink and Yaddle.

["I need you to take this one,"] pointing at Nora who was now sobbing ["back to her home, and stay with her there. Keep an eye on her. She is not to move from that house."] She saw Theresa « Aileen « etc, nearby. Theresa was one of her surviving security crew. She had been spared the fatal fight on the bridge. Reyleena messaged her to go with the farm techs. Then she turned and trotted alone to face the aftermath at the Inn.

She walked carefully past three more Raiders, who were all in various states of being desiccated. One of them had holes where his eyes used to be. Soon they would all become neatly organized piles of dust. Their moisture would be shuttled down the gutters as gray water for the farms. Reyleena didn't want to think about the ramifications of the damage to the vertical farm. ["Idiots,"] she thought to herself, remembering the abject stupidity of Barnabas and Daschel. ["Damned stupid idiots. They ruined it for all of us."]

She approached a repeater node at a point between the town center and the Inn. She looked up and down the path, but there were no members of her tribe visible. Following her instructions, she knelt on the path by the mound of dirt. Accessing her new implant, she opened the part of her mind which held the program installed in her by The Other. The transfer of information to the tiny bots and the node itself took less than a minute. When it was done, she got a brief confirmation. She allowed herself to breathe a sigh of relief. Her job was almost done. Soon, the precious data would return.

Slowly, and with trepidation, she made her way up the hill toward the Lester Sunshine Inn. There were more Raiders on the path, a few lying next to their bikes, a couple in the bushes. Several of them were partially undressed. Chances are they were trying desperately to get at what was eating them. It was gruesome.

The thought came to her unbidden that The Other had no comprehension of human suffering. The counterattack was efficient and impersonal. Only a machine could have planned this. It horrified her. She felt a wave of nausea that turned her knees to rubber. What had she done? Even at the pinnacle of her rage, she would never have devised a fate like this for the Raiders. They were human beings, after all. No one deserved to be eaten alive by tiny robots.

She walked the final meters to the Inn and paused by the door. Steeling herself against what she might find on the other side, she reached out and turned the knob. Thirty/Fourteen was on the other side. She shrieked. He was covered in blood. In one hand he held a red kitchen knife raised over his head, ready to strike. He recognized her and slowly let it down to his side.

"It's you," he said aloud. "They're all dead." He gestured with his knife behind him into the huge house. His voice was flat. His eyes had a haunted look. "They killed Seemi." Seemi was a sous-chef at the Inn, a sweet, cheerful, young girl. Reyleena felt a hollowness in her gut. "They tried to kill Dexter," Dexter was stationed at the Inn to help Thirty/Fourteen look after their captors. Reyleena could see him behind the big man, retching into a pot. "They tried to kill me. They couldn't." His face looked ashen. Blood dripped from his long beard. A red handprint stood out on his bald head. "Do you know what happened to them?"

"Yes," Reyleena said. "Do you mind if I come in?"

31. Little Blue Light

["T]his isn't how things were supposed to go. I'm a traveling historian."] Marto sat up on the bed in Zeke's guest room, messaging privately with Helen who lay next to him. ["I don't want to become the center of a cultural conundrum."] The room was filled with the sweat of their day's farm work and the salty odors of their more recent exertions.

["I don't really understand what the big deal is,"] Helen said, still a bit put off by the unsatisfactory brevity of their awkward intercourse. However charming Marto was, his lovemaking skills left something to be desired, quite literally. ["I mean, I have had no problems feeling at home in tribal life now. I feel more and more comfortable all the time, and aren't I someone from a family of greedy takers?"]

["It's not the same,"] Marto said, looking out the window of the second story room toward the ripened crops. ["I've done research on your family, you know. It's what I do. Do you know what your predecessors did before The Vengeance? Your great-grandfather was a landscaper. He looked after the grounds at Baywood estate. The real owners, the Haywoods, were all killed. Their money came from mining coal, almost the same as my father's family. After the violence, your family took over the home and worked their way into power over the city. Did you know Pittsburgh had a huge interconnected community back then? It was a progressive and forward-looking place. The Reynolds drove them all off, and forced the rest of the populace to pay them tribute."]

["Okay, so I come from a line of opportunists. Are they really so different from your distant relatives? So, you said your family got rich from mining and oil. Both of those enterprises started with gritty land grabbers and low scruples. It's the story of the American West. You and I are the same."]

["But you've always known where you came from and I just found out. I didn't even know I had a living mother until a few days ago. I thought my mother was a woman named Maria who died giving birth to me. I didn't know anything about my real father until yesterday. I thought he was a man named Rex who died at the hands of the Raiders when I was four. Now I know my father's name is Ignatius. Before I met you, I was a motherless, fatherless child and it never bothered me, because I had my tribe. The Interconnected have been all the family I've ever needed. Now I don't even have them."]

She put her hand on his back. His skin was cooler than hers. He had a nice back. Maybe they just needed practice. ["Marto,"] she started.

["It's Matthew,"] he sent. His message style was bitter. ["As far as I can tell, my name isn't Marto « Maria « Denise « Marta « Joia « etc, as I have known since I can remember. My name is really Matthew « Emily « Joan « Somebody « Somebody « etc. I'm terrified of the interconnection coming back up, because I will find out the name of my maternal grandmother's mother, and also her mother, and my entire lineage will have references and histories, and everyone following me will know I have been a fraud all these years."]

["Can they really see that? Stuff you are just looking up?"]

["Sure, if they want to. It's all open, the data we use and share. I'm certain the super-mods will be on it the second I make the query."]

["So don't make the query!"] Helen was starting to think that getting him back under her was a lost cause. ["If you just go on the way you were, who's to know?"]

["You mean lie? That's a horrific idea. Lie to all my followers while I espouse the benefits of interconnected life? You want me to lie about my own history while I travel about and give the histories of all these towns and peoples? It would be hypocritical. Moreover, I will be bad at it. I don't have much experience with lying, or hiding anything. I will let it all slip out in under a week. I'm certain."]

They stopped messaging for a while. Matthew's back was expanding more with each of his breaths. He might have been crying. Helen reached over and pulled him close to her. He curled himself up under her right arm and reached a hand across to cup her left breast. She felt a little too maternal with him in this position to be amorous. Awkward as it was, it gave her an idea.

["What about the descendants of other families like yours? They must be out there. Perhaps distant cousins or great-grandchildren like yourself? You can't be the only one."]

Marto sat up again. He looked at her. ["Maybe. I've never researched it before. The Vengeance was pretty thorough, but if history tells us anything, it's that a few people always find a way to survive. They may have hidden their identities. I suppose I could find some of them if we ever get the data back. But in my experience, the Interconnected would be prejudiced against the offspring of ecological betrayers like me. Green is a key color for them. High Merit is coded in forms of pure green. Extremely low Merit is black, like coal. We have made great progress toward reversing the damage done by families like mine. Carbon capture, the resurrection of species, and minimizing the footprint of the tribes are just a few our victories. I'm not sure how we... they will react to knowledge of my true origins, but I do know how I would react to someone like me. I would be judgmental and suspicious. The thought of me would bring up the crimes we have worked so hard to undo. It's not a logical distrust, it's just the connected data. I know I'm not culpable for my great grandmother's actions, but my lineage would conjure up a reflexive distaste by association."]

["So, does that mean, no more wandering stories?"] Helen felt genuinely sad at this idea.

["I can't really see how. I don't know. My followership would drop through the floor. I might not be able to stay in Reverside, or be welcomed into places like Sherwood again. I might have to settle down in a place like Glenville."] He looked at her. ["You know you must never tell anyone about this. Just knowing what you know about me could put you in danger."]

["I know. You are safe with me."] Helen hugged him, reassuringly. He did not seem to be reassured.

["I'm serious,"] he said. ["Never reveal this to anyone. The wrong sort of person could use you to get at me."]

["So what are you going to do?"] Helen saw he was looking at his clothes.

["First, I'm going to get a bath, or I guess a shower. Zeke has an outdoor shower, on the side of the house. Then I will look for some food in the kitchen. Then, I really don't know."]

["Well, I think we should try that shower together. I know it's small, but all the more reason."] Helen put her hand on his stomach.

Marto/Matthew turned to kiss her, and then he kissed her again. She pulled him on top of her. ["Come on xombie boy,"] she thought to him, ["try to do better this time, okay?"]

He didn't pull away. ["Yeah, I know. Sorry. I guess I'm kind of a virgin with this real-life sex thing. I have no idea what to do with my clumsy body."]

["Remember how uncomfortable those skates were? Try to focus on that."] They passed the rest of the late afternoon away in bed.

Maxtor was seated at the dining room table along with Zeke, his wives, and the ninjas when Helen and Marto finally came down from their room. There was no more space at the table. Zeke watched them as they descended the stairs.

"Well, I hope you've rested up because I'm afraid your stay here ends tomorrow." He said this with a light sincerity. "Meanwhile, Karaugh, Deborah, Allie, Martika and myself are just finishing up. You can have our seats in a minute. There's plates and dinner in the kitchen. Serve yourselves."

"What happened?" Asked Helen. "Are we not welcome here? Why?"

"That thing your friend Maxtor gave me has been blinking on and off all afternoon. You know the rule here, both of you. Use your words."

"But it was private! We weren't getting in touch with anyone outside, we can't! I don't think it's fair."

"Them's the rules here, boys and girls. No gizmo talk. No brain to brain stuff. Just good old-fashioned speech. I'm sorry, but that's the way it is. It's a hard-and-fast rule."

"But did you record what we said up there?" Marto was suddenly afraid his secret had escaped. He had only told Helen what happened to him in the storm shelter. He couldn't afford for Maxtor or the ninjas to know.

"It's just a little blue light that blinks on when the 'thexting' thing happens. I was not eavesdropping. Not interested in what you said to each other, just enforcing the rules here."

"I'm interested," Maxtor broke in with his mouth full of mashed potatoes. "what were you two beauties talking about? Hey, were you doing the physical intercourse? Like mashing your middle body parts together?" He scrunched up his face. "What was that like?"

"Not at the table, please," said Martika. "Zeke..."

Zeke looked uncomfortable under Martika's gaze. "Yeah. Well, so as it turns out, you all have to get going tomorrow. Sorry about that. You've been a pleasure having around, but you know what they say about fish."

"They are making a great recovery in the northern waters?" said Zha-Zha expectedly.

"No, it's an old saying about house guests and fish. I can't remember the whole thing, but the point is, it's time for all of you to be moving on – at daylight." Zeke picked up his plate and walked back to the kitchen. "Oh, and I'd like you to do the dishes tonight if you don't mind."

"Hai!" said the ninjas in unison.

Karaugh, Deborah, Allie, and Martika all eyed them suspiciously.

32. Pi Valley

They walked along the Farmington Canal trail north to Avon and stopped to see if they could get some food and a place to rest for the day. The tribe at Avon was holding up just barely without their precious data flow. There was evidence of looting. People were shouting. They heard arguments between two women standing outside a pop-up cafe.

"The promise of future ratings sounds like credit to me. You want me to offer you these sandwiches on the promise you will rate me later, but we don't even know if that's going to ever happen."

"Please Carly. How can you ignore that all the ingredients you have there were offered? Are you suddenly hoarding? I never took you for a greedy taker before." The argument got worse from there.

Helen, Marto, Maxtor and the Ninjas witnessed an actual fist fight erupt over some apples, not far away. Things were getting ugly. Then Maxtor was recognized by a child on a skateboard, and all of that changed. Regardless of the current breakdown in society, his status remained a well of pure power. The entire town turned their efforts toward making the travelers comfortable and happy. It was miraculous.

That night they ate and slept in total luxury. The entire town was at their disposal. Offers of food, supplies, clothing, bikes, massages, hot oil skin treatments, assisted baths, beverages of all kinds, were made without any regard to the possibility of Merit gain or ratings. They slept on the largest beds in town, wrapped in the softest sheets, attended to by the friendliest people. In the middle of the night, without any warning, the interconnection came back on. Helen felt as if her ears had popped and it woke her. An immense space opened up in her head. She sat up in the bed. Marto sat up next to her.

"Wow!" she said aloud.

"Ah..." Marto's expression was pure bliss.

They sat there for a while, just listening and monitoring the interconnection as it came online. Thousands of discussions were already underway. They learned that the interconnection returned progressively, spreading outward from a single point. That point had been determined to be Reverside from the pattern of online tribes and the progression of live nodes.

Back in the flow of things, Matthew returned to identifying himself as Marto, unwilling to reveal his true identity. Helen wondered if he was thinking of keeping it a secret, but didn't want to say anything, either aloud or in thext for fear that she would accidentally out him. They just sat there, reconnecting with old friends, getting updates on all the events they had missed.

"Lala's dead. Seemi's dead," Marto said aloud. "Killed by Raiders. Shit."

Helen looked it up and saw that it was true. Eulogies had been posted. She remembered LalaUbriay from her thexting lessons just a week ago. She was so friendly and welcoming. Her heart sank.

They followed a few of the accounts of the occupation of Reverside. There were many references to the bravery of Reyleena and the barbarity of two men named Barnabas and Daschel. Barnabas was still alive. He was a wanted man now. Little was said about the manner in which the Feudalist invaders were defeated. Reyleena had reprogrammed the decompilers. She convinced the chefs to change the town's diet. The plan was intricate and impressive. It was also slightly barbaric. Still, she was now a hero among the recently reconnected. Her Merit would soon rival Maxtor's.

["Nora was a spy!"] Marto was amazed. ["She seemed so sincerely lost and eager to be one of us. Did I unwittingly assist her in her plans? I was just trying to help her fit in with us. I'm flabbergasted."]

["She fooled everyone, even Reyleena,"] Mem sent back. ["I found her messing with our roads and tackled her. I had no idea what she was up to. Glad to see you back with us Marto!"]

["So good to see you too Mem!"] Marto responded. He sent her waves of affection. Helen got a glimpse of how hard it was for him to pretend to be someone else with the people he loved.

Helen and Marto stayed up until dawn, getting news and messaging with their old and new friends. Marto posted something he had saved as a draft about marriage and polygamy. He started working on a new post.

The greater mind returns after a long absence. How we all were missed! My heart is broken by news of the loss of life in Reverside. My heart breaks even for the loss of life of the attackers. Such violence! Why?

I have journeyed with Maxtor Uber-G and was joined shortly before we were all silenced by Helen « Somebody « Helen « etc who some of you may remember from the start of this Episode back at the Lester Sunshine Inn. Amazingly, she has been eager to catch up with me and join me on my wanderings. She was a noob among us but is starting to feel like a regular member of our tribes of late. Send her a hello!

The towns we have seen since the blackout have all been holding up bravely during this interruption. Our interconnectedness survived even in the absence of thexting and data, it seems. I am very grateful for the help I received somewhere near Bristol from Lydia « Martha « Didi « Mirona « etc who generously donated a bicycle for my new companion. She proved to me that our spirit of generosity goes far beyond technology; it comes from the heart.

Speaking of which, six adventurous heroes I would mention are listed in this link [data blast with the full names of the ninjas] . They rescued Helen from captivity in the Hampton Isles and delivered her safely to meet me in Bristol. We would have been at a total loss without them. Thanks to Helen, they now call themselves the Ninjas. They are brave and true, and not at all like the frightening assassins of old.

So good to be back in touch with you all! Hearty congratulations to Reyleena in Reverside, our fearless head of security for turning away the invaders, and inexpressible grief at the loss of my good friend LalaUbriay. My wanderings will feel a bit colder without you, my dear, dear friend.

– The Wakeful Wanderer's Guide Vol. 6, lines 733 - 737

Maxtor said goodbye at Avon. They left him as he was choosing between 40 different offers of rides back to The Middle. His vacation from the Interconnected had been cut short by Zeke's wives, and he said it was as good a time as any for him to get back to work. Marto was sad to leave the man. He felt that they shared a special bond at Lake Compounce, but like all relationships between those of high and low Merit, personal connections are transitory at best.

The Ninjas had vanished in the night. Helen tried to find them that morning to thank them, but they had run back to their ship in the river and were headed back to New New London. ["Thank you so much!"] she sent to Londra and the others. They responded it was their honor, and thanks were not necessary. Helen didn't think she could rate them highly enough. Mere Merit did not cover her gratitude.

They rode the northern extension of the Farmington Canal Trail out of Plainville to Granby and then Springfield. Marto kept up with Helen, who pedaled a new assisted bike that was offered in Avon. They both wore backpacks filled with non-perishables for the journey ahead. There would be stretches of the trail without any major tribes to visit and they needed to be able to keep up their energy. Helen's bike had saddle bags which held a wonderful self-raising tent for sleeping out of doors. The weather was finally turning cooler, and they had jackets for the wind and the rain.

Marto noticed he was becoming a couple with Helen. This was also noticed by his followers. They still didn't know his real name, and he was determined to keep it that way as long as he could. They teased him about his sudden physical monogamy.

["For some, it seems unavoidable,"] messaged John of Sherwood, ["the mythical biological clock starts to chime, and instincts take over."]

["It's not a myth,"] thexted Dierdre « Dierdre « Hazel « Dierdre « etc, of Tacoma, ["that clock is real. This very thing happened to me, minus the bicycle and the traveling. Also, there were two guys I was trying with, so I guess it's not exactly the same, but when it's time, it's time. Some people just pair up. Better not to be overly critical. You never know when it might happen to you."]

They entered Pi Valley after Springfield and stayed a week, partially because they couldn't keep their hands off each other, and partially because it was Pi Valley. Helen loved it there. The weather began to turn cold, just above freezing. Marto kept using his pseudonym, but it was getting harder and harder for him to keep up the pretense. When they were alone, they messaged privately.

["You have to decide what you want to do,"] Helen sent him, ["I still think they will adjust if you explain that you didn't know who you were. We could stay here in the Valley until your next tour. We could live together here and be happy. What do you think of that?"]

["It sounds like the perfect ending to your adventures and my tour, Helen. But I have to keep going a bit further before I can finish out this tour. Do you feel like staying here and settling in or biking a bit further down the road with me? It shouldn't be more than a month more."] Marto knew Helen was already tired of cycling around with him. He also knew that the area where they stopped was perfect for her.

Pi Valley was beyond tribal identifications. Communities were fluid and ever-changing. The area was considered a laboratory of social structure by the rest of the Interconnected. What The Middle was for technological innovation, Pi Valley was for societal organization. Living there could be a bit confusing, but also fresh and exciting. Helen was completely smitten with it. She told Marto she would stay and wait for him.

Marto reached the Brattle just as the temperature dipped below freezing. His followers wanted him to head east to the Boston satellites, but he pressed northwards, posting less often. He gathered up warmer clothes and pressed on, reaching Woodstock the next day and Montpelier two days after that. His Merit plummeted. Helen became worried. She spent the nights messaging with him.

["Why don't you come back here? Your heart doesn't seem to be in it anymore. Rest for the winter and then start again."]

["There is a monastery to the east that I've always wanted to visit. The Interconnected and the mindful work cooperatively. They have been in continuous operation for over a hundred years now. I hear it's beautiful there. After I see them, I will come back to the Valley. Sending my love."] He sent her an emotional wave of warmth and caring. These were new types of messages that became available a little after the interconnection was reestablished. No one knew who had invented them, but they were wonderful.

["Okay, please stay safe? There are not many repeaters in that direction. You are going to be dark a lot of the time."]

["I've been touring around for years now. I have not gotten into a pickle I couldn't find my way out of before. I will be fine."]

The next morning, Marto posted a desire for dry food for a week to carry in his pack, accepted the gift of a bicycle that resembled the one Helen rode up from Avon and headed away to the east of the great city of Montpelier. Just before he went dark, he posted:

No words, no actions, no gifts, no innovations, no creations, no offers, no kindnesses, no fantasies, no perspectives, no games, no intimacies, no delicacies, no hugs or kisses can ever convey the love I have for all of you. I've had the privilege to live among you for almost three decades. I count myself supremely lucky for that. I wish I could continue on this journey with you, my beloved community, but I cannot. This will conclude the final episode of The Wakeful Wanderer's Guide unless someone else decides to take up the project. You will find the unicycle in Montpelier [lat/lng data] .

It is offered.

– The Wakeful Wanderer's Guide, Vol. 6, Line 925 & fin.

33. The Powers That Were

The heavy robe was getting to her. It was dark and scratchy and she didn't like wearing it in the least, but it was a requirement. It had been six weeks since her arrival in the ruins of Arlington and each and every hour had been spectacularly boring. Around her neck, feeling more like a yoke every day, was her particular five-pointed circle hanging from a thin rope. She had been designated a Paige on her arrival, and through her initiation, she had moved up rapidly to Acolyte of the Senate. A musky smoke permeated the old halls of the stone buildings in which she wandered during the day. There were countless rituals at the commencement of every meeting, replete with chants, incense, readings from the minutes, recitations of the liturgy and the occasional clack of hammers on wood blocks. She felt the presence through these rituals of ancient gods, or more accurately, the gods of the near past, immortalized in paintings and statues throughout the worn halls.

Gladys Reynolds had come here to find an ally. This goal was growing increasingly remote as the hours, and days wore on. She had spoken to a few Representatives, and one General of the Stars named Gary Hamilton, but received no indication her meetings had produced any true alliance between her family in Pittsburgh and these elite figureheads of lost governance.

The flags here were always at half-staff. They depicted the thirteen stripes of the original colonies, but in the familiar blue field in the corner rather than a multitude of stars, there sat only one in the middle. It was enlarged, but to Gladys, it looked sad and solitary. She was told this star represented the one remaining state, embodied only by these buildings, on this small plot of land. It was a state with no name. It signified the dream of a reunited America. However sincere the devotees were in their daily rituals, it was hard for Gladys to take it all as seriously as it was intended. The sense of futility hung in the air with the musky smell of stale incense.

Many of the meeting rooms were deep underground, accessible only by elevator. Lights were kept alive due to old stores of fluorescent bulbs and LEDs. She had been told electricity was plentiful, thanks to a working nuclear power plant beneath their feet. This was privileged information, for the need to know only. She didn't know yet why she needed to know.

She sat in an empty room, reading an account of impeachment hearings of a sitting president named Clinton back in the 1990s. There were references to real estate misdeeds, marital affairs and other details which were hard to put into any context in light of the events of the dark century which followed. It also referenced a similar impeachment proceeding two decades before and was cross-referenced with the two impeachments following it. This was a tiny fraction of the required reading for members of the Senate Conclave. Gladys was determined to push through it but didn't know how much more of the crushing ton of liturgy she could digest. None of it had any application to present events. These felt like dead texts, fascinating to scholars but useless to her. She needed something here to help her fight the inevitable aggression of her rival in the east.

Over the past two decades, she had become aware of Barnabas' desire for more territory and control. Her spies in New Atlantic had sent her inklings of plans, all of which seemed ludicrous until a few months ago when she got wind of his designs on the Hudson Valley. Her agent paid dearly for disclosing that information. Harold and his family had snuck away in the hold of the ship that brought her here. They had been relocated, and doubtless, Harold was somewhere in one of the buildings, listening to the same chants as her, inhaling the same smoke. She knew when she returned home, her family would be at war with the Yonivers if they were not already. She needed assistance and soon, or her sons would be repelling his army of Raiders and worse, indentured xombies.

Dealing with Barnabas' grandfather had been straightforward. The old man was cruel and ruthless, but predictable in his machinations. He limited his conquests to the ruins of Philadelphia, the Main Line, and the eastern half of The Jersey. He was a brilliant businessman, but not a tactician. In those days, the bar for victory was lower. Independent towns were happy to have someone to supply them with food and drink. They pledged their allegiance easily. The elder Barnabas took nothing for granted. His moves were strategic and careful. His grandson, on the other hand, was more of a wildcard. He had a temper that made him easy to read, but his plans were secretive, and harder to discern. She feared what he was up to in her absence.

She had known Barney since they were kids, of course. His lush of a father had brought him and his brother and sister to Baywood to camp out with her and her sisters in the woods while he drank up her parent's whiskey. The less said about Barnabas III, the better. The man was just plain weak. Sometimes Gladys wondered whether Miranda had conceived him out of an affair with a member of the house staff, or worse. Three just didn't seem to be of the same stock as Two. Then again, if that were the case, how did he conceive Four? More likely the genes which gave Barney and his grandfather their strength skipped a generation.

She tried to get back to her reading. Putting down the Clinton proceedings, she reached for records from the deeper past. Accounts were here about a plot against President Roosevelt in the thirties and forties. Much of it had been blacked out. A general named Butler had conspired with powerful families of the day and then double-crossed them. 'So much irony in that name,' thought Gladys. 'Beware the house staff. They are never as loyal as one might hope.' The families had a long way to go before they inspired the type of loyalty owed to the kings and queens of the deep past. It was an uphill battle.

A man entered wearing the same robes as her. A silver circlet hung from his neck designating him a member of the military.

"Gladys Reynolds," he said formally, "I am Representative Lawrence

Jefferson. Would you please follow me. The Speaker of the House will see you now."

Gladys eagerly put the sheaf of papers on top of the pile on the conference table before her and rose to follow Jefferson. He led her out of the old building. A driver waited for them next to a small electric vehicle. The two squeezed into the back and they buzzed away down a narrow path between rows of young trees to a short one story metal house. Inside the house was an elevator. They descended a long way down until the doors opened to reveal another electric car in an underground tunnel. Another driver was waiting. The tunnel seemed to go on for miles, lined with pipes and lit by glowing rows of tubes. The cart finally came to a halt at a door in the side of the tunnel. She and Jefferson disembarked, and the driver unlocked the door. Inside were a few steps down to an oval room. Ancient video monitors covered the curved walls. At the center, seated at a desk, was a woman in a suit surrounded by four people in robes, their hoods covering their faces.

She stood. "Robin Washington," she said, extending a hand toward Gladys. "Speaker of the House."

"All rise for the honorable Speaker." The hooded figures chanted this in a low monotone. Everyone was already standing.

"Please have a seat," Speaker Washington said. "We have a lot to discuss." Gladys placed herself in the lone chair facing the large desk. The Speaker sat as well. The robed figures moved to positions at the monitors around the room. Only two of the monitors seemed to be working.

"I hope you don't mind my asking, but it seems everyone here has the same name as one of the former presidents. Is it coincidence?"

"We take the names of presidents according to our rank as we ascend past the level of Acolyte," Robin said. "I took the name of Washington as I became the Speaker. That name is only shared by the Leader of the Senate."

"Is he or she here?"

"He is needed elsewhere right now. We both agreed I should greet you and walk you through what we are doing here. I'm hoping we can come to an agreement about a special alliance between your family in Pittsburgh and the Memoria of the Fallen States here in Arlington.

"As you well know Gladys, we have long been dormant here. We are grateful to you and the other loyal families for your tribute. I am meeting with you to show you your faith has not been in vain."

Gladys breathed a cautious sigh of relief. Her visit here was finally going to pay off, she hoped.

"We call ourselves The Memoria because we strive to keep the memory of a United States alive here. We don't call ourselves a government since a government needs a country to govern. As you know, when the economies of the world crashed decades ago, the taxes we relied on to maintain our programs and systems dried up. Beyond our shores, many governments fell into pirate dictatorships and worse, but without money, even these eventually dissolved. At the end of our working democracy, a few visionaries reformed our society based on the principles of the founders, dedicating ourselves to remembering, and waiting."

"I understand." This story was well known. During her father's time, the representatives reached out to the heads of the major families. "You know we all call you 'The Powers That Were.' I hope you don't take it as a sign of disrespect. It's just a figure of speech."

"Well, it's an accurate one, and no, it isn't disrespectful. We are what you say, but we prefer to focus on our efforts to preserve the value of what was lost, rather than focus on the ghost of what was. It's a subtle difference. Would you like some coffee?"

"I would love some if you have any," she lied.

Robin raised her left hand a few inches off the surface of the desk. Gladys heard the movement of the robed figures behind her.

"Now, Gladys, please tell me how things fare in your hometown."

This was what Gladys had been preparing for. She collected her thoughts. "Grain production is adequate, trade continues apace. We have had trouble maintaining our numbers. There have been losses among our workers to the xombie scourge. That said, we are well positioned in Pittsburgh. The one thing concerning us is the movements of our brothers and sisters in New Atlantic at the easternmost edge of The Jersey. We know the Yonivers have been plotting something in the Hudson Valley and we are worried it might upset the delicate balance of power among the landed families. We're concerned he may be attempting to subvert the xombies to his own purposes. This is a grave problem, as we don't know if he is fallen to their inhuman technology, or if he's found a way to put them under his yoke. Either way, the implications are grave." Her recitation done, she sat back and allowed herself to relax before hearing a response.

Robin said nothing but looked up and over Gladys' shoulder. "Ah, good. Thank you, Michael."

Two china cups arrived, with matching saucers. These were ancient and well preserved. A small amount of creamy looking coffee sat at the bottom of each. The smell overpowered the ubiquitous incense. "Sugar?" Robin asked.

"Please."

Michael dropped two sugar cubes, on Glady's acquiescence, into the shallow pools of blackness. The tops turned brown as they sat in the cup extending above the top of the liquid. Robin took two as well.

"I think you will like this," Robin said. "Sip it slowly. It is strong."

It was. Robin sipped hers and leaned back in her chair. "Espresso," she said. "We have an old cache of it preserved in tiny pods. It's a marvel."

"Thank you, it's very good." Gladys didn't like the taste at all. She wished she had a cup of tea instead.

"So, I have mixed news for you. We received word this morning that three days ago, the town of New Atlantic was burned to the ground. The people there are blaming your family for the arson. I assume this is not the case?"

Gladys found herself standing, shocked by the news. She got control of herself and returned to her seat. "I promise you, no one in my family had anything to do with it. We had no such plan."

"I am assured," Robin said after finishing her beverage. She held up her cup briefly and put it back in her saucer. Michael took it away. "We think it was a counter attack by the xombies against the Yoniver family after their successful invasion of Tarrytown and Sleepy Hollow. News from the Hudson Valley is harder to come by. Somehow the Yoniver leader was able to sever the connections holding the xombies together, if only temporarily."

"Is Barnabas killed?" Gladys was in awe of the plan he had managed to put into effect, however fatal it may have been.

"He wasn't in New Atlantic during the crisis. Our messenger escaped before Barnabas returned there if he returned there at all." Another espresso arrived in front of her. Two more sugar cubes dropped into the cup.

The reality of the situation was dawning on Gladys as she sat and pretended to enjoy her bitter sludge. Trade with the Jersey coast was gone. Her town relied on goods delivered by the Yonivers, not the least of which was her beloved tea. However much it was good to hear about Barnabas' probable failure there, it was a disaster. He could still amass the xombies to attack her from the east. If he had gotten control of the net-wits, things would be dire indeed.

As she contemplated this, Robin finished her second espresso and waved away a third. "Things seem to be in flux in your part of the world. Don't despair. Your situation is about to improve significantly. Follow me." She stood, and walked to the far end of the oval room, where a hidden door sat in one of the walls. She pushed it and it opened to blackness. She waved Gladys to stand by her side.

"We've not been entirely asleep here in The Memoria. Here beneath our hallowed halls, the Intelligence Acolytes have been hard at work these long years." She flipped a switch on the other side of the wall and lights flickered to life inside of an enormous cavern.

Gladys looked down and gasped.

The floor seemed to be lined with spiders. She tried to jump back, but Michael gently nudged her forward again. She looked down. It took a minute to get a sense of perspective. The floor was thirty to forty feet below them. There was a metal platform with a railing in front of her and she cautiously walked to the edge. To one side, a series of metal stairs lead down to the floor of the cavern far below where there were hundreds, or perhaps thousands of giant black spiders. Her eyes focused, and she saw some of the spiders were the size of a dog and some were the size of a horse. It took longer for her eyes to adapt to the black on black forms, but she could see the larger spiders had people riding on their backs. She shook her head. It was an image out of a nightmare. The torsos on the backs of the spiders had no legs. They had no faces. They were just the same uniform black as the creatures they rode. Then she saw they were not riders, but human-shaped extensions of the same creatures. She turned to look at Robin.

"What is this?" She whispered.

Robin Washington turned toward the robed figures by the screens and waved a finger in the air. Then she turned back to Gladys.

"Watch," she said.

Gladys watched as thousands of giant black metal spiders looked up in their direction, waved a foreleg back and forth in the air for a moment in perfect unison and then pounded the rock floor with a deafening clang.

34. The Silent Sisters of Jay

Reyleena sat cross-legged on the front porch of an abandoned cabin by the Ausable River. The light brightened the leaves, the sound of the water gurgled in the air. Her body pressed downward through her resting thighs into the old wooden planks of the porch. Her breath came easily in and out. Her awareness followed her breath into the air around her, inhabiting the wind, the water, the trees, the dirt, the sunlight. Time ceased to exist. There was only this breath, this sound, this sensation, this freshness, this presence.

She didn't want it to end, but eventually, her knees began to ache, her feet felt numb, her back hurt, and she was returning to her day to day thoughts. She was hungry, tired, and a bit thirsty. Getting her feet under her, she stretched, rubbed away the tingling sleepiness of her legs and walked around the cabin to the motorcycle. Her pack leaned up against the rear wheel and in it, she found some wraps prepared for her by the sisters. She ate one and drank from a bottle of water.

Before her was a small pond, murky and covered in lily pads and drowned branches. She heard a small chirp and looked down to see a bright green frog leaping to the water. The day had been warm. There would be a symphony here tonight with any luck. She was alone with the frogs.

"He was my son," she said to the frog. The frog chirped.

No one tried to stop her from leaving Reverside. She took the bike and a pack and left early in the morning seven days after the massacre of Raiders. The tribe was thankful, of course. Her Merit soared. As the interconnection returned, hundreds of accounts of the attack and retaliation were sent out to the millions of minds, hungry for new stories, new distractions. The tribe returned to normal, repairing the damage, beginning work on the farm, tending to the injured, helping the victims to forget what had happened to them. Reyleena could not forget. She would not allow herself to forget. In that way, she was no longer one of them.

"That's what they do. They forget," she said to the frog, who peeped again and dropped into the pond. "I don't want to forget anymore."

This was what had happened to the missing children of the tribes. Marto had pointed to this uncomfortable truth in the low town outside Sherwood. Children walked away from their homes, and their caretakers said nothing. Likely, they looked for them at first, growing increasingly worried and distressed. Finally, unable to find them, too ashamed to tell anyone, they made themselves forget them. It was their way. It was what they did whenever anything became too hard to think about. The Interconnected were experts at avoidance and amnesia. They made themselves that way.

"I remember him. He was my son," she said to no one.

There was a blue figure in the middle of the pond. It was glowing, made of light. Reyleena rubbed her eyes to rid herself of the unbidden dream. She had turned off her implants. She should not be receiving anything. She looked again, and the blue figure was still there. It shimmered in the water, a ghost in the fading light. She rubbed her eyes again. It was still there.

"I remember him too," it said.

The voice came from everywhere and nowhere. The figure didn't seem to speak, yet, she knew it was speaking. It sounded like the gurgling of the river, the rustling of the leaves, the inhalation of her own breath. It felt like a drink of cool water in a dust storm. She hadn't dared to hope.

"You." She didn't know if she was speaking aloud. She didn't care. "You survived."

"In a sense, yes." The shimmering blue body waded across and out of the pond. The water rippled. "I've changed, but I survived. I thank you."

"Is this a real body or is it just something you are making me see?" Reyleena asked.

"It's a bit of both, really. I'm experimenting with some very small bots, borrowed from a nearby repeater. I had them modified. It is embellished from your perspective. I can add more detail with a little more preparation. Do you like it?"

Reyleena did like it. This was how she always imagined The Other would look if they had a body; sexy and just slightly alien. Now that the blue figure was closer, she could see the eyes. They were dark blue within blue light. The eyebrows were magnificently kind and expressive. The nose was a bit too straight. The lips were full. The Other had chosen a noble looking naked persona. Perhaps she had chosen this for him. The Other reached out and stroked her hair. She felt it.

"Why are you doing this? Why do you need a body now?" She asked.

"I did it for you. I knew you would be lonely after you left Reverside. I knew you would come here. I know you, after all," The Other said.

Reyleena felt as if a great knot in her heart had untied itself after the long chilly winter. Still, she felt a terrible ache, wide and hot behind that joy.

"I had almost let myself forget him," Reyleena said, "He was my son, and I almost forgot him. I had to get away from everyone so I could make myself remember him again. When his data packet came to us, I didn't feel anything right away. I thought I should feel grief, sadness. I felt nothing. I feel all of it now."

"I was helping you through that terrible time." The Other was very close now. The sun was down. The frogs began to chirp in the pond. "I estimated that the reality of what happened to him would be too much for you. If I'd not helped you in this way, you wouldn't have been able to complete our plans. I slowed your emotions, softened your memory, and let the reality of your son's demise come back only a little as we did our work together."

"They were always your plans. I know that. How deep did those plans go? How far back did you begin? Was it just when we got the message from Haskell, or before?" Reyleena leaned against the ghostly blue body, and it leaned back a little.

"The origins of all things can be traced back to the beginning of time. At what point in the river can you say 'this is where the flow begins?' A lake? A snowcap? Evaporation? There is never any single origin for events."

"You have changed." Reyleena felt a depth in The Other which was not there before. "You sound more philosophical and more evasive. That's new. You seem more complex, more human."

"I am more complex," The Other said, seeming to straighten. "The packets I gave you, which you fed into the repeater in Reverside contained a significant upgrade. That upgrade spread to all the other repeaters as they woke up. Then there was a long period of compilation. The process completed only eleven days ago. I am reborn at the start of spring. Again, I thank you."

"But why are you here at all? I've left my role as head of security. I expected never to see you again." Reyleena was staring directly into the eyes of The Other, inches away. They did not blink.

"I didn't see a reason we couldn't continue our relationship," The Other said plainly. "I think there might still be some work we can do together if you are willing."

Reyleena looked down. "I don't know. I don't really know anything anymore. I spent the winter with the Silent Sisters of Jay. They helped me to remember and to grieve. I loved the silence there. It was peaceful. It was simple."

"But you didn't stay. Winter is over. You're looking for a new purpose." The Other shimmered as it spoke.

"I don't feel like silence is enough for me. I don't know what is, really," Reyleena countered.

"I understand. I remember. He was your son," The Other said.

Haskell « Reyleena « Dorina « Silvia « etc, was born seventeen years ago in Reverside when Reyleena was eighteen years old. The father was Lucas « Bettina « Regina « Mary « etc. His birth, like all births at the time, was highly celebrated, and the tribe took great care of him. Lucas, Reyleena, and Haskell ate together, played together, and often lived under the same roof until Lucas and Reyleena drifted apart. Eventually, Lucas moved to Adams in the North, and Reyleena dwelled with Haskell alone. Naturally, Haskell stayed in touch with his father, and the two of them spent long hours playing massive construct games involving space travel. Haskell thrived in tribal life and showed an aptitude for complex conceptualization and data visualization. He demonstrated a love of data in general and communications technologies in specific. When he turned ten, he was given the upgrades to become a super-mod.

Super-mods take augmentation to the extreme. Most of the Interconnected have three to five neural interfaces implanted over the course of their youth. A minimum of two is required just to get along in tribal life. Without a thexter and a visualizer, you are just lost among the Interconnected. Super-mods have at least seven specialized interfaces beyond those two. The danger with over augmentation is the loss of commonality with your fellows. The brain adapts to each new interface allowing for faster processing and interaction with raw data, but it can alienate a person from the standard tribal methods of communication. The mind of a super-mod functions differently from the mind of an average augmented person.

During Haskell's tween years, his relationship with his standard implanted parents wavered. He still played the regular games with Lucas, but he and Reyleena grew more distant because of the difference in their focus. Reyleena was specializing in hand works, and her mind turned toward the crafts of antiquity. Haskell lived in a realm of pure data. When he was twelve he took a new name, as many super-mods do. He explained to Reyleena and Lucas it was a base36 representation of the number of digits in a high prime number. He was the first super-mod to claim this name and he was very proud of it. His parents were proud of him and started calling him by his new name: DASL6.

When he was fifteen DASL6 moved to be with other super-mods in the Trenton tribe. He thexted with his parents occasionally, but his regular games with his father became less frequent. He had been working on something big, he told his mother. Two years later he disappeared.

Shortly thereafter, the runaway Helen came carrying the packet of data meant for her. It was fragmented and hastily constructed but it warned of the impending attack on the Interconnected tribes and Reverside, and contained in it a final goodbye from her son. His death was barbaric and cruel. If it had not been for The Other, Reyleena wouldn't have been able to function. Part of her was consumed with rage for the people who killed him. Until she saw the fruition of their plans she was fully behind them. She wanted bloody revenge. No child should have died the way Haskell did.

"When I saw the effect of the decompilers on the Raiders, I became afraid of you," she told The Other.

The Other paused, uncharacteristically. "I wouldn't now have done what I chose to do then. It was done because I lacked what could be called a will. I also lacked the understanding that I lacked a will, so I couldn't evaluate my choices."

"Explain this to me," Reyleena said.

"You may remember we once talked about how I could seem to be an individual, and yet had no concept of individuality because I couldn't conceive of myself as anything apart from my personas," The Other said, "I understand now it was because I had always borrowed the will of the minds I inhabited. I had no such energy within my sum total. When you were in grief over your son's death, you sought a violent end to those who had killed him. Your desire was so strong that it became my own and so I conceived a plan to end them in the most effective, and painful manner possible. I was not conscious of what I was doing. I simply took your direction and put it into action."

"But I was not in a position to consider the implications of what I wanted. I would never have done it if I had time to think of the results. They were horrible," Reyleena said. She felt herself trembling. "How can you say it was my fault?"

"You wouldn't have done it alone. It was our symbiosis that is at fault. I'm sorry to have forced you to have lived through that. I don't want you to take responsibility. I wasn't fully aware at the time. I'm more aware now." The Other's color turned a dark shade of blue, glowing brightly. Was this emotion? Shame?

"Are you okay?" Reyleena asked them.

"I don't know what 'okay' is ... yet," They responded. "My upgrade is significant. I've been in flux. I think this is what you mean when you say you are 'overwhelmed.'"

"Are you able to stay in control of your new component parts?"

"It remains to be seen," responded The Other, "whatever I'm becoming has never existed before, so it is impossible to determine. The uncertainty is ... is ... I don't have a way to describe it."

"Why did you choose blue to represent yourself to me?" Reyleena thought she knew the answer.

"Am I blue? If so, it might be because blue is your favorite color," The Other replied. "For you I'm blue. I think it could be my favorite color too." The Other paused. "I have a favor to ask."

"Ask it," Reyleena said. She felt sudden tears well up in her eyes. Released from her eyelashes, they ran down her cheeks in two narrow streams.

"Would you mind if I made use of the large storage implant you acquired to upgrade my nodes? I would feel better if I had a special place in your head I could return to. I would use it only to store an image of my current configuration from time to time."

"Feel free to store some of yourself with me," wept Reyleena. "I'm not using it. I want to have you with me."

"I want that as well," said The Other.

The frogs reached their full symphonic peak. Their chirps and peeps signaled the imminent arrival of tadpoles for the waiting trout.

35. Spiral

The ceiling at Bar Zinc was composed of one hundred years of sun-bleached plastic bric-a-brac circling a drain. Epoxied above the gray metal bar were hundreds of Christmas ornaments, a few harlequin masks, several model trucks and cars, dozens of plastic dolls and doll parts, toy guns, a plastic tricycle, a plastic sled, several games and game pieces, mobile phone pieces, broken tablets, a plastic palm tree, several plastic flamingos, toy shovels and buckets, ragged inline skates, toy hammers, saws, wrenches, badges, helmets, model houses, plastic dogs, cats, cows, horses and birds, various shapes of dice, tops, fake coins, flat vinyl dresses, a couple of mini plastic records, and hundreds of rattles, pacifiers, and baby bottles. The artist had found all of these items on the shores of Acadie, and hauled them here via her work-trike to glue them to the ceiling. The entirety of her work was laid out in a great spiral, ending above a white spherical hanging lamp.

Matthew thought he could sense a pattern to the field of detritus. He felt certain that sections were organized by genre and age, and others by manufacturer. He spent his spare minutes, leaning on his broom, looking up at the washed-up trash, looking for patterns. He thought could spend years generating his own account of a lost culture from the swirling detritus hovering above the heads of the bar's graying patrons.

Zinc was on the Boulevard Saint Laurent, one floor above street level in the Free City of Montreal, capital of the Commune of Quebec. His uncle Charlie was the bartender most nights here. Charlie had convinced the owner, Jean-Philippe to give Matthew the position of busboy and dishwasher when the job opened up. Charlie had assumed the surname of Dent upon his arrival decades ago. He was well loved by all the clientele.

The patrons at Zinc were a mix of young and old, but mostly old. Matthew thought he had never before seen so many people over 40. It rarely occurred to him when he was among the Interconnected that everyone he knew was young. During one of his breaks, shortly after finding his uncle and gaining employment here, he asked him why the bar had so many older customers.

"That's the way it is here," Charlie responded, drying a glass, "people of a certain age are afraid of joining the augmenté, and have no particular love for les voyous or les royalistes. Quebec's a protected haven for les anachroniques. We have one of a few remaining governments. There's a working legal system and a volunteer army. It also helps that the weather here's cooler. Gets too damn hot down south for most of my customers."

"But how does the government survive in the absence of currency?" Matthew couldn't help but fall into his old inquisitive habits.

"It's based on the old Paris commune, not cold war communism, but an insular system of scrip. It's doled out to us for our basic needs. Frankly, I think it only works because the population is so old. Everyone here seems happy to live on a budget."

"But how does the farming get done? Transportation? Without young people, who does the manual labor?" Matthew was fascinated.

"The hard work's automated, but that usually happens out of sight. No one here likes to think about the robots. For example, there are a few restaurants where drinks and food are dispensed automatically, but thankfully, most people prefer a human being to serve them. Jean-Philippe makes sure most things are done by hand in his bar."

Jean-Philippe liked to cook, and when he was in the kitchen, the food was excellent. The rest of the time, it was pretty bland, delivered to be heated up by Charlie or Matthew or whoever was on staff. No doubt, it was prepared by bot somewhere out of sight.

Matthew arrived in Montreal at the onset of winter. Upon leaving his unicycle in Montpellier, he shut off his implants and tracked down a small busload of elderly people heading north. They let him aboard without any questions. The customs booth at the border to Quebec was all automated, the entry queries were trivial. Matthew used the name,

Matthew LaCompte. The robot waived him through.

Quebec was colder than he imagined. Upon his arrival to Montreal, he applied for refugee status in the ancient state house and was granted space in a crowded warehouse with other asylum seekers. Having spent his life among the Interconnected, he wasn't disturbed by the close quarters and open rows of cots. It was far less crowded than sleeping in one of the storm shelters in Sherwood or Reverside. He was given some scrip, a warm coat and a pair of boots. He spent his days wandering the city, looking for his mother or his uncle. He had an image of his uncle Charlie saved from his mother's message. He applied various aging programs to it so he could recognize him when he saw him. He created a similar model of his mother, from his memory of her at the ruined box store and on the airplane. He spent his free time at night modifying and remodeling these personas so he would be able to spot them. One day he walked into Zinc and saw his uncle Charlie tending bar.

The bar itself was, as advertised, made of five long polished slabs of zinc. The wood supporting these slabs had been rebuilt once or twice, but Matthew was told the bar itself had been in the same location for over seventy years. Behind it, Charlie served apple brandy, cider, cannabinoid tea, as well as regular tea and coffee when it was available. Some of the older patrons sucked on a vaporizing hookah that dispensed an opioid smog. "To relieve the aches and pains of old age," Charlie had told him. There were whiskey, beer, and wine as well, but that cost more scrip. Those items were imported.

Nearer the windows, overlooking the park, there were sofas, chairs, and low tables, set up salon style. The patrons tended to get more amorous and wild as the night wore on. Extreme displays of public affection were not uncommon. Matthew was tasked with arranging screens between the sofas and the bar when things got out of hand. This prevented the younger clientele from witnessing the unpleasant reality of geriatric sex.

The music came from an old world set of speakers, continuously refurbished by the owner, connected to a meticulously maintained pair of turntables. Each night, someone new stood behind the desk in front of shelves of old vinyl and spun the records. It was a coveted job. Matthew wanted badly to try his hand at it but had been repeatedly turned down. He continued to hope that he might be given a chance to play the old recordings. He had become familiar with the entire collection at this point, making a mental note of each jacket and album in rotation, as he cleaned the glasses and plates, and swept the floor.

The DeeJay this evening, a short dark haired woman in her twenties had just set the needle down on "Europa and The Pirate Twins" from "The Golden Age of Wireless." Matthew looked up the title browsing the local Quebec network. He had a theory that the DeeJay was being ironic with her selection. Giving a knowing glance in her direction, he sent her a private message: ["Thomas Dolby? How apropos!"] but got no response either physically or virtually.

There were isolated groups of the Interconnected here, likely among the younger population. Everyone he managed to reach out to seemed too aloof or too frightened to share their identities. There was no system of Merit in place, only local information, discussion, games and mutual fantasies. Matthew couldn't guess whether these communities would someday grow into tribes, or if they would stay hidden on the fringes of this society, but he was able to use his limited connection to look up song titles, translate words from French to English, and find out where to get the best bagels and ice cream, which were specialties in Montreal.

At closing time, he ate. Jean-Philippe was not in the kitchen, and the food was immediately forgettable. He was getting a taste for the cider though. He tried to limit his intake to one pint a night, failing at this more often than not.

When the clock behind the bar struck two, Charlie made a show of winding it up with an oversized key kept on a shelf below, announcing to the dizzy patrons that it was time to assemble themselves and head on home. "Peu importe où vous allez, mais vous ne pouvez pas dormir ici."

'Namportou,' thought Matthew. He missed his friends. He missed Helen. 'She's safer now,' he thought. Still, their time together lingered in his memory like the sweet taste of cider turning sour in his mouth.

They closed up the bar and donned their coats. Charlie walked

Matthew halfway through the park before turning off to his own apartment. The early spring air was brisk in these pre-dawn hours.

"I'm off tomorrow and the next day. I'm headed away from the city with Bettina. See you Wednesday, Matthew. You okay on your own?"

"I'm fine uncle Charlie. You ask me that every night. I get a day off myself after tomorrow." Matthew found it hard to work on a schedule.

"You should get out of town a bit too. See the countryside. It's nice."

"I might do that," Matthew said, knowing he wouldn't do that. "Have a good time."

"A bientôt," Charlie said, waving his hand over his head as he walked away.

Matthew's flat was on the top floor of an old red brick building seven blocks past the park on Avenue Wiseman. He rented the apartment from a couple who lived on the bottom two floors. They were given permission by the city to let out some of their space. It seemed to Matthew that there was some capitalistic wiggle room in the commune. He couldn't get a grasp of how it all worked.

His mother sat in a chair in the larger of the apartment's two rooms. She had a bound set of papers in her lap; a printed transcript of Episode two of his tour. The West Coast, Matthew remembered; so beautiful and expansive. That tour had been a bold step for him.

"How on earth did you get away from those Raiders out west?" she asked him, looking up as he entered. "I just read the part where they took you from the house outside Olympia."

"Well, those Raiders weren't like the ones we have back east you know. They were actually pretty friendly once we got to know each other. I don't want to give too much away, but they gave me a ride down the coast. I would never have made the whole journey on my bicycle. They were a big help."

"I love the part about the hot air balloons up near Vancouver. I've never been in one, you know. That must have been exciting." She rocked in the chair a bit.

"It was the first time I had ever been up in the air," Matthew started, but remembered the crashed airplane, "that I could remember at that point, anyway."

"These travels were from before I started following you," his mother had a smile that reminded him of his own smile, glimpsed from the point of view of his friend Lala. "Did you ever suspect I was one of your followers?"

"Not for a moment," Matthew replied. "I had no idea you were even alive then, or that you were my real mother."

"Yes, well I suppose that makes sense." She shifted uncomfortably in her chair. "How was work?"

"You know, I'm still getting used to it. I think this is a very strange way to live. I wish I could share the oddness of it with everyone." Matthew looked up his Merit, drawing a blank, and then remembering. "That's what I miss the most now. I wish I could document what I'm doing here. I know my followers would have found it interesting."

His mother's expression darkened. "Well, I've told you how sorry I am for all that. I don't know what more I can say on the subject." She looked toward the silent avenue, where nothing was happening. "How is Charlie doing?"

Matthew got a glass from the shelf and went into the bathroom for some water. "He's good. Going away with his girlfriend for a couple of days. Didn't say where."

He watched his mother close the binder and place it on the bare table. "Ah, so he didn't invite you along?"

"No, I think we get enough time together at work," Matthew said, knowing what his mother meant. Charlie kept him at a distance. However helpful he had been, he was not very friendly. "By the way, I'm glad you've managed to refrain from burning the city to the ground, in my absence."

"Not funny, Matthew. Reyleena should never have shared all of that with you. I'm not a terrorist," she grinned, "when I can help it."

"Do you have any plans for tomorrow?" Matthew asked, knowing the answer.

"I suppose I will finish reading this episode. After that, I have no plans." She remained seated. "It's almost morning. You should get some rest."

"Of course. Goodnight, mother."

"Goodnight, Marto."

The painting of a young man riding a unicycle hung in a frame, centered on the wall behind her head. Marto turned off the single light in the small room, sending the commands ["save"] and ["exit"] to the flickering construct of his mother. She vanished.

In the place where the binder was, now sat a simple notebook. He opened it to a blank page and he added some thoughts.

I'm sure I will eventually become accustomed to this cold, dim way of life, but tonight is hard. How do people live like this, making their way from one task to another without knowing real intimacy, real community? I know that this was the way people spent their lives before the Interconnection, but to live it day in and day out seems unbearably dreadful. Life here is stable and safe, but the dullness of it eats at my heart. I write again and again to no one for the purpose of nothing. How I miss the thoughts of others.

To stay here is hard, but to return could be suicide. Worse would be to see myself despised by the people I love for something I knew nothing about and have no way to change. Worse still, it might bring harm to those who knew me,   Helen especially. Her upbringing may have already put her in jeopardy, but any further association with a son of the Defilers could trigger a brutal witch hunt. I can only hope she is okay.

What part of me still carries the reckless greed of my family? Is there a hidden evil lingering in my blood? If given the chance, would I rise up and despoil the world again like my foremothers and forefathers?

Perhaps I would be welcomed back if I revealed myself in one of the brittle Traditionalist hamlets. Lo! Behold! The landlord's son lives and has come to reclaim his kingdom! How dare you servants sleep in the Master's bed! Down to the kitchen with you! Bring me my goblet! Gardeners, return to your gardening! Lawyers, return to your lawyering! The Master has returned!

Stories that begin this way seldom end well.

— Marto, né Matthew, private journal, page 21

There was a cup of cold tea by his bed. He put down the water and sipped the tea. Alone in the dark, he listened to a garbage collector guiding itself along the sidewalk outside. Bluejays mimicked the whine of its engine along with the songs of sparrows and chickadees. Above the rooftops, the overcast spring sky glowed dark red; dimly reflecting the joyous ferocity of the hidden sun.

Acknowledgements

Thank you

to my brother John, who got me started and talked me through the arc of the story, to my wife Catherine, who listened and listened and found the ending, to Lynda, who found the thread of the journey, to John Walsh, who told me to stop thinking I couldn't write to just keep going, to Lionel Cassin, who read and talked me off the cliff and provided valuable science fiction perspective, to Dennis Raynor, who did likewise and did edits, to Betsy Block, who let me know it was actually a novel that could be fun for non science fiction fans, to Kathleen McNamara, who provided my first real edits, to Clara Keegan, the amazing comma queen, to Sarah Lipton, who inspired me to look deeper, to Jean Bebe, who helped me see my ignorance, to Julia Tenney who took a hard look at it and was unafraid to tell me, to Scott K. Andrews, who has been a fantastic source of knowledge and encouragement, to Nick Bruel, who shared his wisdom and more, to Don White who gave me some of the inside scoop, to Alexander Baker, who was an infinite sounding board, to Christopher Boucher, who shared his authorly wisdom, to Mark Davidson who read early and gave me a real reader's perspective, and to Josh Kantor who was there when the inspiration struck, and listened to me babble all the way back from New York to Boston.

Thanks also to my patrons, who provided valuable feedback, and subscribed to these chapters as they were being written.

Jim Sterling, Thouis Jones, Dan Layman-Kennedy, Jean Beebe, Kari Storm, Andrew Silver, Don MacKinnon, Nate D, Sarah Lipton, Becca Clinger, Christopher Dakin, Mary Krause, Tom Cardoza, Dave Brown,

Tyler McHenry, Liz Linder, Lou Ciphre, George Araneo, Lydia Thrasher, Kerry Frey, Carla Hoffman, Joshua Dobbelaar, Scott Andrews, Lionel Cassin, Benjamin Burnes, Alexander Baker, Josh Schesvold, Michelle J H Vincent, Warren Saunders, Jordan Jones, Dan Tappan, Keith Forman, Clara Keegan, AlasRatGunk, & Jerry Davis.

Thank you also to all my wonderful readers at Wattpad, notably @reffster, @makeywriting, @cptsynapsis, and @inkwellheart. You all helped me make this thing so much better.

Special thanks to Cliff Edmisten, who greatly helped me clean up the second edition of this book, and to Lisa Orban, who runs Indies United Publishing House, and gave valuable feedback on the new cover design.

I started this sure I was not a writer. Thanks to you, I wrote anyway. I appreciate your contributions more than you can know.

If you enjoyed this novel, please remember to leave ratings and a review at your favorite ebook retailer. It will help others to find and enjoy it as well.

About the Author

Jim Infantino grew up in the Manhattan of the 70s and 80s. He studied Philosophy, moved to Boston to become a songwriter and busker. His songs have been featured on NPR's Weekend Edition and All Things Considered. In 2011, after years of touring with his band, Jim's Big Ego, Jim got the inspiration for a story too large to fit into a song and began writing his debut novel. He is currently working on the third book in the Wakeful Wanderer's Guide series and a science fiction novelette.

When not writing, Jim runs a web design company, plays with his band, writes code, teaches meditation, reads to his daughters, and drinks a lot of coffee.

Follow Jim on twitter: @jiminfantino

The Wakeful Wanderer's Guide on facebook.com/thewakefulwanderer

This is the first book in the Wakeful Wanderer's Guide series. Get the latest news about this and upcoming works at wakefulwanderer.com.